THE VISCOUNT AND THE VICAR'S *Daughter*

MEARA PLATT

Print Edition

Cover Design by Dar Albert

ISBN-13: 978-1-945767-17-3

CHAPTER 1

Ardley, England
June, 1823

ALEXANDER DAYNE, THIRD Viscount Ardley, emitted a roar as someone dumped a pail of cold water over him while he lay flat on his back in…where in blazes was he? *Blast.* He was beside the vicarage house of St. Martin's Church again. He coughed and sputtered, trying to clear his fogged brain as he sat up with a groan and raked his hands through his hair to brush back the strands that had fallen over his eyes.

When he looked up, all he saw was the lavender sky of breaking dawn, the golden sun burning through the last tendrils of mist and clouds, and the highly irritating Miss Viola Ruskin casting her slender shadow over him. Her presence boded no good for him, but at least her lithe, little body shaded him from the glare of the early morning light as she hovered close. "Do you have a death wish, Miss Ruskin?"

"No, my lord. But obviously, you do," she said, her voice as soft and lovely as a summer breeze despite her irritation.

He wiped the last of the droplets from his eyes and glowered at the pretty perpetrator who happened to be the local vicar's daughter. She was also known as the Ardley Angel, not only for her good deeds but also for her exquisite looks. However, she was quickly becoming the devil's bane of his existence.

"What have you to say for yourself?" she asked in a schoolmistress voice that sounded surprisingly gentle to his ears because there really was no evil in this girl, just an irritating primness that he, much to his horror, was finding quite to his liking lately. Her stunning, brandy-colored eyes were ablaze as she shook her head in disapproval. A lock of her dark brown hair had fallen over her forehead and her cheeks were flushed as though she had just exerted herself.

"Need I remind you that I am a grown man and do not need you to act as my mother." But he sank back onto the soft grass and groaned again, for the sky and ground seemed to be spinning around him and tossing him off balance. "Did you move me off the roadway?"

"Yes, my lord. It is the third time this week."

It galled him to be obliged to the girl, but he hadn't sunk quite so low yet as to deny she had now saved his hide more than once. For a sprite of a girl to drag his big body safely aside was no small feat. "Thank you."

She knelt beside him and put a delicate hand on his shoulder. "I do not need your gratitude. What we all need is for you to come to your senses and behave in accordance with the honor of your title."

Behave?

Other than drink himself into oblivion, he thought he had held himself together fairly well in the two years since his world fell apart. Hardly misbehaved at all. Which probably explained why he was noticing Miss Ruskin's lush, pink lips within dangerously close reach of his.

They were incredibly attractive lips even when pursed, for she had a lovely, generous mouth.

Her bosom was also generous.

She must have noticed the lowering direction of his stare and gave him a disrespectful shove before scrambling back to her feet. "This is exactly what I mean."

He rolled to his feet, ignoring the jolt of pain that shot into his skull as he did so, and took hold of her hand before she could storm away. "If I wish to drink myself into a stupor every night, that is my business and none of yours."

The impertinent sprite was not in the least intimidated by him even though he now stood a full head taller than her modest height. She wasn't small, but of average height, and yet there was something in her appearance that reminded him of a kitten, something small and worthy of a cuddle.

He was not about to cuddle this pillar of innocence as she stood there tossing daggers at him with her eyes.

"None of my business?" She gave a huff that raised her chest magnificently. "It is entirely my business when you insist on passing out in front of the vicarage like some destitute vagrant for all the parishioners to see."

He did not care what he looked like.

It was the way she looked that troubled him, so much beauty wrapped up in so much innocence. He groaned inwardly, irritated he had been studying her and inexplicably finding her irresistible.

This wasn't like him at all.

Why her?

And why now?

"There is no danger of your father's parishioners seeing me. It is early yet, not much past dawn if the glint of sunlight is any indication. You are the only one out here at this hour."

"Fortunately for you. But you may not be so fortunate next time." She shook her head and emitted a sigh of exasperation. "You are Viscount Ardley, lord of the big manor overlooking our small enclave. Most of the villagers are dependent on you for their livelihoods. How do you think they would feel if they were to see you passed out in a ditch? Well, what have you to say for yourself?"

He arched an eyebrow and gave a careless shrug. "Since I seem to be landing in that ditch with some regularity, I suppose it is a good thing for me we've had no rain to drown me."

She placed her hands on her hips and once more gave a magnificent huff. "This is all you have to say?"

He looked down at himself, realizing he wore no jacket or vest…or cravat, for that matter. Indeed, he had on nothing but a white shirt of good quality lawn that he hoped had not been ruined by the dousing she had just given him, and buff breeches that were relatively dry since she had dumped most of the water on his head.

The soaked shirt was plastered to his body and made a *thwacking* sound as he peeled it away from his skin. "No rain," he said with a fierce frown, "and yet I seem to have gotten drenched anyway."

"And I will do it again if I catch you inebriated in front of the church again. Do not be glib about this situation. You were stretched out in the road and might have been run over by a passing coach. Would serve you right…meaning no disrespect, my lord."

He burst out laughing. "No disrespect? You have insulted me in every way possible."

"Hardly. There is a lot more I would say to you if I were given leave to do so."

He ought to have been furious, but Viola Ruskin had a way with people. Everyone liked her, even though she was the most buttoned up, self righteous little thing, and always the first to comment on his bad behavior.

So what if he was drinking himself into oblivion nightly?

Did he not have good cause?

He stared at her for no reason other than she had the most beautifully vibrant face. An alive face is what he would call it, for this is how he thought of everything now…as either alive or dead.

She was the sweet breath of life.

He was dead inside.

And yet, not quite as dead as he thought since he could not seem to tear his gaze away from her.

The little apple in her throat bobbed. "Let me help you inside," she said more gently. "I'll put the kettle on to boil."

"For tea? Do not trouble yourself. I'll take a brandy."

"You will do no such thing. You already reek of it, and your eyes are so bloodshot it is a wonder you can see anything out of them. Indeed, you are so soaked in spirits, I'm afraid to light a flame anywhere near you for fear you will burst into flames yourself. It shall be tea for you and nothing stronger."

"Do you dare contradict me?" He was a bloody viscount, after all. He could bloody well do any bloody thing he wanted, especially to himself.

"If by 'contradict' you mean save your life…then yes, I dare it." She tipped her chin up in defiance, but he could tell by the little bob of the apple of her throat that she was not as confident as she wished to appear.

He had a sudden urge to kiss her slender throat, but he would never do it. Was it not enough of a betrayal that he was lately having these lustful feelings for this girl?

Viola Ruskin was an infuriating mix of prim and sultry, and this seemed to hold an insane appeal for him. He could not understand why, especially since it was the last thing he wanted to feel. In truth, he meant to spend the rest of his days completely numb to all sensation. He wanted nothing but ice in his veins and steel in his heart. Indeed, he needed to be rid of this raw and incessant ache in his heart before it drove him to ruin.

Viola pursed her plump, pink lips in disapproval, then sighed and led him into the vicarage kitchen. The vicar's residence, a small but stately manse, was built of ancient stone and situated beside the church which was also built of this same ancient stone and had magnificent stained glass windows and a soaring spire.

The kitchen was not very large, but there was sufficient light coming in through its windows and the open door at this hour of the morning to give the room a golden glow. She motioned for him to sit on a stool beside the long table.

He stumbled to it and sat heavily, letting out a breath. When he inhaled, he caught the scent of freshly baked bread…or pie…or something delicious that made his stomach growl. Perhaps it was her delicate, fruity scent that was so tempting. But he said nothing and merely watched as she added water to the kettle and then put it on to boil.

She cast surreptitious glances at him while she worked, next frying up eggs and slices of ham with practiced ease. They sizzled in the pan, releasing a heavenly aroma that made his mouth salivate and caused his stomach to growl again. "Do you not have a cook to attend to this chore for you?"

"Mrs. Bligh will be here shortly, but you need nourishment now. Besides, I am not ashamed to know my way around a kitchen. It is quite a useful talent."

"What do you mean?"

She turned to him with a wry arch of her eyebrow. "You really have no idea, do you?"

"No idea about what?"

She turned her back to him a moment to put the eggs and ham onto a plate for him. "What do you think will become of me once my father passes? You know his health is failing. I am doing my best to tend him, but nothing seems to help. He will be gone soon," she said with a soft tremor to her voice, "and another vicar will be appointed to take his place. He is all I have in the world. When he is gone, I shall have no one. Nor will I have a roof over my head, for the new vicar's family will certainly push me out when they move in."

He inhaled with a gut-felt ache. "Forgive me. I was callous and did not think."

"Why should you concern yourself with me?" She set the plate before him, and then added a scone from the basket sitting on the table and covered in a cheerful cloth. A heavenly aroma drifted toward him as she lifted the cloth. Those scones were obviously freshly baked. She must have been up quite early to have already prepared this batch.

Yet it could not have been something she did regularly, for her hands were delicate and not at all roughened by this sort of labor.

"I know you are too caught up in your own misery to think of anyone but yourself." She sighed and took the stool beside him. "I'm sorry. That was harsh of me and unfair. I know how dearly you loved your wife and daughter."

"Do not mention them," he said in a low growl.

"I'm sorry," she repeated, but he caught the edge of irritation in her voice. "We all lose loved ones. Do you think I am not struggling with the impending loss of mine as well? I never even knew my mother. She died giving birth to me."

He was about to reach for her hand to give it a light squeeze in apology, but she moved away to pour him a cup of tea. She now set the cup down beside him and settled once more on her stool. "That wet shirt must be uncomfortable for you, but I don't think any of my father's shirts will fit you."

"I'm fine. The weather's warm enough. I will survive it." He still wanted to take her hand, but the moment had passed, so he picked up his fork instead and began to eat. "This is delicious."

"Thank you. I am hoping to find a position for myself as a cook…when the need arises."

He glanced at her in surprise. "Why would you bury yourself in a kitchen where no one can see you?"

She cast him a wry smile. "It is the safest place for me, surely that is obvious. One of the few positions for which I would be hired. No wife will take me on me as governess for her children or as maid for her household."

He nodded. "Because you are far too pretty."

Blast.

He hadn't meant to let that slip, but she did not appear to be taking it as anything more than a factual comment.

"I am not blind to the way men look at me."

"You could use your appearance to best advantage and find yourself a husband."

"Yes, I could. But I cannot bring myself to do it, at least not yet. I wish to make a love match, if possible. I do not want to marry merely for the sake of convenience. I am not afraid of hard work. My life does not have to be easy, but it does have to be happy."

He gave a disdainful snort. "Happy?"

If only he could remember what that felt like.

"And what is wrong with wanting this? Why should I have to cringe every time my husband reaches out to touch me? Any man would expect rights to my body in exchange for providing a roof over my head and food on the table. But I am not made this way. I…I cannot give myself to someone I do not love." She blushed furiously. "Oh, this is more than you wanted to hear. Much more than I should have said."

She moved away and pretended to busy herself putting away supplies.

"Miss Ruskin, do not be afraid to come to me if ever you are in need of assistance. I may be wretched in many ways, but not to the point I would ever forget my duty to those who reside in my village." He set down his fork and stared at his empty plate, for he had devoured every last crumb.

She stopped fidgeting about the kitchen and turned to regard him with a thoughtful expression. "You would help me?"

"I know I have not been worthy of any of you these past two years, but I do understand what you mean about happiness. I have felt the loss of it acutely ever since Jillian passed. Then to lose my little Molly to the same illness mere days later. It was more than I could bear."

He saw tears form in her eyes. "I know, my lord. If I am severe with you, it is because I know that the man I have been finding drunk outside the vicarage this past week is not who you are or were ever meant to be."

He snorted. "Pretty wretched, I know."

"We are all very proud of who you are. A war hero, a loving father and husband, a good and kind man who cares for those under his protection. But you've lost your way so badly at the moment. I have every confidence you will set yourself right and find your true path."

In addition to being physically beautiful, Viola was also intelligent and compassionate. He had behaved poorly, especially toward her, and now felt quite contrite. He was not an ogre but had been taking out his grief and frustration on others for too long. "I thank you for an excellent meal. I promise to do better for all of you."

She shook her head. "It is most important that you do this for yourself."

"I know. It has been two years now, and yet I feel as though I am getting worse instead of better."

"Because you are not permitting yourself to move on. May I speak my mind, my lord?"

He cast her a wry grin, for Viola was an opinionated little thing. Perhaps this is why he had been stirring awake only to find himself in front of St. Martin's Church these past few days. Was he seeking her out? "Go on."

She took a deep breath and returned to the seat beside his. "A part of you is ready to move on and this angers you."

"Why should it anger me? In truth, I am desperate for it."

"Yes, but you also believe moving on is a betrayal of Lady Jillian's memory. Yours was a love match and her loss has left a gaping hole in your heart. You want to find someone who will fill that emptiness, but at the same time you hate yourself for even considering someone else as your wife. You think it will somehow diminish all that Lady Jillian meant to you."

She was right, but it did not make him any less angry to hear the truth from her lips. In fact, having it set out so plainly hurt more.

He rose and raked a hand through his still wet hair.

Blast.

Droplets still streamed down his neck and into his chest thanks to her dumping that water on him. "Thank you for breakfast, Miss Ruskin. I shall endeavor to pass out in the village green next time rather than disturb you," he said with an icy sarcasm that was completely unprovoked on her part.

But the truth struck like a spear through the heart and he was not yet ready to hear it.

She was right, but it did not mean he had to accept what she was saying. Nor was she the only one shoving this obvious dilemma in his face. His father's letters had been filled with pleas to stop living in the past and find himself a wife. His father was the Earl of Trent and he was the earl's heir.

No one was letting him forget this.

Everywhere he turned, his duty as eldest son was being flung in his face.

She placed a hand on his arm as he started to turn away. "What now, Miss Ruskin?"

"If you are going to rant and rage at me, then you may as well address me as Viola. Why maintain formality when what you really want to do is forget I exist?"

"That makes no sense."

"Let us not keep up a polite pretense. You are in a very bad way and slowly killing yourself. I am glad if I make you angry because it is time you dealt with this problem obviously plaguing you. You cannot stay buried in this dark well of misery you have dug for yourself. At least try to poke your head out and see what a little bit of sunlight might have to offer."

"Such as?"

"You are a viscount and heir to the Earl of Trent," she said, repeating his own thoughts. "Your estate is well-managed and healthy, and you are still young and handsome. Why not venture in–"

"Do not dare say the marriage mart! I have no interest in remarrying." Which is what he had told his family as well and received much the same reaction as he was now receiving from impertinent Viola.

Her father was the vicar.

She was just the sanctimonious vicar's daughter.

What right did she have to pass judgment on him?

He groaned inwardly, knowing he was being a complete and utter ogre to her.

She placed her hands on her hips and frowned at him, ignoring that he towered over her and was twice her strength. "You know I am right. This is precisely why you are angry at yourself…in addition to barking at me. Stop behaving like a trapped and wounded dog. Bark all you like, but it will not fix your pain. Only moving forward will ever help. Start slowly. Do not venture into the marriage mart until you are good and ready. I am not suggesting you dive into those waters right away."

"Merely dip in a toe?"

She nodded. "You have friends, do you not?"

"I don't know. I've chased most of them away by now."

"The true ones will return upon your invitation. You still have your brother and parents, too."

He did not know why he was listening to her. Perhaps because she was making sense. And yet, the last thing he wanted to do was be sensible. "Your point?"

"Throw a weekend house party."

"Have you been corresponding with my mother?" he muttered with the same icy sarcasm in his tone as before.

"No, but your family has obviously been imploring you to do this or else you would not be looking at me as though you wish I would disappear into Hades along with the other demons burdening your soul. But this is my home and you are the trespasser here, not I. So it is you who should be on his way. And what is so wrong with the suggestion? It is just a party and need not be anything more. Your brother's wife and your mother will gladly help you make up an invitation list."

His groan was more of a low growl. "My mother? And Daisy? I am not a little boy who needs their guidance."

She looked him up and down. "You are certainly not a little boy. But you are behaving like one. Is it not obvious you desperately need a woman's hand in this?"

"If you are suggesting my mother and Daisy are to decide upon which sweet young things to invite, then forget it."

"Fine, you select them. I'm sure you will make a disastrous mess of it."

"Will I now?" He lifted her up and held her up at his eye level.

He saw the sudden panic in her eyes, for he must have looked like something wild and unmanageable at this moment.

She grabbed onto his shoulders for support and her eyes widened a little more. "Put me down, my lord. This isn't funny."

"Neither is your suggestion." But he set her down because he did not need her shrieking in his ear. His head was still pounding like a hammer being swung atop a nut to crack it. "I will do it…hold a house party, but under two conditions."

"What are they?"

"That you spend the weekend cooking for me. I have never tasted anything as splendid as this breakfast you just made for me. Not that I should be surprised since parishioners have been attending your father's Sunday sermons by the hordes because of the pies you bake for refreshments after his service."

"They come to hear him speak. It is ridiculous to think they attend merely for my pies. You never do. In fact, you tear out of church the moment his sermon is over. Why?"

"Because I prefer to retreat to my bear cave and lick my wounds."

She cast him a confused look.

"I tried staying afterward once, but all anyone would talk to me about was Jillian and Molly. It was too much for me." He sighed brokenly. "Cook for me, Viola. I shall pay you handsomely for your trouble."

"But you have Mrs. Stringer to run your kitchen. She has been in your service for almost a decade."

"She is not up to the task of preparing meals that require flair and delicacy. I shall give her the weekend off to visit her sister and let the staff know you will be assuming her role while she is gone. It is you…it must be you…or you can forget about the house party."

She groaned. "Gad, have you always been such an ogre and did we just not see it? All right, *if* Mrs. Stringer is amenable, then I shall do it. This will also be helpful to me in gaining your recommendation regarding my cooking abilities when the time comes. I'll need your word that I shall have your letter of recommendation."

He nodded. "If your meals are half as good as the scones, ham, and eggs you whipped up for me just now, you have my oath on it."

She let out a breath. "What is your second condition?"

That you share my bed for the weekend.

Oh, blessed saints! No! This was the brandy in him talking.

He quickly suppressed the errant thought.

The last thing he would ever do is hurt someone as kind as Viola. It was not her fault she was also luscious and lively, not to mention far more pleasant company than anyone outside of his own family. Nor was it her fault that he – when drunk and obviously delirious – desired her in this crass way.

Jillian would be so disappointed in him.

In truth, he was disappointed in himself, and quite detested himself for having such thoughts about the girl whose only intention was to help him. But he was a man, and had deprived himself of those needs far too long. There was no explanation for it other than his grief had gotten jumbled up with his anger and frustration. To put it in mathematical terms, grief plus anger and frustration had somehow equaled lust.

But why for Viola?

She was not the sort of girl he would ever touch.

"My lord? What is your second condition?"

Indeed, she was the decent sort he ought to be protecting, especially from him.

"That you help me select the young ladies to be invited." He studied her as her lovely eyes widened in obvious surprise. "It must be you, or I will not go through with it. Are you willing?"

CHAPTER 2

VIOLA SHOOK HER head and emitted a soft trill of laughter, unable to believe this brandy-soaked viscount knew what he was asking. "Me? Help you? I do not know the first thing about these society darlings. Truly, your mother or your sister-in-law will be far more adept at guiding you."

"But I want you," he said with a soft growl that shot warmth into her cheeks.

"To help you?" She shook her head again. "Fine. But do not blame me if you find them all unsuitable. The fault is squarely on you."

He crossed his heart, drawing her attention to his broad chest and the light ripple of his solid muscles visible beneath his wet shirt. "Blame falls entirely on me. Then we are agreed?"

"Dear heaven," she muttered, knowing this could turn into the biggest mistake of her life. What was she doing? For that matter, what was he thinking? He was a big, gorgeous brute of a viscount and so far above her station that she dared not even dream of a possible match between them.

Truly, not even dreams of him were safe.

He was out of her reach in every way possible.

Her answer to his request had to be a resounding no.

What she ought to do is chase him out of her kitchen before this went any further.

She took a deep breath and slowly let the air out as she said, "Yes."

Dear heaven again.

What had just come out of her mouth?

She had meant to refuse.

Oh, Viola. What a ninny you are.

His smile was genuinely openhearted. "Thank you."

She could not recall ever seeing him smile like this in the two years since his Lady Jillian had died. Perhaps this was a good step forward for him, but what about her path? He was climbing out of the deep well he had dug for himself and she seemed to be jumping right into it.

She shook her head.

All would be well if she remained sensible.

Was this not her best quality?

Nor had her father raised her to turn her back on those who sought their help. Even if the house party proved to be a disaster, it did not matter. What mattered was the viscount's willingness to take this important first step toward his recovery.

Her father was dying and she could do nothing to prevent it.

So why not help someone who could be saved?

She breathed a sigh, feeling better now that she had made this decision. After all, it was only a weekend house party, and they would have no need to see each other during it or ever again after it.

Indeed, if it turned out to be successful, he would likely return to London and begin accepting invitations to all the elite society affairs.

She would be forgotten, assuming she even entered his thoughts.

He seemed pensive now that he had made this first leap forward. Pensive and pleased, for his entire appearance seemed to lighten as he began to unburden himself. "My family and friends have been hounding me about getting back into circulation for over a year now. My parents, especially. They don't stop. I cannot bear to open their letters anymore. I know what each one is going to say."

"They write because they see you have gotten yourself stuck and worry about you."

"I know. This is why I have been drinking more heavily than usual. They are right, it is time I gave it a try. However, I am not sure I will ever be able to move on."

"The path does not have to be smooth. Indeed, I expect it will be quite bumpy. But at least you are now taking a first step."

"And yet, I cannot help feeling as though I am betraying Jillian." His eyes were a deep, turbulent blue as he leveled his gaze on her. "I have stuck you in the middle of the fray, haven't I?"

"I can always bow out of the planning if it looks as though my assistance is not working out."

He shook his head. "No, Viola. You are never going to be the problem. I think my stumbling to your doorway three nights this week is no coincidence. I did not come here to unburden myself to your father. It is you I wanted to see. You, with your sharp tongue and brutal honesty, is what I need. Think of yourself as my guardian angel."

"No, my lord." This was too much of a responsibility for her. She wanted to stay on his good side because she needed to think of her future and wanted a solid reference from him if she hoped to find a position as cook in a fine household. But to have him think of her as his very own angel? Someone to nourish his aching soul? "You are feeling generous toward me because I have just provided you with one of the most delicious breakfasts you have eaten in years."

He laughed. "All right, that must be the reason."

She hoped so for both their sakes.

She was not blind to how men responded to her, although she truly did not think she was prettier than any other young woman in Ardley. She dared not think he was looking upon her as his angel for unmentionable reasons, that he was famished for some form of nourishment other than an occasional breakfast from her.

She silently prayed she would be able to handle him. He knew how to behave in a civilized manner, but on the inside he was a raging beast because he was so hurt and angry.

A wounded bear.

And yet, he was so handsome on the outside, he made her heart ache.

Viola cast him a pained smile back. "When do we start?"

"As soon as possible. This is the right decision and I do not want to think too long about it or I will change my mind."

"I agree. The sooner we get underway, the better. Let me tend to my father first, see that he is fed and made comfortable after he gives his morning sermon. Then I will come up to Ardley Hall. Is that all right? Shall we say about noon today?"

"Yes, that will do." He appeared to want to say more, but merely gave a nod. "I had better make myself presentable for your visit."

She watched him stride out of her kitchen, and then hurried to the window to watch him make his way through the gate and onto the road to his home. Presentable? Ha! That man would look magnificent even if he were dressed in rags.

His home was a grand manor situated just up the hill from the vicarage, a cozy house despite its size and elegance. She had visited several times with her father over the years, more so when Lady Jillian was alive, and fully understood why the viscount missed his wife so much. She had made Ardley Hall a happy place for him and all who visited.

"Oh, Viola. What are you doing?" She closed the kitchen door and went on about her business, trying to finish as many chores as she could manage in order to take her mind off him and this house party she had foolishly agreed to help him plan.

She assisted her father in readying himself for the morning's church service, and then made certain he was comfortably settled in his study after the service. It was his habit to immediately work on the following day's sermon while that spiritual fervor was still fresh on his mind. "Papa, I won't be gone long. Mrs. Bligh will bring in your lunch shortly. Do you want me to wait until she does?"

Her father cast her a doting smile. "I shall be fine, child. Go run your errands."

She tucked a shawl around his shoulders and made certain his tea and freshly baked scones were within easy reach. He had grown so feeble, she wanted something nourishing always within his grasp. It did not matter that his midday meal was on the way.

He hardly ate anything these days, so he needed all the encouragement possible. "It isn't so much an errand as a stupid agreement to help out Lord Ardley. I don't know how I let him talk me into this foolishness."

Her father laughed. "You ought to feel honored. It means he trusts you above all others."

She rolled her eyes. "Then he has terrible judgment, doesn't he? I don't know the first thing about society or the marriage mart."

"But you understand people, Viola. This is what he is relying on you for. Is this not what you told me? That he needs to be set on his right path."

"With the right woman by his side." She shook her head. "How can I know who is the proper mate to his heart? This is someone he must choose for himself. What if he already found her in Lady Jillian and will never find this same bliss again? Is it wrong for all of us to force him into someone else's arms?"

"Child, you are not forcing him. He is the one seeking a way out of his misery and has asked for your help. Who knows? In helping him, you might also find your own path forward. He is not the only one stuck and refusing to move on."

"Papa, are you referring to me?"

"Yes, as you well know. Squire Haworth's son has shown quite a bit of interest in you. Why are you so resistant to his advances?"

She sighed. "No man is going to steal me away from you. Not George Haworth or Lord Ardley. Oh, Papa. I do wish I had refused Lord Ardley's request."

He patted her hand. "Is it so bad that your path and his are intertwined at the moment?"

"No, but it is quite disconcerting."

"You must do this for yourself, Viola. A recommendation from the viscount about your excellent cooking will get you hired by the finest houses in England. Truly, this is your best choice if you decide not to marry young Haworth. However, I do wish you would consider his offer more seriously. His father is a wealthy squire and George is his heir. He would give you a good life."

Her father was right. But cooking, not George Haworth, was

the way to securing her future and the viscount had promised to help.

Poor George.

She liked him, but did not desire him in the way a wife ought to desire a husband. He was a good man who deserved better than a tepid wife.

She kissed her father on his forehead and then hurried to Ardley Hall under a gloriously gentle breeze and bright sunshine. The church had been built over eight hundred years ago and so had the older parts of Ardley Hall. But Ardley Hall had been upgraded over the centuries by the ruling family whereas the church and vicarage remained as originally built.

Oh, what she would give for a modern amenity or two.

She passed by the viscount's sheep pasture and waved to Mrs. Bligh's son who tended his flock. "Good morning, Jeremy!"

"Good morning, Miss Viola. Are ye headed to the big house?"

She nodded. "I am."

"Try to keep out of his lordship's way then. He has been in a foul temper this past week."

"Oh, I'm so sorry. I'm headed there to see him now, but he won't dare be impolite to me."

Jeremy laughed. "That's true. Ye have the Almighty on yer side and he ain't about to mess with that."

A light breeze whipped the hem of her gown about her ankles as she strode through the impressive gate and walked up the drive toward the grand manor house. The thick stones walls had been painted a cheerful white and the shutters were a deep, forest green. The garden was beautifully maintained, and it would not be long before red roses burst into bloom along the trellises.

She was about to walk up to the front door, then realized perhaps she ought to go around to the back. She was hardly a distinguished visitor. But just as she was about to head to the servants entrance, the viscount himself happened to walk out of the stable. A slant of sunlight followed him as he marched toward her with a manly stride. Dear heaven, he looked every bit the Viking warrior with his head of golden hair and powerfully muscled body.

Even in dry clothes, he looked magnificent.

She blinked her eyes as he approached, trying hard to expunge the memory of his wet shirt clinging to his every muscle and sinew.

"No, Viola," he said with a light frown, startling her out of her wayward thoughts. "You are always to come to my front door."

"But–"

"I'll allow no protest. You are my guest."

"But you have engaged me to be your cook."

"I haven't yet. The party list comes first."

"But I am still–"

"Stop." He cast her a wry grin, his gorgeous eyes, the fathomless blue of an ocean, now shimmering with amusement. "How about we compromise?"

"Compromise?"

"You wish to go in through the servants entrance."

She nodded. "Yes. It is the only–"

"Oh, Viola. You are such a stubborn little thing. You insist on entering through the kitchen and I demand you come in through the front. Neither of us will give in, so here is my compromise. I'll give you a leg up and you can climb in through that window." He pointed to the bow window to the left of his front door.

His grin held devastating appeal as he fashioned a step out of his hands. "What do you say?"

She laughed. "Not on your life. You win, my lord. Front door it is."

"And this is how it shall always be for you." He held out his arm, obviously intending to treat her as a lady and escort her inside.

"Oh." She glanced at his forearm a moment before setting her hand on it.

Her insides curled.

The man was not only handsome as sin, but he was treating her as a fine lady.

Remember your place, Viola.

You are to be his cook.

But he led her into the parlor and offered her a seat in one of the elegant silk chairs before ringing for his butler. "Are you certain we ought to–"

"Yes, I am certain. We have work to do and it is best done here where my staff can see us and know we are doing nothing improper."

"When will you take me to the kitchen?"

"After we have made our guest list. I am not going to introduce you to my kitchen staff before we are certain there will be a weekend house party."

She cleared her throat. "All right, but just note that it is your guest list and not mine."

He arched an eyebrow. "Fine, I stand corrected. *My* list, not yours. I see that you are carrying a bag with you. May I ask what's inside?"

She nodded. "I've brought along several London newspapers known for the gossip they report."

He cast her another devastatingly attractive grin. "Why Miss Ruskin, I had no idea you indulged in their lurid tattle."

"Actually, it is my father who is the gossip fiend," she said with a merry lilt as she drew them out and handed one over to him. "These papers assist him in preparing his sermons. Fertile fodder, he calls it. There is always something sinful to be found in them. Adultery mostly, but also theft, hubris, dishonoring thy parents, an occasional Upper Crust murder. But they also hold useful information, such as who are this year's *ton* diamonds."

"Ah, that is helpful. We are to pore over this list of diamonds and then invite several of them to tempt me out of my grief?"

She nodded. "Yes, just a few this time. To invite them all would overwhelm you, I should think."

"Especially since I don't want any of them here." He raked a hand through his hair, obviously not liking the chore. "Who do you suggest?"

Her eyes widened. "Me? I don't know the first thing about these debutantes or their families. You are the one who has been out in society."

"I am the wrong person to trust with that decision. At the moment, I do not know what is up or what is down. I intend to leave the decision to you, for you have good intuition about people."

"I do not have special powers," she said with a vehement shake of her head. "If I did, I would be playing the horses at the Newmarket races and setting aside my winnings for a comfortable future for myself."

He chuckled at her jest. "Do not dismiss your instincts. They are quite excellent. Do you think I have not noticed?"

They paused in their conversation while his butler, one of her father's regular congregants, a kindly, older gentleman by the name of Mr. Greaves, scurried in. "My lord?"

"Tea and refreshments for me and Miss Ruskin."

"At once my lord," Mr. Greaves said, hurrying off before Viola had the chance to greet him.

But it was not long before he returned, rolling in a large tea cart. To her surprise, it was quite finely laden with an assortment of cold meats, cheeses, fruit, and cakes, in addition to tea. The cups, plates, and silverware set out were of the finest quality.

Perhaps too fine for her.

"Good afternoon, Mr. Greaves. You scurried away before I could properly greet you. How are you today?"

Apparently, it was not done to speak to the servants, something she realized when he looked upon her in obvious surprise and then turned to the viscount for guidance as to whether or not he should respond.

The viscount nodded.

"I am quite well, Miss Ruskin. I hope you enjoy the refreshments set out."

"I'm sure I will." She smiled at the man as he quietly backed out of the room.

"You startled him," the viscount said with some amusement.

She sighed. "You are treating me as you would an honored guest, but I am merely the vicar's daughter. Obviously, I do not know the rules in a fine house."

"I suppose we do have our rules, but kindness is always permitted. I do not fault my guests for being polite or showing courtesy to those in my employ." He poured her a cup of tea as he spoke, and then placed strawberries and a lemon cake on her plate. "We grow our own strawberries in the conservatory. Have you ever seen it?"

It felt so odd to be served by him, but he appeared to be quite comfortable in performing the task. "No, never. I have only ever been in this visitor's parlor and your back garden where Lady Jillian held her tea parties."

"Never been given a tour of my home?"

She shook her head. "Never. But I would love to see the conservatory, if I may?"

He nodded. "I'll show you this house from top to bottom before we are done with this project of ours. Let's get to work now, shall we?"

"Yes, but do you have a *Debrett's*? I'm sure you must. Having it close at hand will help."

"What for? To tell you who the noble families with a long lineage are as opposed to the crass and presumptuous *nouveau riche*?"

By his tone, she knew he was speaking with light sarcasm. "My lord, there is nothing wrong with *nouveau riche*. They bring fresh blood into the noble lines. I also suspect these interlopers with their new blood have been infiltrating the aristocratic bloodlines for centuries. Girls were often betrothed during childhood to men they never would have chosen for themselves. So they discreetly sought their…you know…elsewhere."

"Pleasures?" He grinned. "You are blushing quite profusely, Viola. I thought you were forthright and confident about everything."

"Not all things."

"I am merely teasing you. You may kick me if I provoke you. You are a little know-it-all, but there is an innocence about you I find quite refreshing. This makes you irresistible to tease."

"You had better stay on my good side, my lord," she said, grinning back at him, "or I might select utter crones for you and make your weekend party a misery."

He laughed. "You will never do it. You are far too softhearted and want very badly to set me on the right path. This why you are perfect for the task. Earnest, honest. Caring. Ah, you are blushing again."

"I am not used to such compliments."

"Accept them as facts, for these are your qualities. Everyone thinks so." He took a sip of his tea, the delicate cup looking quite out of place in his big hands. They were nice hands, his fingers long and well-proportioned, but not smooth as one would expect from a gentleman of leisure. Well, he was often out in the fields with his farmers and did take interest in his mills, stables, and other enterprises. The only duty he really shirked from was in finding another wife upon whom to breed heirs.

"My lord, I think we should stop talking about me and concentrate on the qualities you seek in the young lady you would take as your wife."

He grimaced. "My head will explode if I am required to give it thought. Can you not simply decide for me?"

"Absolutely not!" Her eyes widened in horror. What was wrong with this man? She would kick him if he weren't in such obvious torment. "I know this has to be difficult for you."

"It is excruciating. Is there not another way?"

She took a deep breath.

Why was he making this so hard for both of them?

"All right. What if…that is…" She took another deep breath. "Should I…perhaps…should I assume you would like her to have the same qualities as Lady Jillian?"

"No!" He raked a hand through his hair. "I am not looking for a twin of my wife. Do you understand what I am trying to say?"

She nodded. "The young lady must bring her own unique qualities to the marriage."

"Yes, Viola. That is it exactly. You instinctively understand this. And this is why you must be the one to help me."

He seemed so convinced of it, she knew it was a waste of breath to attempt to dissuade him. "Let us start with another question, better phrased than the first. What qualities in general attract you?"

"Do you mean the physical attributes of a young lady?"

"No, these *ton* diamonds are all going to be beautiful. But I refer to the less obvious qualities. Do you prefer someone quiet and thoughtful? Or someone cheerful who enjoys company? How intelligent does she need to be? Must she have musical talents? Must she enjoy a domestic life? Or a society life? You know, constant parties, teas, other social affairs?"

She was trying to be serious, but he simply looked stunned.

Perhaps it was too much to toss at him all at once.

She sipped the last of her tea and resumed the conversation from another angle. "Let us forget about these ladies for now. How about we make a list of the friends and family you wish to invite, get those squared away first."

He cast her a wry smile. "You are treating me like a little boy again."

She shook her head and laughed softly. "No, my lord. I shall never mistake you for that."

Little boys did not have rugged, manly faces or eyes that bore straight into a girl's soul.

"Would you care for more tea, Viola?"

"Yes, thank you. My throat is rather parched since I have been doing far too much talking. I shall stop now and give you the chance to speak your mind."

He filled her cup with a jasmine tea that was her favorite and too expensive to ever purchase for herself. Perhaps the viscount's cook, Mrs. Stringer, had prepared it especially for her. Or Mr. Greaves might have suggested it when he ordered the refreshments.

Her father had been vicar in this parish for decades and she had grown up knowing all of these congregants and their families, often visiting their homes when someone took ill, or simply delivering food if they hit a rough patch in their lives.

She knew them as well as one would know one's own family. "My lord? Do you not like the idea of starting with a list of friends and family?"

To her frustration, he continued to say nothing for the longest while.

Was he going to back out of this endeavor?

She clenched her teeth and forced a smile, wanting to be

patient with him but not about to sit around and pamper him. As the silence persisted, she set down her cup and rose. "Perhaps you might ponder these questions tonight and send word to me tomorrow once you are ready to talk."

He emitted a low growl. "Sit down, Viola."

Goodness, that sounded commanding.

She plopped back in her chair.

"And stop tossing me those impatient looks. I do not need your assistance with the others on my guest list, only with the young ladies to be invited. The select *few* young ladies to be invited."

She gripped the sides of her chair to calm herself down, for he had never used this tone of voice on her before, not even this morning while drunk and hating himself. It was quite daunting. "Um, how many is a few?"

"Let's start with three."

"Only three?"

"I do not want them all descending on me like a plague of locusts."

"Well, that is going to charm them," she said dryly, wishing she had better control of her sharp tongue. She understood this was difficult for him, but that did not give him the right to take it out on her. "They'll sense at once this is all you think of them."

"They might, but none of them will care. I am wealthy in my own right and next in line to an earldom. They will overlook just about any failings in me."

"You are quite cynical. I am sure the parents of any of these girls will want to see them happily settled to a man who will not demean their precious daughters. What good parent would ever want to see their children unhappy?"

"No, Viola. What any good parent wants is to see their daughter well settled. Whether she is content or not is up to her. The marriage does not have to be a love match, but must provide comfort and financial security for her and her offspring. The rest of it, what she makes of her life, is up to her."

He had gentled his tone, and although he still spoke with irritating cynicism, she could not deny that much of what he said was true. "Seems you understand this game far better than I do.

Why am I even here? You have dismissed all of my ideas."

"I have not dismissed them or you. The truth is, I have no idea what I want. All I know is what I don't want, and that is someone who is a pale imitation of Jillian."

She groaned. "You are going to hate me again."

He arched a golden eyebrow and cast her a wry smile. "I do not hate you at all. What do you wish to ask me?"

"I did not know Lady Jillian very well."

"And now you want to ask me about her traits? What qualities she had that should not be repeated in my next wife?" He shook his head. "Do not stress yourself about it, for it is not something I can ever answer. Let's just start with physical appearance. I do not want someone who could be a sister to Jillian in looks."

She munched on her lemon cake, swallowing the bite before continuing. "That does make it easier for me, my lord. These newspapers do offer a general description of these debutantes. Very general. But as I said earlier, they are all considered beautiful, so you should not be too disappointed. As for their temperaments, that will be a little harder to decipher from these news accounts."

He leaned forward now and gazed at his boots as he spoke. "Obviously, I do not want someone quiet as a mouse or someone who chatters incessantly. But there is a wide range in between. Nor is it important whether she enjoys the country or prefers London, for she can set herself up wherever she pleases once I have my heirs."

Viola shot to her feet again. "Let me make one thing clear to you, my lord. If you think I am going to help you find a young lady you intend to toss aside once she pops out sons for you, then we are done here."

Dear heaven!

Why had she said that?

Who was she to impose her own love requirements on anyone, certainly not the viscount and his diamond of a bride?

He growled at her again. "I am going to tie you to your chair if you keep bouncing up in indignation every time I express a thought that is not to your liking. You are not the only one permitted to express thoughts here. Sit down, Viola."

She cast him a defiant glare, but sat down.

Then she wiped the stupid bit of defiance off her face.

Obtaining a good reference as a cook was vital to her.

This was a chance of a lifetime and she was kicking it away. "I'm sorry, my lord. I was in the wrong."

"No, you weren't. And stop apologizing to me every time we disagree." He had a remarkably commanding air about him, a tone that ought to have sent cold shivers through her body but instead her shivers were quite hot.

"I'm sor–" She shook her head and laughed. "All right, I'm *not* sorry."

His smile sent more improper shivers through her.

"Let's get back to business." His voice was calm and even, but there was unmistakable steel beneath his words.

He leaned forward once more and rested an arm upon his thigh. "I've frightened you. Never be afraid of me, Viola. I shall never hurt you. I want your opinions, but I do not want you hopping about like a chicken on one leg every time I say something that displeases you. Is it not obvious I am struggling to figure out what I want?"

"Yes, it is. Just as I am struggling to figure out why you should want my help. I have never been married, never even had a beau."

"What about George Haworth?"

She blushed. "He is not my beau."

He arched an eyebrow. "But the poor man obviously hopes to be. He is besotted with you."

How would he know this?

Well, it did not matter. "My lord, I was not raised in elegant society and do not even fully understand the rules of our more casual country society. I know my wish to hold out for love may be viewed upon by some as foolish."

"No, Viola. It is not foolish to want such a thing. Unfortunately for many women, it is simply impractical. They would starve unless they found a protector. But you are quite unique and have the means to carve out your own future."

"Thank you, I'm glad you think so. Still, it makes me very

uncomfortable to undertake this project with you. I do not understand why I am really here."

This genuinely surprised him, she could see it in his expression. "Do you think I have a nefarious purpose in mind? You are a pretty girl, but it is your intelligence and good sense that I seek. Nothing else."

She nodded. "You do not make me uncomfortable in *that* way. But I am no more clever than the next person. What do you see in me that singles me out?"

"You do not give yourself enough credit. I cannot say precisely what it is about you. But I am a good judge of character and know you are someone worthy of my trust."

"That is a great compliment, my lord."

"It is the truth." He leaned back in his chair. "Another truth is that I really have no idea what I want in a wife. It is easier for me to factor out love because I don't know if I will ever find it. So I am better served concentrating on seeking someone who will be a tolerable companion."

"Merely tolerable is unacceptable." She clutched the arms of her chair, willing herself not to leap up again.

He cast her a wry smile, knowing exactly what she was feeling.

But he said nothing, remaining silent for an agonizingly long moment before he spoke. "Intelligence and common sense are important to me. So you see, this is why I chose you to help me. I want those qualities in a wife as well. Tenderness, not just toward me but toward others in general. I saw enough suffering during the war to last me a lifetime. I will not abide a wife who uses her status as my viscountess to step on people."

He continued to regard her, his gaze not leaving her face. "I want someone with opinions, but not a jumping frog who will leap out of her seat every time I express one she does not like."

Viola wanted to leap out of her seat again, for the barb was aimed straight at her. "I shall make sure she has all the qualities of a sloth."

He chuckled. "Nor do I wish to wait a hundred years before I get an opinion out of the woman. Can we not settle somewhere between jumping frog and moribund sloth?"

"All right. I shall look for a chipmunk."

He burst out laughing, something she did not think he had done in years. "Gad, you are not going to make this easy for me, are you?"

"No, nor do you want me to or else you would have asked someone who would toady to your every whim."

"True enough. Just look for someone with qualities similar to yours. A little less opinionated, perhaps. But clever. Kind. Quick witted. Also, she must have a cheerful aspect. I already wallow in my own self-made gloom. But I do not want someone who will chirp at me all morning. A man likes quiet when he reads his morning newspaper and drinks his coffee."

"I will do my best, but you must realize it is an impossible feat for me to discern the right young ladies to invite when all I have to go on are these gossip rag accounts."

"I know. Select three and we shall invite them up with their families. I'll make a list of family and friends to be invited. Leave that to me."

"I still think we ought to write to your mother and ask for her comments on our proposed list of young ladies before invitations are actually sent out."

"No, I am not asking my mother."

"You are behaving like a stubborn, little boy again. How about your brother's wife, Daisy?"

"Even worse. She is clever and wonderful, but she is also a Farthingale and will immediately have all her relatives meddling in my matrimonial affairs."

"How about asking your brother?"

"Gabriel? My younger brother? I am not asking my little brother for advice on women."

"Good grief, you can be quite irritating. He is a full grown man now and happily married, not to mention his being as much of a war hero as you are. Your parents must be so proud of both of you. I would give anything to have had siblings to turn to in my time of need."

"Girls do this. Boys do not."

"How about your grandmother then? You always speak so

fondly of Lady Eloise."

"No, it would be rude to seek her opinion when I do not plan to invite her."

Viola gasped, started to leap out of her chair again, but caught herself in time and sank back. "You are not going to invite your own grandmother?"

He leaned forward once more. "It is too much of a trip for her."

"A day's ride from London? Is she in poor health? Then let us put off discussion of this house party. You ought to be visiting her instead. It will be the best medicine for her."

"I will visit her soon, but that will not get in the way of our planning."

"If you go now, you might also have a firsthand look at your *ton* diamonds. Is this not a far better idea? Then it is a simple matter of inviting the ones who appeal to you."

"No, I shall have this house party first. The moment I step foot in London, the deuced invitations will start arriving. Nor will I put it past my well meaning parents, or Daisy and her family, to contrive occasions to match me up with some peahen they deem suitable for me." He regarded her steadily. "It is a matter of battle tactics, Viola."

She tipped her head and regarded him in confusion. "What do you mean?"

"I do not control the London battleground. So I need to bring the enemy into my territory where I shall have greatest advantage over the outcome."

"Finding a wife is not a battle, my lord."

"This is where you are wrong. Has the marriage mart not been described as exactly this? I am in command here and in full control of my surroundings. Here is where I shall live with my wife, so it is important for me to see her in what is to be her home. I want to know how she behaves around my servants. I intend to get a full report from my housekeeper, Mrs. Lester, at the end of each day."

"That is quite devious of you."

"Not at all. It is a matter of protecting myself."

"And what of your friends and family? Will you ask for reports from them, too?"

He shook his head. "No, but they will toss in their opinions anyway. They will deem it important that I should know their thoughts. However, they will only see the false face any of these diamonds want them to see. It is the opinion of my staff that will matter most to me, for they are the ones who are likely to be dismissed and mistreated. Servants do not count as people, you see."

"That is awful."

"It is the way of the *ton* and why I prefer to live in Ardley. Any potential wife of mine had better like it, too. I do not intend to change my ways and settle in London."

She cast him a wry smile. "Another reason why I am so wrong for this task. I have never been to London. Oxford and Coventry are the extent of my travels."

"We'll have to remedy that."

"Oh, I suppose I will get to London eventually. It will be a while yet. I do not dare leave my father. Besides, it is beautiful here. Why should I ever want to leave?" But she would have to settle elsewhere eventually. Perhaps her next position would be as cook in a London household, or she might seek a situation in a grand estate overlooking the sea. She'd heard from several parishioners that Cornwall was lovely.

She hoped not to have to think about this for a very long while.

But once her father was gone…where would life take her?

And would she ever see Alexander Dayne, third Viscount Ardley, this man of her dreams, again?

CHAPTER 3

"LADY SYBIL'S FATHER is a duke," Viola muttered, scribbling notes on a sheaf of paper while seated at the small writing desk in a corner of Alexander's parlor several days later. The task of whittling his choices down to three was proving harder than expected, especially since he was enjoying Viola's company far too much and was in no hurry to see their time together end.

"Is this supposed to impress me?" Alexander drew a chair close and now studied her as he settled in beside her. She looked quite pretty seated there, so earnestly attending to their project. The desk had belonged to his grandmother, Lady Eloise, purchased when she was young and newly married to his grandfather, both of them residing in marital bliss at Ardley Hall.

"Your offspring would have a duke for a grandfather. One of them might even inherit his title."

"Do not be impressed by titles," Alexander said, picking the *Debrett's* up from the small writing table and perching it on his lap. They had been pouring over the gossip rags and whatever books on heritage and heraldry found in his extensive library for several hours now. "Lady Sybil's father is the Duke of Preston, an intolerant blowhard and an arse, pardon my language. All that can be said of him is that he is a boor to everyone, nobleman and servant alike."

"All the more reason his poor daughter must be eager to get out from under his thumb."

"Or she might have inherited his ogrish ways."

"Invite her to your house party and we shall see."

"But that would require inviting her parents as well."

Viola turned to him, her dark eyes wide and so prettily framed by long, dark lashes. "Oh, I see your point. Well, let us set her name aside for now. But I do want to return to her before we finalize your list. I hate to think of her as having been browbeaten all her life by a bullying windbag of a father. She might thrive under the guidance of a loving husband."

Alexander knew he should keep an open mind, but there was no way in hell he was going to attach himself to the Duke of Preston. "Who's mentioned next in that gossip rag?"

"The Earl of Chartoff's daughter, Marianne. That is a lovely name."

"The man is an utter dimwit. So is his wife. Not a functioning brain between them. I hope his daughter does not take after them."

Viola sighed, set down her quill pen, and turned to him once again. "There are fifteen diamonds on this list I've put together. We have gone through seven so far and you have found fault with every one of them. Are you sure you do not want to go to London and simply have a look at these young ladies for yourself?"

"Absolutely not."

She cast him a delicate smile. "My lord, you do realize you are behaving like a stubborn, little boy again."

He grunted in amusement. "Yes, but so what? It is my prerogative to be as thickheaded as I like. By the way, I think you ought to call me Alex when we are in private. I am confiding my heart to you and it seems ridiculous to maintain formality now that I am…in effect, I am trusting you with my very heart."

She paled, the delicacy of her features quite obvious as the color drained from her face. And it was a beautiful face, for Viola had softly arched eyebrows and an equally soft, rounded chin. Her nose was slender and slightly on the long side which he liked better than those little, squashed noses others deemed adorable and delightful.

Her lips were full and generous, and her entire face lit up when she smiled.

She had finely sculpted cheekbones and little, rounded ears.

Atop it all was a head of chestnut hair that resembled dark silk and would be exquisite to the touch. So would her body be exquisite if he ever dared put a hand on the girl…which he would not. "Fine, don't call me Alex. Keep to the ridiculous formality, if you prefer. As for those seven struck off the list, that still leaves eight to review. Out of those eight, we only need to find three."

She glanced at the clock on the fireplace mantel. "Would you mind terribly if we resumed this discussion tomorrow? I really must get back to my father."

He shut the *Debrett's* and rose along with her. "I'll walk you home."

She shook her head. "I am fine walking on my own. I'll leave those juicy gossip rags with you to peruse at your leisure."

"Must I?"

"Yes, you must," she said, sounding like a prim schoolmistress again. But there was a softness to her voice that he found immensely attractive and gave him naughty thoughts.

He tamped those down immediately.

"I'll tuck those gossip sheets away or poor Greaves will be scandalized." He took her gently by the arm to lead her into the entry hall. "You are not going to walk home, and certainly not on your own. Give me a moment and I'll have my carriage readied."

"That is ridiculous. I am only going to the vicarage which is just down the hill. It is a lovely day and the walk will do me good."

"Very well, but I'll escort you. No protest, Viola."

She looked up at him with her big, soft eyes. "What will everyone think?"

"Nothing at all, unless you behave as though you have something to hide. Do you?"

She blushed furiously. "No, of course not."

He released her arm. "Then there is no problem. Greaves and Mrs. Lester already know that you are helping me organize a house party and choosing which eligible young ladies to invite. Greaves knew it within minutes of your arrival because he is an incorrigible snoop and not at all discreet. Neither of them think anything of our meeting regularly in my parlor, open to anyone's view. They know it is all business, and will not even raise an eyebrow in surprise when they learn you are also to cook the specially crafted meals for the event."

He hoped that sounded convincing.

He would deal firmly and swiftly with any harmful gossip that arose.

They strolled out the front door and toward the massive, wrought iron gates visible in the distance that served as the entryway to his property. He glanced at Viola, noting her sturdy walking boots and her practical gown. It was not fancy at all, just a dark green muslin devoid of all adornment. Yet, she looked elegant despite the gown's lack of any lace trim.

Jeremy, the local boy who tended his sheep, waved at Viola and was about to call out to her, but suddenly stopped when he noticed who was walking beside her. "My lord," he said, his eyes wide and questioning as he bowed.

Alexander took a moment to acknowledge the young lad and ask after the flock.

The boy's gaze kept darting between him and Viola, who was blushing again. Blessed saints, the girl needed to learn how to hide her expressions. Why was she embarrassed? They had done nothing wrong. "Miss Ruskin, come along. Your father is awaiting our return."

"Yes, my lord."

She scampered by his side. "Um, you do not need to walk me to the door."

"Yes, I do. It is only polite that I stop in and greet your father." No matter that he hadn't been at all polite the other the day when drunk and sprawled out in front of the vicarage. "As for you, I shall see you at noon tomorrow. I'll have Mrs. Stringer prepare a proper luncheon for us."

He glanced up at the sky and the gathering clouds. "If it is raining, I will send my carriage down to pick you up. No discussion on this, Viola. I can tell you for certain that walking around with one's clothes soaking wet is not pleasant."

She tried to stifle a grin, but failed.

Two pink stains now marked her cheeks. "I'm sorry."

"Do not apologize to me. I deserved the dousing. However, don't ever do it again."

She could not have missed the steel in his voice.

"I won't. I give you my word of honor."

They spoke no more as they reached the vicarage and he was led in to see her father. Viola ran into the kitchen to hide out with Mrs. Bligh, the woman who served as cook, maid, and general housekeeper in their small home.

Vicar Ruskin looked quite tired, but he greeted Alexander with a cheerful smile. "I hope my daughter has not plagued you too badly."

"No, she is extremely helpful. I assume she confided my plans to you."

Her father nodded. "She tells me everything. I hope these first meetings have proved productive."

"They have. She will join me tomorrow at this same time, if that does not inconvenience you."

"No inconvenience at all, my lord. I ought to be thanking you for getting her out of the house. Once her chores are done, she has nothing to do but worry about me. We've had to cut back quite a bit on our activities because of my health. It is not good for her. In truth, you are doing me a service."

"Let me know if I can do anything for your comforts." He glanced toward the door to make certain it was closed. "As for your daughter, I do not want you to worry about her future."

The man's face lost all cheerfulness and his eyes began to cloud with tears. "How can I not? She will be all alone in the world once I am gone. It is my greatest fear and my greatest worry. The little I have set aside for her to inherit will not go far, at best allowing for a few luxuries if she scrimps and saves on everything else. It is not nearly enough to provide security and independence throughout her life. Yet, she will not relent and agree to marry George Haworth."

"You cannot force a girl like Viola to give her heart to someone she does not love."

"But I fear so greatly for her if she remains on her own. The world out there can be cold and hard."

"She will not be unprotected. I shall see her safely settled in a good house. She thinks to work as a cook. I've tasted her food and it is quite excellent. She has talent, but I believe she is more suited to be a companion to a dowager rather than to be toiling in a kitchen. Perhaps my grandmother or one of her friends will take her in. I will make the arrangements when that time comes. Upon my oath, I will not abandon her. Consider her under my family's protection. I hope it will not be needed for a good long while yet."

The old man cast him a shaky smile. "That would ease my mind greatly. Thank you, my lord."

Alexander placed a hand on his arm. "Just work on getting yourself better. Do not worry about Viola. My family will look after her. We will never let her come to harm."

He purposely included mention of his family because he understood very well the vicar's concerns about him, an unmarried viscount, and Viola being lovely and vulnerable. To tell the vicar he alone intended to take personal interest in seeing Viola safely settled would cause the man to worry even more about his intentions.

Indeed, Viola was young and beautiful, but her family was not even of the landed gentry in rank. Not the sort of woman a man in Alexander's position could ever marry without raising eyebrows. But she was just the sort a man in his position would take on as his mistress.

This had to be the vicar's greatest fear, especially since his daughter was too independent for her own good. She would settle for nothing less than a love marriage, which meant she would have no husband to protect her.

The old man could not even marry her off to a good man like George Haworth before he passed.

Viola would not hear of it.

Alexander could see the vicar was tiring rapidly. "I'll be on my way now. Your daughter has given me work to prepare for tomorrow. She is a hard taskmaster. I had better return to my studies or risk being ordered to sit in a corner and wear a dunce cap."

That made her father chuckle. "I shall ask her to go easy on you, my lord."

He nodded. "Much appreciated."

He left the vicar's study and stuck his head in the kitchen in search of Viola, but only Mrs. Bligh was around.

She noticed him in the doorway and immediately set aside her mixing bowl to bob a curtsey. "My lord."

"Good day, Mrs. Bligh. Where is Miss Ruskin?"

"Out back taking down the laundry, m'lord. Shall I fetch her?"

"No, just let her know that I have returned to Ardley Hall." He strode out, keeping his eyes on the road and not glancing back at the vicar's residence. Viola was still in his thoughts, but he was not going to seek her out again today.

It was ridiculous to consider that he already missed her company.

In his own defense, she was remarkably comfortable to be around. Perhaps it was something in her manner that put him at ease. She wasn't noisy nor was she irritatingly quiet as a mouse. She was just…there. Perfectly there and ready to engage him but not chew his ear off.

An odd feeling of contentment flooded through him whenever they were together, especially the occasional times she would look up from scribbling her notes at his grandmother's old writing desk and smile at him. It felt as though she belonged there, as though the room was not complete without her in it.

"Bloody hell," he muttered, raking a hand through his hair.

The girl was too much on his mind lately.

What was that about?

He returned home and went directly into his study to catch up on the day's work he had neglected because of his attention to the house party planning. He also called for Mrs. Lester before he became lost in those documents piled atop his massive desk. His was much larger and sturdier than the decorative writing desk used by Viola during their sessions.

"My lord, you summoned me."

"Yes, Mrs. Lester. I wanted to advise you that Miss Ruskin will be dining with me at midday tomorrow. Kindly let Mrs. Stringer know I will be having company. If the weather is nice, we shall dine on the terrace. Otherwise, the summer dining room will do. Set her place next to mine. It is not a social occasion. We shall be working as we eat."

"Very good, my lord."

He spent the rest of the afternoon reviewing contracts relating to Dayne family business matters and then addressing village of Ardley requests with his estate manager, a good man by the name of Charles Wilson. "What else, Wilson?"

"The recent storm damaged the roof on several cottages. Those roofs need to be repaired before the next heavy rains arrive."

"All right. Put our men to it immediately. What else?"

"Some trees fell across the roadway, no doubt their roots were loosened by the storm. We've started clearing them off, but the surrounding trees need to be checked to ensure their roots are firm. Also, portions of the road need to be repaired."

"Finish clearing the trees first since the road needs to remain unobstructed, then attend to the cottage roofs. We'll look to check out the upright trees and patch up the damaged road last, assuming it is still passable."

"It is. Just rutted. I'll advise the merchants and farmers to drive their wagons with care over that strip."

Alexander finished his work by early evening and retired to his bedchamber with every intention of reading while sipping a particularly fine brandy. One glass was all he would allow himself. No more drinking himself into oblivion. Viola was not going to find him sprawled on the road in front of the vicarage tomorrow morning or any other morning ever again.

The evening was warm, so he stripped out of his clothes, washed up, and wrapped a towel around his waist before settling into one of the cushioned armchairs beside the unlit hearth. He'd placed the small pile of gossip rags Viola had brought along today atop a small table beside his chair.

Settling in, he began to read by lamplight. "Who is Lord M? And Lady B?"

He had been so out of touch with all that was going on outside of Ardley, he did not pick up on who these misbehaving individuals were. Yet, human nature never changed. The names might differ over the years, but the transgressions were always the same. Adultery, debauchery. Gambling. The occasional illegal duel where the stupid sods, assuming they survived, had to flee to the Continent until the scandal of it died down.

As the midnight hour came and went, Alexander set aside the batch of gossip papers and strode onto his balcony to study the stars. But there were almost none to be seen amid the gathering clouds. The air had turned damp, no doubt a harbinger of rain to come.

He felt the sticky breeze against his skin, and hoped the rain shower would pass quickly during the night. He did not want it lingering through the morning, for it would only delay repairs that needed to be made. Working in the rain was miserable, and he'd had much experience with it during the war years, trying to move artillery over muddy ground, the hours it took to pull a single cannon over a hillock.

The scents of war came flooding back to him as well. The wet wool of their uniforms. The acrid scent of smoke in the air. The mix of mud and blood and grass.

The awful scent of decayed flesh.

He shook his head and returned to the present.

But his present thoughts were all on Viola.

On winter days, when the trees were bare of foliage, he was able to see all the way to the vicarage and beyond to the town of Ardley. But at this time of the year, the trees were lush and green, mostly obscuring his view. He saw little more than an occasional torchlight burning in the distance as the wind shifted the branches to allow for the briefest opening.

A gust rustled through the leaves as he stood looking into the night and he noticed a light glowing through one of the vicarage windows. An upstairs window, which meant one of the bedchambers.

Viola's perhaps?

"What are you doing?" he muttered, thinking of her again and not in any polite way.

He closed his eyes to imagine her removing her gown and

running a damp cloth over her delicate skin as she washed up for the evening. He imagined her taking off her chemise, her hair unpinned and her body naked in that moment before she put on her nightgown. It had to be a cotton nightgown because young ladies as prim as Viola did not wear silk.

It was of no matter since the goal of any hound was to get the lady in question naked.

He groaned, imagining Viola in this way on his bed, her long, dark hair fanned out in waves against his pillow, her breasts full and waiting to be cupped in his hands.

Those lush mounds would taste so sweet on his tongue.

His body responded, blood pumping hot through his veins. What he truly wanted was to pump himself into Viola. It was a terrible thought to have about her, and a terrible ache he dared not ever fulfill.

The fault was his entirely.

Was he thinking of her simply because she had been with him today?

He blamed this inexplicable lust on his prolonged celibacy, for he had not been with a woman since Jillian's passing. In truth, his celibacy had begun years earlier, after Jillian had given birth to Molly. The experience of childbirth had frightened his wife so badly, she never wanted to undergo it again.

The arrangement had not pleased him, but he accepted it because Jillian had not denied him intimate pleasures in other ways. He had not reached the point of seeking another woman to satisfy him fully.

But not to have more children?

Perhaps never to have a son?

This had crushed him.

Yet, he and Jillian had been friends since childhood. He could not see himself abandoning her for someone else. What was the point? He would never have divorced her, so any children sired outside of marriage would have been illegitimate. Even if he supported them, which he would have done without question, they would never have been rightful heirs.

Besides, he had pledged to love and honor Jillian.

He had never broken that vow.

Perhaps because he was moving forward to seek a wife, those sexual urges were now flooding back with breathtaking force. Still, he could have conjured any woman in his bed, so why Viola? He'd certainly bedded more than his share in his university days. Lush, robust young women with big breasts and hearty appetites for sex.

But no, his thoughts were on the vicar's daughter.

He did not think the girl had ever been kissed.

He would have seen a knowing look in her eyes when mentioning George Haworth. But no, the poor, besotted man had gotten nowhere with her.

He did not know why this gave him so much satisfaction.

George was no milksop and had to be aching over his unfulfilled desires.

That was another thing…how many of those *ton* diamonds were still virgins? It would not be hard to tell. A woman's eyes always gave her away.

Viola was achingly clueless.

He set aside the towel and climbed into his empty bed, feeling particularly tense and tortured tonight.

He awoke at his usual early hour, washed and dressed, and then spent the rest of the morning pacing and grumbling, so that his staff ducked under the furniture or behind doors to avoid him whenever he strode their way. "Greaves! I see you hiding behind that door."

His put-upon butler sighed and stepped forward. "Yes, my lord."

"Do you see her walking up the drive yet?" It was two minutes to noon and he had been fiddling with his watch fob, pulling it out to check on the time and then sticking it back in his vest pocket, since ten o'clock this morning.

"My lord, is there a reason you are pacing like a jungle cat? You will frighten Miss Viola if you greet her with that glower on your face."

He sighed. "It is this house party business that has me on edge."

Greaves retained a stoic expression, giving no hint of what he thought about holding a house party at Ardley Hall. The man had seen what he and Viola were reading these past few days and must have overheard some of their discussion. "What do you think of the idea?"

Greaves looked like he wanted to dig a hole in the floor and sink into it. "It isn't my place to say. Nor would I ever listen in on your and Miss Ruskin's private discussions."

"That is utter rot," Alexander said with a jovial laugh. He wasn't trying to keep it a high level secret and did not care that all his staff knew of his plans by now because Greaves was an impossible tattletale, worse than any woman in his employ. His *trusted* butler must have spilled the news to everyone seated at the staff dining table on that very first night and continued to fill them in ever since.

"I mean it sincerely, Greaves. What do you think? Should we hold one?"

The man cast Alexander an indulgent look. "It will be nice to have the house filled with music and laughter again, my lord."

He raked a hand through his hair. "Everyone seems to think so. Am I the only dissenter?"

"It is your house and your life to do with as you wish. But I do believe it has already done you some good. Just the planning of it with Miss Ruskin has put you in better spirits. Perhaps it is Miss Ruskin who is cheering up your day, for you seem to walk around like an angry bear whenever she is not around."

"Speaking of the little devil," Alexander said, unable to hide his grin. "Here she comes."

Greaves hurried to open the door as Viola approached the house.

She strode in, her cheeks pink and her eyes alight, just as the clock struck the noon hour. "Good day, Greaves," she said merrily. "I believe I am right on time."

Alexander now stepped forward to take the bag she was carrying out of her hands. "More London gossip rags?"

She nodded. "I had no idea my father hoarded so many. These are last year's batch to add to this year's gossip rags I brought with me earlier. It cannot hurt to expand our list of marriageable diamonds."

"Because you think I am going to find fault with the last eight on this year's list?"

She cast him a heartwarming smile. "Oh, Lord Ardley. I do not merely think it. I know you will."

He could not help but chuckle at her impertinent remark. "Oh, ye of little faith."

She was probably right since he had no enthusiasm whatsoever for this project. Greaves' words rang true. He was enjoying Viola's company more than any planning for a house party.

She followed him as he led the way into the summer dining room. The sky was still overcast and boded rain within the hour.

"My lord, how did you sleep last night? The air was so hot and thick, I found it impossible to fall asleep. And did you hear the thunder and lightning in the wee hours? Startled me right out of bed. I was sure one of those bolts was a direct hit on the church spire. But I went up there this morning and all appeared fine."

He paused. "You went up to inspect the spire on your own?"

She nodded. "Of course. Who else was to do it? Certainly not my father."

"Viola, why did you not send word to me? I would have had my estate manager take a look. Wilson's an excellent man."

"But he is your man. Not mine. I could not impose."

"Yes, from now on this is exactly what you must do. What if some of the stones had loosened and you were hurt?"

She arched an eyebrow. "Oh, then I would not be able to cook for you and your elegant guests."

"I do not care about those guests or your cooking for them," he said with marked exasperation. "This has to do with your safety."

"I am duly admonished," she said, sitting in the chair he now held out for her beside his own. "When do you think to send Mr. Wilson to us? I ought to be there to show him the way up. You see, there is a simple trick to dangling on–"

He was standing beside her and now turned her chair around so that she faced him, startling her as he easily lifted her along with it and then place his hands on either side of her chair's back to trap her in. "You are not to go up there on your own again."

That delicious little apple in her throat bobbed up and down. "Perhaps not again today. But someone must attend to it. That someone is usually me since neither Mrs. Bligh nor my father is in any condition to manage it."

"Not anymore, Viola. Promise me. Never again. I will take responsibility for it from this day forward." His face was inches from hers, too close.

He eased away, dangerously aware of her body and her deliciously fruity scent. What was it? Peach? Apple? Strawberry? All his favorites. Perhaps a mix of all three. He didn't know and didn't care. He just wanted to lose himself licking her.

Oh, Lord.

He set her and the chair back in their proper position.

She was a light, little thing.

Probably delightful to carry in his arms.

"Why are you being so apishly protective over me? Afraid to lose your party planner? I have been climbing the stairs to the spire and walking on the roof for years without incident." She nibbled her lip as he continued to scowl at her.

He emitted a low growl. "You are not to walk on that roof."

"Admonished again. All right. Done. No more climbing for me, at least not until your man checks it out."

"Nor afterward. Did you not hear what I just said? My responsibility. From here on out, you send for me."

"Fine."

He breathed a sigh of relief, not quite sure why he was behaving like a protective ape, just as Viola had accused. "Let's talk about the last eight young ladies on the list. I did some research into each of their families last night."

"Truly?" She looked at him in surprise.

"You assigned this homework to me, did you not?"

"Yes, but I did not think…excellent. And?"

"It is a good thing you brought more names over today."

She groaned. "What is wrong with those eight?"

"Must I detail each one for you?"

"Yes, because it is obvious you are trying to find fault with all of them instead of considering them with an impartial eye. Are you certain all of them must be ruled out?"

"Two might do," he grudgingly admitted. "Lady Charlotte Nevins and Lady Aurora Gaston."

"Lovely names, Aurora and Charlotte."

He shrugged. "Their families are decent. I know the fathers and brothers. All decent men."

"Excellent. We are making progress. The parents must be invited, but I think you should also add their brothers to the guest list. This way, the young ladies you dismiss may set their cap for one of those brothers and not call the weekend a complete and utter disaster."

He cast her a wry smile. "Thank you for that vote of confidence. It so happens, I intended to invite the brothers."

"That is one issue easily resolved. You are not as hopeless as I imagined you to be." She smiled at the footman who now entered with their soup course, a light, marrow broth. "Good afternoon, Horace," she said to the young man as he served her. "How is your mother?"

Alexander nodded to the lad, allowing him to answer.

"Doing much better, Miss Viola. Thank you."

"I'll come around to see her tomorrow."

"I'll let her know. She'll be pleased."

Young Horace darted back to his position against the wall immediately behind Viola's chair. Two other footmen also entered and now stood beside Horace.

Viola smiled at both of them. "Good day, Charles. Wallace."

"At your service, Miss Viola," they each said in turn.

Sighing, Alexander shifted the topic to general Ardley matters since he was not going to discuss the matter of finding himself a bride while others were in the room. He and Viola spoke of the Midsummer Fair planned by the Ardley shopkeepers council, then moved on to discussing the condition of the schoolhouse and what repairs were needed.

Their main course was trout served with potatoes and onions in a cream sauce. It was a heavy meal and he knew Viola would have prepared something far better. He watched as she nudged the cream off to the side of her plate, liking it no better than he had.

He dismissed the footmen once the main course had been cleared and their tea and ginger cake brought out.

"Let's get back to this bride hunt business," he suggested now that they were alone.

"Yes, let's. I was thinking you really ought to invite five young ladies to better your odds of finding one or two who are suitable."

"No, three will do. It is all I can handle. And I think perhaps I do not want to invite my parents. I would rather not have them hovering over me, holding their breaths every time I dance with one of those diamonds. Nor do I need them pushing me toward one of their favorites."

"Assuming they decide upon a favorite."

"Oh, they will. My parents are not subtle, especially not my father. He hounded Gabriel to distraction, tossing one horrid prospect after another at him every chance he got. Blessed saints, he has the worst taste imaginable."

His look of mock horror made her laugh. "Even so, you must invite your parents. It is the first party you've held in over two years. They would be devastated if you snubbed them. I gather you have no such hesitation about inviting your brother."

"None whatsoever. He's an excellent brother and Daisy is delightful. I'll introduce you to them once they arrive."

"No, I'm the hired help."

"You are not. Besides, you need to meet them for completely practical reasons. Gabriel and Daisy are the perfect ones to help settle you in a respectable household if you choose to find a position in London."

"I see." A shadow fell across her eyes. "Of course. I must think of my future."

He placed his hand over hers. "I've given your father my word that I shall help you in every way possible. You'll have my entire family to assist you in finding the right place for yourself. You will not be alone and you will never be destitute."

"Thank you, my lord. I'll do my best not to be a burden to you or ever let you down."

He gave her hand a light squeeze when he felt it tremble within his. "You won't let me down or ever be burdensome, Viola."

He was reluctant to let her go, but dared not hold onto her slim fingers any longer.

They worked at the dining room table, reading through the remaining gossip rags. Finally, after cross-referencing the families in *Debrett's*, they decided upon a third young lady, one from last year's batch of diamonds.

Viola cast him a triumphant smile. "Congratulations, my lord. Your party is officially underway."

The prospect did not appeal to him at all. "Kindly do not look so cheerful as I am led to my doom."

"For pity's sake," she said with a roll of her dark, gorgeous eyes. "It is a party not a battlefield. Let's finalize the invitation list next. I still think we ought to ask your mother's advice on it before invitations are sent out."

"We are not asking my mother." He cast her a wry smile. "I think you keep raising the suggestion because you like to irk me."

She laughed. "No, I assure you. I want this party to be perfect for you. It is so easy to make a mistake, and I want this to be right. You deserve to be happy."

"I suppose."

"That is the most unenthusiastic response I have ever heard in my life." She was still laughing lightly and her eyes sparkled.

Well, at least he'd made her happy.

"We still have a few minutes before I must return to the vicarage. Do you want to start planning the menu?"

"No, let's leave the final invitation list and menu planning for tomorrow." He rose and held out her chair to help her up. "I'll walk you home."

She offered no protest, probably knowing it was futile.

He was not leaving her to walk home alone.

It was bad enough she walked up here on her own, but she would have hit him over the head and accused him of being an insufferably protective ape if he had insisted on picking her up at the vicarage to bring her over here every midday.

She walked briskly, obviously eager to be rid of him since he had given her a hard time in selecting that final diamond. He had settled on Lady Alicia Simmons, daughter of a marquess, for no reason other than he wanted to get the selection over and done already.

Now, he had three prospects, Alicia, Charlotte, and Aurora. All of them diamonds. All from noble families with impeccable bloodlines. All with spotless reputations, if the gossip rags were to be believed.

He was not so dimwitted as to ever believe them.

Lord help him, would he find any of these young ladies to his liking?

CHAPTER 4

VIOLA WAS ABOUT to leave for Ardley Hall the next morning when she heard a commotion outside her door. Her father was settled in his study, so she and Mrs. Bligh ran out to see what was happening. "Good heavens! My lord, what are you doing? Come down from there at once!"

The viscount was perched atop a wooden ladder leaning against the church wall. Standing just above him on the rooftop was his estate manager, Mr. Wilson, along with several other men who seemed to be inspecting the roof. "Good morning, Miss Ruskin," he called down, looking far too pleased to be dangling up so high. "You said the church roof might have been struck by lightning. We're checking on the damage."

"But, my lord! I did not mean for you to climb up there yourself!"

He said something to the men atop the roof and then slid down to greet her, his thick work gloves protecting his hands from splinters. "Forgive my casual attire, but I wanted to see for myself what needed to be done," he said, removing the gloves and handing them off to one of his workers. "There is some damage to the cornices. Not too bad though. Mr. Wilson will take care of it."

"Thank you." She looked up at him, sincerely grateful to have one less worry weighing upon her father's shoulders, for he was barely managing to make it through his daily sermons. For several months now, she had taken over his morning calls to ailing parishioners. She had already done her rounds this morning.

"Are you ready?" he asked, making her go weak in the knees as he stood beside her looking irresistibly rugged and manly. "We shall walk back to Ardley Hall together."

She nodded as a light breeze blew around them, carrying the subtle scent of sandalwood and the delicious heat of his skin toward her. "I'll just grab my shawl."

She ran inside and took her favorite, a slate blue wrap of softest wool. She also took a moment to pin a few loose curls in her hair. After checking her reflection in the mirror, she pinched her cheeks to put a little color in them and hurried back down. "Ready, my lord."

Her heart was in a flutter as she walked beside him.

He felt approachable, dressed casually as he was.

However, she was not so foolish as to believe he could ever be someone within her grasp. This could never be so.

He was heir to an earl, even though he was dressed in workman's clothes consisting of a sturdy cotton shirt open at the throat and dark brown trousers. His boots were a dark brown leather that appeared worn from use but were obviously of the finest quality.

The cut of his shirt made his shoulders appear quite broad and his arms solidly muscled, although that might have been all him and nothing to do with his clothes. He was a big man and walked with a confident stride.

Looking at him in these natural surroundings, she could not imagine him elegantly attired, his collar points stiffly starched as was the style in London. No wonder he did not wish to go there. However, the ladies would swarm all over him, like bees to a honeycomb, the moment he arrived. How many eligible men were as devastatingly handsome as he, even in a city of that size?

In truth, he was the sort who would fit in anywhere and look magnificent whether he was dressed in black tie and tails or coarse work clothes.

They walked down the lane in an easy silence.

She waved at young Jeremy who was watching over the sheep.

They boy cast them a beaming smile and waved back. "Good morning, my lord! Miss Viola!"

"Good morning, Jeremy," she called back.

"That's one happy boy," the viscount muttered, arching an eyebrow as his expression turned wry.

"Yes, he is. Unlike you, my lord. We are merely planning a party, not all out war. It is not the end of the world if this weekend affair does not work out as you hope." She was used to walking briskly and had no trouble keeping up with his long strides as he quickened them.

"I still dread it." He finally slowed as they reached the massive gates to Ardley Hall. They were big and dark, and trimmed in gold, which served as a reminder he was far out of her reach, even though there were times he looked at her in a way that gave her hope there could be something between them. "I think I must have been in a daze these past two years not to feel the emptiness of my home."

She nodded. "It happens when you lose loved ones."

He stared at the grand manor in the distance. "If it weren't for Wilson occasionally joining me, I would dine alone most nights. I always breakfast alone. Wake up alone. Spend most of my days alone. The house must have thirty rooms and I use perhaps two on a regular basis. I keep a staff to dust rooms I haven't been in for months. There are fifteen bedchambers in my home and only mine is in use. The nursery is abandoned."

He shook his head and emitted a ragged sigh. "With Molly gone, there are no children to put in the nursery or to yell at when they run up and down the stairs in their muddy boots. No nannies to chase after them. I still hear Molly's giggles sometimes...well, the memory of her happily running down the hall into my outstretched arms."

Viola's heart ached for him. "That is a treasure to hold for a lifetime."

"I would rather be holding my daughter." He walked on, obviously falling into a dark humor. Working on this party he did not really want to hold was stirring up the past. She understood how badly he wished to turn back time and have his daughter with him again. He hadn't mentioned his wife, but Viola knew he had to be missing Lady Jillian, as well.

Fortunately, he was in better spirits by the time they reached his manor and sat down to their midday meal.

The room they were in was referred to as the summer dining room, but Viola thought it would have been more appropriately named the winter dining room, for the table was small for a house of this size, seating only six while his main dining room table easily accommodated twenty or thirty.

Summer was a season when everyone traveled and houses were filled with guests attending weekend parties such as the one they were planning. Winter was the season of seclusion, when one holed up in one's nest and waited for the weather to turn warm.

"Today's main coarse is game hen," he said, wincing as Horace, the young footman, brought it out for them. "Dear heaven, what is it swimming in?"

Viola laughed. "Another of Mrs. Stringer's questionable experiments, I would say."

She dipped her fork in the liquid and then closed her mouth over the tines, drawing the fork out slowly while she figured out what ingredients his cook had used. She also closed her eyes, the better to savor them. When she opened them, she was surprised to find the viscount staring at her with the oddest expression on his face. "Lemon, butter, garlic. Onion. Pepper. Sage."

He cleared his throat. "Obviously too much butter. No doubt too much pepper since my nostrils are flaring and I am going to sneeze."

That explained his odd look.

She had mistaken it for desire, but it was merely his desire to sneeze.

That made far more sense.

The man was kind to her, but would never be interested in her.

Why should he be when he was going to find himself a diamond for a wife?

She dipped her fork again, closed her eyes, and put the fork to her mouth, this time lightly licking it with her tongue.

She heard him moan. "Stop, Viola. I don't need to know every ingredient."

"All right. But I think she should have cut back on the butter and perhaps the garlic. I did not find it overly peppered." She opened her eyes and smiled at him.

His expression was still odd.

She couldn't be sure, but he seemed to be staring at her lips.

Not for long, though. He dug into his food and refused to look up until he'd left nothing but chicken bones on his plate. The seasoning was not dreadful, but Mrs. Stringer had put far too much butter and the meat felt boiled rather than roasted and crisp. "You seemed to enjoy this recipe. You hardly looked up while you were eating."

He cast her a wry grin. "No, it was rather awful. Do not think to use any of Mrs. Stringer's recipes. In truth, I do not recall a single meal she has prepared over the past two years that stood out for me. They were not dreadful, just unmemorable. Although, a few might have been dreadful and I simply did not notice."

"Her cooking is perfectly fine, just not delicate. She has a tendency to overly sauce her meats but otherwise she does a splendid job. Shall we start on the invitation list? You have fifteen bedchambers, you say? Does that include yours?"

He nodded. "I still owe you a tour of the house. Let's make up this list, then I'll show you around. Tomorrow I'll have you work with my housekeeper to decide on who should be put into which guestroom. I suppose there is no rush for that since it will depend on who accepts the invitation."

"They all will. I may not be *ton,* but I do know a little about how they think. Not one of them is going to miss your party. The handsome, wealthy viscount come out of hiding to search for a wife? It will be a coup for those who receive your invitation. The three diamonds selected will be all the rage, putting all the other eager debutantes to shame."

"Wouldn't it be nice if my invitation enticed other gentlemen to offer for them?"

She laughed in exasperation. "That would entirely defeat the point of your party. You want one of them to marry *you,* not some other nodcock."

He groaned.

"Let's get to work." She reached for the supplies he had

brought in and set on the other end of the dining table.

They now shifted over to that end of the table and Viola took a sheaf of paper off a pile. "The bedroom arrangements will be tight. But I suppose your bachelor friends can double up, if necessary. So can the young ladies, two of them can share quarters. Or is this simply not done?"

"The men will share. I'm not sure how the diamonds will feel about sharing quarters with their competition. But I think there will be room enough for the ladies to each have their own bedchamber. Don't fret too much about it. I'll also need your help developing an itinerary for the day's activities."

"And the menu, don't forget."

"Yes, the menu is most important."

"When will you speak to Mrs. Stringer? We ought to get her consent before–"

"Consent? Viola, she works for me. I shall speak to her kindly, but you will be put in charge of the kitchen. She shall have the choice of remaining to work under you or taking the few days off to visit her family. I have every expectation she will choose to visit her family, especially since I will pay her for those days."

"You will?" She smiled in approval.

He smiled back. "You would be up in arms if I offered anything less."

Was he being kind to Mrs. Stringer for her sake?

Warmth flooded through her, even though she knew it could not be so. She was not special to him, merely assisting him. He admired her intelligence and probably thought her pretty, but nothing more.

She wrote down the names of those to be invited since her penmanship was better than his. "I count twenty-one guests in all. It will be a tight fit."

"Cross out my parents," he said with a grin, no doubt aiming to get a rise out of her.

She laughed. "I will do no such thing. Everyone in your immediate family is on this list, including your grandmother, and shall remain on here. I am adamant about this."

"I will be made to feel like a dancing bear, all eyes on me while

I perform."

She ignored his comment and began to rattle off those named on the list. "Your parents, Lord and Lady Trent."

"I know who my parents are." He was leaning back and grinning, so he obviously was not put out by her insistence.

"Your grandmother, Lady Eloise Dayne and–"

"I know my grandmother's name."

She sighed. "Your brother and his wife, both of whom shall remain nameless."

He chuckled, but his mirth soon faded. "The nursery is available if they choose to bring their children with them. It is time to see those little beds and the playroom occupied again."

"I think that is an excellent idea, my lord." She cleared her throat and continued before tears clouded her eyes and upset him further. That he would even suggest making the nursery available was an exceptional step forward.

She wanted to hug him and congratulate him for it, but the gesture would draw too much attention onto him, and he might change his mind. "The three diamonds," she said, staring down at her paper again. "Their parents. Each diamond has a brother who will be invited. Your cousin, Lord Graelem Dayne and his wife, Laurel. She was a Farthingale before her marriage to your cousin. She is Daisy's sister, is that not so?"

He nodded.

"Is there perhaps an unmarried Farthingale we can add to this list? Your brother and cousin fell in love with girls from that family, so–"

"No, they are all taken."

Goodness, he wasted no time in dismissing the notion. Well, it was none of her business if he wished to be a snob about it and attach himself to an aristocrat's daughter instead of a clever and beautiful commoner. These Farthingale women were obviously a cut above the other debutantes, even if their blood was not blue. "Do Lord Graelem and Lady Laurel have children?"

"Yes. Again, the nursery is available if they decide to bring them."

She felt a tug to her heart.

This house was made to be filled with little ones.

She returned to the list. "Last are two of your bachelor friends, Lord Chesterfield and Lord Hythe. If they agree to share a room, then everyone will be comfortably settled, the young ladies having their own rooms. Of course, this assumes the parents of each young lady will agree to share marital quarters. Do you think they would be amenable? It would only be for a few days."

"I have no idea. Nor do I care."

She sighed. "That is not fair. I want your party to be perfect, but this is precisely the sort of thing your mother would know and be able to advise me on."

"This really bothers you, doesn't it?"

She nodded. "It is just the sort of mistake that will earn you ridicule. I can see the gossip rags reporting it now. *Viscount A's titanic blunder!* And it is so easily avoided. Don't forget that it is your parents who will be left to face the embarrassment."

"Their hides are tough."

"Perhaps not as tough as you think. Why put it to the test? Also, should there not be more society paragons invited? I do not mean young ladies and gentlemen, but older, married couples."

"No."

"But–"

"No. That list has already exceeded my limit of tolerance. My parents can remedy any *faux pas* on my part by throwing their own parties. They have a very elegant London townhouse and a delightful country estate known as Trent Hall. In fact, they are holding a grand ball to celebrate their thirty-fifth wedding anniversary in a month's time in their London home."

"Oh, how lovely. And all the more reason why we should put this list past your mother."

"No."

"Then your–"

"No."

"So I am to put this list past no one?" She began to fret her lower lip, for he was not taking this party as seriously as he ought to be doing. This was a product of her endeavors as well. Perhaps she was being too prideful, but she wanted everything to be perfect.

Oh, there were likely to be mistakes.

But it should not be ones easily avoided just by asking for help from those in the know.

He sighed and ran his thumb over her lower lip. "Stop chewing on it or you will make it bleed. I shall write to my grandmother. She is the only one with an ounce of discretion and one of the most sensible ladies I know."

Her heart was in her throat.

No one had ever touched her in this intimate way before.

The light rub of his thumb against her lip had felt so soft and exquisite, it shook her to the core. But she knew he meant nothing by it, nor did she dare reveal how much it had affected her. "She sounds wonderful." She hoped he did not notice the wobble in her voice. "I look forward to meeting her. Of course, I have seen her once or twice over the years when she visited Ardley Hall, but we were never introduced. However, I feel her warmth in this house. Do you think it is odd that I should sense so much of her presence here?"

"No, one feels things and those first instincts are often our best guide."

"You mentioned she and your grandfather lived here when they were first married and he held the courtesy title of Viscount Ardley."

He nodded. "She decorated most of the rooms in this house."

"This explains why I am sensing this strong connection. I've only seen a few of the rooms on this floor, but her touch is obvious, down to every nook and cranny, the soft colors, the pieces of furniture. The house is grand and yet feels charming and cozy."

"I shall tell her you said so, Viola."

She blushed. "She won't care what I think."

"I have every expectation that she will." He leaned forward. "Let's talk about the menu next. I can include your dining proposals in my letter to her as well."

"Would you? That is perfect. How elaborate should these dishes be? Is there anything specifically not to be included?

Something considered too common to be served. Any foods you detest? Or that you know members of your family detest? We still have not gotten around to touring your house, but I would love to see the conservatory first. I can make something quite grand depending on the fruits and vegetables you are growing there."

"Your eyes are alight. You really enjoy cooking, don't you?"

She nodded. "I know it is frowned upon for a gently bred young lady to be seen in a kitchen, but what is more splendid than a meal that waters your mouth? I doubt you will complain when I test the recipes out on you."

He laughed and rubbed his belly that had not a bit of fat on it. "I look forward to it. You would do this?"

"Yes, of course."

The man was hard, toned muscle.

Actually quite surprising because Mrs. Stringer's food was heavy on cream sauces and her vegetable dishes were often boiled to mush and dripping in butter.

"I'll have to take stock of your larder to make certain you have the necessary ingredients. Also, we'll need to supplement your staff. I hope Mrs. Stringer decides to stay because four days of feeding twenty-five people no less than three or four meals a day requires military precision and a trained team to carry it out. I have done this before with our vicarage benefit dinners, but those were one meal, one event at a time, even if they were for a much larger crowd."

He shook his head. "You are young and softhearted, Viola. Mrs. Stringer is used to being in charge in my kitchen and will undercut you if she stays. Not necessarily on purpose, for she may not even realize she is doing it. But she will feel demoted and it will affect your authority. The kitchen maids will naturally look to her because she has been in charge of them for all these years. However, if she is not there, they will look to you without question. I am going to encourage her to leave. Not that she will require much encouragement, if any at all."

"It feels cruel. Don't be angry with me if I start crying. I don't want to hurt her feelings. It will upset me as much as it upsets her."

He leaned forward and cast her a wry smile. "That woman will let out a whoop of delight and be out of my kitchen like a shot the moment she knows I will pay her for those days."

"I hope so," she said with a light laugh.

"She will. By the way, I hate eels. Nothing slimy is to be put on the menu."

"Dear heaven, wouldn't think of it." She scrunched her face in displeasure and gave a mock shiver. "Consider eels and slime struck off the list."

He took her hand to help her to her feet, but released it as soon as she was up and steady. "Take a walk with me, Viola. I'll show you the conservatory, and then I'll take you through the rest of the house."

The day had warmed, so she left her shawl in the small dining room along with the piles of London gossip rags and followed the viscount into a more formal salon that had large glass doors leading onto the terrace. "This is the ladies parlor where Jillian usually entertained her family and friends."

"Did she decorate this room? It very much resembles your grandmother's taste."

"Because it is my grandmother's design. Jillian thought it was too pretty to change." He opened the glass doors and waited for her to finish perusing the salon.

"I think so, too. She did such a lovely job. The floral patterns on the settee and chairs seem to draw the garden into this room and make it feel cheerful all year round."

He smiled as she stepped onto the terrace. "I'm glad it meets with your approval."

"Well, I don't suppose my opinion matters in the least. But it might be interesting to know what your three diamonds think of your home."

"They'll think the house is too casual," he said, his expression now stubborn. "But I like it just as it is and no one is going to change a single drape or stick of furniture. I won't allow it."

"That will certainly ensure a successful start to your marriage." She rolled her eyes and spoke in a dry manner that did nothing to hide her opinion of his stubbornness. "It will be your betrothed's home, too. She will want to make it her own. Perhaps if you allowed her a room or two? Those she would use to entertain her friends?"

He did not seem to take offense, for his eyes lit up with mirth. "You think I am behaving like an unreasonable little boy again. Perhaps I am. I've been alone here for the past two years. Would you make any changes?"

"No," she said with a final glance around. "I don't think I could improve on your grandmother's decorations. They are very much to my liking. But you cannot go by my opinion. Compared to the leaks and well-trampled floors of the vicarage, this place is a beautiful palace."

They reached the conservatory which was a large, plant-filled room completely walled in glass. The glass trapped the heat, making the air quite dense and hotly dank. His gardeners had obviously watered the plants recently, probably were in the habit of watering them several times a day, so it was no surprise moisture permeated the air. But Viola did not mind at all, for this abundant indoor garden completely fascinated her. "What you have done here is wonderful. Incredible."

She walked along rows of unusual flowers and fruit-bearing trees. A variety of vegetables and herbs were growing in raised soil beds along the walls.

The viscount did not follow her around, but merely stood beside the door and watched her with his arms crossed over his chest. She felt the heat of his gaze upon her, but tried to dismiss it as mere curiosity on his part.

However, she could not shake the sense that her approval mattered to him.

Each soil patch was clearly marked so anyone would know what was growing in each section planted. Some patches had indistinguishable shoots only now starting to push through the fertile earth, but others were already well along. She could see onion bulbs and leeks, as well as turnips almost ready to be picked.

She caught the scent of strawberries as she neared a row of plants along the back wall. By late next month, they would also grow wild among the hedgerows in his garden and in many other places around Ardley including the vicarage garden. But this crop had already started to mature, and ideas began to whirl in her head about the many wonderful desserts and jams she could make with them for his house party.

She walked down another row that held lemon trees and fig trees.

Then another row of cucumbers and peppers.

She returned to his side, no doubt looking as though she had just been on a magical ride through a land of enchantment, but this seemed to please him because his smile was as broad as hers. "Who tends these plants, my lord?"

"I have a staff of gardeners, but my head man is Walter Burrows."

She nodded. "Is he new? I don't think my father or I know him. He is a marvel. Would you mind if I consulted with him as I formulate my menu?"

"He's been with me for years, but keeps mostly to himself. I do not mind your talking to him at all. I'll introduce you to each other when you come up tomorrow."

"Thank you, my lord."

"Bother it, I do wish you would call me Alex."

She shook her head vehemently. "No, it is not my place."

"But are we not friends? We are working closely on this house party and you know I have trust in your judgment. Not to mention, I let you get away with dumping a pail of water over my head."

She winced. "You will never let me forget it, will you?"

"No." His eyes glittered with mirth.

"I have tremendous respect for you and am enjoying our time together immensely. This project is a delight for me. But how can we ever be friends? We are from different worlds." They left the conservatory to walk back to the house.

"Not so different."

She frowned at him. When he spoke like this, he unwittingly gave her hope there could be something between them.

"I have spent much of my life in Ardley," he continued, "save the years I was on the Continent battling Napoleon. You were born and raised here. Both our lives have been shaped by these same surroundings."

"Not at all the same. Yours have been quite a bit finer than mine. Your childhood was not only spent here, but in an elegant townhouse in one of London's finest sections. Is it Mayfair or Belgravia? I don't suppose it matters since I have never been to London and could never afford anything so fine. There is also your father's country estate, Trent Hall. I expect it is even grander than Ardley Hall."

"It is."

"I also expect you were at Eton for boarding school and then Oxford for your university studies. So you see, my lord. We are from very different worlds."

He did not look pleased.

Indeed, he was frowning back at her as though she had given him a set down when this was not at all her intention. "I think it would be very dangerous for us to be friends," she continued. "I feel remarkably comfortable in your company and enjoy it far more than is wise."

That seemed to mollify him, although he still looked grave. "I think you are the most pleasant part of this odious project. You make it bearable for me, Viola. I cannot tell you how much I detest the idea of a house party. I feel as though I am to be a prancing bear put on display and made to show my tricks."

"The young ladies must also be feeling this same way. Perhaps you shall commiserate over your mutual woes and put each other at ease."

He grinned. "You are being too sensible again when all I want to do is feel sorry for myself. Come on, I'll show you the rest of my home."

He led her from room to room, but when they went upstairs to tour the bedchambers, he insisted on having Mrs. Lester accompany them. The woman was quite kind to her, but most of the staff in the viscount's employ were local residents who attended their church, so she knew them personally. "You maintain the house beautifully, Mrs. Lester," she said once the tour ended and they returned downstairs. "Would you mind if I consulted you on the room assignments for his lordship's house party?"

"Not at all, Miss Ruskin," she said with a genuine smile. "I would be happy to help."

"Thank you. That is a great relief for me."

"Miss Ruskin will also require a bedchamber for the duration of the party. I cannot have her going back and forth to the vicarage. She needs her own quarters here." The viscount now turned to her. "By your count, thirteen rooms will be assigned, plus mine which I occupy. This makes fourteen. I have fifteen bedchambers in this house. You'll take the fifteenth."

"No," she and Mrs. Lester said at the same time.

"My lord," the woman said in a shocked tone. "Miss Ruskin is to be your cook, not one of your party guests. To put her on the same floor as you…it will not look right at all."

"That is utter nonsense."

Viola shook her head. "Not nonsense at all. It will be my reputation ruined if this is where I am put. Mrs. Lester will make room for me with the staff."

"No."

He was being irritatingly stubborn again. "Then put me upstairs in the nursery with the nannies."

"No."

"Then Mrs. Stringer's room by the kitchen, if she chooses to leave."

He folded his arms across his chest, looking quite indignant. "And if she stays?"

"Then I shall sleep in the barn if I must, but I am not staying with you and your guests. Are we clear on this?"

"Stubborn nuisance," he muttered, not pleased at all. "Fine. Sort it out with Mrs. Lester later. Let me walk you home."

She grabbed her shawl but left the gossip rags since they might need to refer to them again if more diamonds needed to be chosen. There were no guarantees the parents of these first three would accept his invitation, although there really was little doubt they would.

The viscount said nothing as they marched from the house toward the distant gates. When they reached the gates, she finally broke their silence. "Why are you so angry? Do you think I would not love to be your friend or be assigned one of those beautiful guestrooms for myself? But I would be a duck among swans. I do not even own a silk gown or silk dancing slippers."

He groaned. "I am not angry with you, mostly with myself. I like being around you, Viola. You are easy to talk to and I feel I can be myself with you. My stubborn, boorish, demanding self. But you seem to deal with me well enough. I like that you stand up to me. You're clever and engaging. What of these other ladies? I dread having to smile and be polite to them, or talk to them when they have nothing in common with me."

She gave a curt laugh of disbelief. "You have everything in common with them. Your upbringing. Your aristocratic heritage. The ladies will be polished and talented, trained to rule a household and understand how to raise little viscounts."

He groaned. "Dear heaven, that sounds horrific. I want my daughters climbing trees, something they cannot do in silk frocks. And I want my sons to be adventurous and daring, not straightlaced stiffs in silk cravats, top hats, and waistcoats who look down their noses at everyone."

"You would be the father, so raise them exactly as you wish to form their character. Children learn from watching the behavior of their parents. You will lead by example."

"But so will the diamond I choose. What if she teaches them to be frilly and flighty and disrespectful of others?"

"Then it seems you will have chosen poorly, doesn't it? If these three are not to your liking, then go find another three. And then another three, until you meet the perfect one. Oh, there's Jeremy tending your sheep."

She waved to the boy, relieved for the distraction.

Assisting him in this search was already difficult on her heart. To be asked to help him again would be impossible. The sooner this was over and done, the better. She could then move on and try to forget him, although she was not certain a heart could ever forget so easily.

They walked on, once again in silence after greeting the cheerful lad.

Despite how much she enjoyed being in the viscount's company, she was relieved to escape him now. He was trying to turn her into a friend, and she wished so badly to be that and more to him. It was kind of him to want to treat her as an equal by offering her one of the elegant guestrooms, but he was not seeing things clearly.

He could twist it any way he wished, but she would never be of his class. Attempting to thrust her in the midst of his family and friends would be an utter humiliation for her.

Did he not understand what they would all think?

Or was he perfectly aware of what he was doing and trying to turn her into his mistress? She dismissed the possibility as soon as it arose, for this simply was not in his character. Alexander Dayne was not a womanizing cad.

If only he were, then she might easily dismiss her growing feelings for him.

But he was quite the opposite, a man a girl could dream on. Kind. Loyal. A bit of a loner and a curmudgeon when it came to having company.

He was not the sort to love a good party.

But he was the sort to provide for and protect the woman he took as his wife.

It would never be her.

But what if she was wrong about his intentions and he wanted her as his mistress?

She would have to refuse him.

But would she regret it for the rest of her life?

CHAPTER 5

ALEXANDER PACED BACK and forth in his study, the newly arrived letter from his grandmother held tightly in his hand. He ought to have opened it, but Viola would be along at any moment since it was nearing the noon hour. For some odd reason, he wanted to read the letter with her.

His thoughts had been on Viola too much lately. He felt her absence whenever she left his home, and eagerly anticipated her arrival at the noon hour each day, much as he was doing now. He tried not to make too much of it. Was it not easier to blame his feelings on everything but the possibility that he liked her and she might be the right one for him?

But the planning of this party had gone too far now that his grandmother was aware. He also wanted to see it through for himself, to be certain Viola was not merely someone convenient for the moment, a comfortable companion to get him through the summer.

He did not think she was someone temporary.

It would be so much easier if this is all she was to him.

He turned at the knock on his study door and strode across the room to open it. "Greaves, is she here?"

"Yes, my lord. She is ensconced in the parlor, as usual."

Viola was standing in wait beside the settee when he walked in. She looked so lovely in a simple gown of russet and her hair done up in gentle curls. He noticed the trim of lace around her collar and wondered if she had added it just for him. She never adorned her gowns with so much as a ribbon, but he liked this look. The delicate white lace looked pretty on her and seemed to bring out the soft rose of her cheeks. "I have something for you, Viola."

He held up the letter.

She inhaled sharply and her dark eyes widened. "Is it a letter from your grandmother?"

He nodded. "Sit beside me and we shall read it together."

"You waited for me before you opened it?"

"Yes. We are in this together, are we not?"

She blushed, obviously pleased.

They settled on the settee.

At first, Viola tried to keep a prim distance, but she soon gave up and scooted closer. Her shoulder rubbed against his arm and their thighs touched as she leaned over to read along silently. It struck him that he could have read the blasted correspondence aloud, but then Greaves would have overheard and reported it to the entire staff.

He liked their proximity, the soft press of her body against his, and realized this is what he had been missing these past two years. A touch.

This closeness.

Of course, he was feeling stronger urges than mere caresses toward Viola. The need to have a woman in his bed was plaguing him nightly as he emerged from his fog of bereavement. To his frustration, the woman in his dreams always seemed to be Viola. The physical ache was there, but he was also feeling the need to have someone to share his thoughts and confidences, and she fit that role as well.

Viola read to the bottom of the page and smiled up at him. "She's complimented you on your selection of these *ton* diamonds. Well, it sounds like a compliment. *Your choices astound me.* Or do you think she is being sarcastic and laughing over how terrible they are?"

"No, she would have warned me if she thought they were poor. You're the one who deserves the compliment. I could not have accomplished this without you."

She laughed, her eyes shimmering as she looked up at him with mirth. "Those gossip rags deserve the credit. It is my father and his fascination with sin that we must thank."

Once again, she had him smiling, and he was beginning to wonder if any of the diamonds could make him feel this way. "So be it. But the menu is all yours and my grandmother thinks it is excellent. See, she says it right here. *I cannot improve on your choices and look forward to tasting each course.*"

"The proof will be in the tasting."

"I have no doubt it will all be delicious."

"Thank you, my lord. By the way, I cannot stay long today."

His merriment immediately fled. "Why not?"

"Now that your grandmother has approved our food choices, I plan on experimenting with the recipes. I do not want to be underfoot in Mrs. Stringer's kitchen, so I'll gather the ingredients and make them at the vicarage. I plan on baking a game pie this afternoon."

"Already sounds delicious."

"Just wait, for I'll be mixing in apricots, raisins, honey, and cinnamon, among a few other aromatic spices. I'll also add carrots and potatoes."

"Am I invited?"

She nodded. "Yes, of course. Would you mind joining my father and me for an early supper? I hope the recipe does not prove too sweet for your palate. I will cut back a little on the ingredients next time, if it is. Then tomorrow, I plan on trying out several recipes for fish."

"Fine with me. Can you make enough for my staff as well? I mean about the fish for tomorrow. And you ought to cook it here at Ardley Hall. Or is it too big of a task to prepare a meal for my entire staff? I suggest it for tactical reasons. You will have them in your thrall if any of these taste half as good as they sound. Also, you will have to get used to the workings of my kitchen. I shall speak to Mrs. Stringer and smooth everything over."

"Shouldn't I speak to her as well?"

"No. She is part of my staff. She'll take her instruction from me."

"Yes, but…all right."

"Viola, you can do what you do best once you are in her kitchen."

"And what is that?"

"Make everyone like you."

She blushed, once again looking quite pleased. "Oh."

"I know you will find a way to make Mrs. Stringer feel important even while you take charge." He stretched out and placed an arm along the back of the settee, quite looking forward to tasting Viola's dishes.

She spoke with such heartfelt enthusiasm and had a beautiful sparkle in her eyes. He felt her love of life wash over him as well. He was no longer surprised, for the girl always put him in better spirits.

"All right, I will prepare the fish in your kitchen and for all of you tomorrow. You and your staff shall be my critics. I cannot do it today with the game pie because I did not gather enough ingredients for more than two or three pies. My plan for all the meals will be to keep them simple, but artfully decorated and flavorful."

"You'll have no quarrel from me." He glanced at the letter again. "My grandmother suggests early July as the date for the house party. How does this sound to you?"

She nodded. "Perfect. The Midsummer Fair will be over by then and I will be completely free to devote my time to your endeavor. Although, I think we've now done most of the work. All that is left is to send out the invitations and arrange for nightly entertainments. Do you think it should be dancing every evening or will you toss in a music recital or two? Also, the older guests will want card tables set up for them every night, I should think."

"Yes, card tables for those who wish to play, and our village musicians to provide music for those who wish to dance. Forget the musical recitals. The men detest them and the women would rather spend a night dancing with potential husbands than listening to some stranger sing shrill songs at them. As for me, I would like nothing better than to have them all disappear into thin air."

"Ah, excellent," she said with a gentle, trilling laugh. "I see you are warming to the idea of this party."

He grinned back. "I forbid you to be sarcastic, Miss Ruskin."

"I cannot help it. Your attitude is atrocious. I almost feel sorry for these young ladies. How will they ever please you?"

He once again thought of several ways a man might be pleased, but those were not to be discusssed with innocent Viola. "Don't worry about those ladies. Your cooking shall put me in good humor and they'll declare me a most amiable fellow."

She rolled her eyes. "Doubtful. I am coming to know you too well, my lord. The best we can hope for is an occasional smile out of you. Your endurance will be sorely tested, I'm sure. But you must not run away from your company. You are the host and must be present at all times."

"That's where you are wrong. My meddlesome parents will be quite useful, taking over host duties while I contrive any excuse to escape into the kitchen."

"Don't you dare! Your kitchen staff and I will be running around like chickens without our heads, cooking for you lot. The dishes will be quite good. Many of the herbs and vegetables will have reached maturity and we'll be able to pick them fresh from your garden. But do not doubt I will chase you out with a rolling pin if you dare step foot inside my domain."

"Yours, is it? I had no idea you were such a tyrannical task master."

"I am not. If I am stern, it is for your own good. You must give these young ladies a chance to get to know you."

He lolled his head back, banging it lightly against the back of the settee.

She giggled. "You are strong, my lord. You will survive the house party weekend."

"It will be a close thing, I assure you. Let's finish up with whatever needs to be done here, then I'll walk you back to the vicarage. Do you mind if I stay and watch you cook?"

Her eyes rounded in surprise. "Don't you have more important things to attend to? I assumed you would just come back down in time for supper."

"No, I'd rather stay and watch you. I have nothing else pressing."

"Very well. Shall we leave now? Or work on the invitations?"

He arched an eyebrow and laughed. "Afraid I'll back out? I won't, Viola. I'll take care of those tonight when I return from supper."

"You are going to write them on your own?"

"The invitations will be formally engraved, of course. I'll send a sample to my grandmother first thing in the morning. She will have them done in London and sent out for me. Is there anything else that needs to be done here?"

She shook her head. "No, I suppose there isn't. Nothing urgent, anyway."

"Good, I'll walk you home."

It did not take them long to gather the last of the supplies Viola needed from his larder, and then head off to the vicarage. "I'm back, Mrs. Bligh," Viola said, entering through the kitchen. "As you see, I have brought an assistant."

"Your lordship!" Mrs. Bligh bowed and began to fuss with the ties of her apron. "Shall I prepare tea and refreshments for you in the–"

"No, we shall be working in here," he said, tossing her a grin. "Kindly ignore me. I am determined to help Miss Ruskin."

Viola grimaced. "I could not shake him off, Mrs. Bligh. He insists. So we shall put him to work on the game pie I told you about."

"Oh, dear. Are you sure about this, my lord?"

He nodded. "Quite."

"Well then, I shall not intrude. The chicken is plucked and quartered, just as you asked, Miss Viola. I have dusting I can be doing while your father naps…unless you wish me to stay."

"No, his lordship and I have it all in hand. He cannot get into too much trouble while he is up to his elbows in flour." She turned to him. "You'll be more comfortable without your jacket. You'll also need to roll up your sleeves. I'll give you an apron to protect your elegant waistcoat. Wouldn't want it to get soiled."

Mrs. Bligh regarded him in bemusement. "Are you really

going to cook, my lord?"

"Yes, Mrs. Bligh. Do not look so alarmed. I shall surprise you both, for I am quite adept. We often had to fend for ourselves on the battlefront. Miss Ruskin, I am at your service. Tell me what to do."

Viola laughed. "Mrs. Bligh, we must make a note of this and perhaps order a commemorative plaque put up in our kitchen. *On this spot Viscount Ardley cooked a game pie for his subjects this day of Our Lord, 20th of June, 1823*. What do you think?"

The older woman chuckled. "I think you had better get started on the pie or you shall never get it done in time for supper."

"Right," he said, removing his jacket, waistcoat, and cravat before taking the apron and putting it on.

Viola scooted behind him to tie it properly, then helped him to remove his cufflinks. She then tucked them into the pocket of his jacket along with the stickpin he had left on his cravat. "You should not be so casual with your finery. That stick pin looks expensive."

"It is."

She tossed him a stern, schoolmistress look as she now helped him roll up his sleeves. "I am not a little boy, Miss Ruskin," he said in a husky murmur. "Quite capable of tending to this myself."

"I know, my lord. But it is faster if I help you out." She then donned her apron and expertly tied it behind her. Her sleeves were only elbow length so there was no need to roll them up. "Give me a moment to set out the bowls, knives, and other implements."

He helped her when she attempted to lift a massive pan onto her stove. "What are you doing?"

"I need to put the chicken on to brown. Would you chop up those onions? Those will go in with the chicken."

He nodded and set about the task. In the meanwhile, she added oil to the pan. While it heated, she took out a glass jar which appeared to hold a blend of spices. She rubbed this blend onto the chicken and then tossed the chicken parts onto the skillet. Breasts, legs, and thighs landed with a sizzle and a release of steam that smelled wonderful as it began to permeate the room. She then grabbed the onions he had cut up and tossed them in the pan. "All right, next will be the potatoes and carrots."

He peeled them, surprising her with his deftness. But he'd learned to be good with a knife during his war years, and carving up a potato was much easier than fighting off an enemy soldier looking to stick his bayonet into you.

She tossed those in, then handed him apricots and figs while she lifted out a pot of honey and another jar of spices that smelled exquisite as she opened the lid. Once those were tossed in, she stirred them in with the chicken to blend them thoroughly. When the chicken was sufficiently browned, she removed it and began to carve it into little pieces to separate the meat from the bone. "You are surprisingly good with that knife, Viola."

Apparently, he wasn't the only one with carving skills.

"No better than any other woman who cooks for her family." She tossed the small pieces back into the pan and once again stirred them in.

He leaned closer as he watched her work. From time to time she tasted the contents of the pan, inhaling the aroma as she added a little more of the blended spices. When she considered the mixture done, she gave him a taste. "Blessed saints, that's good."

"It is the blend of spices that gives this pie filling its flavor. This is what I purchase on my trips to Oxford."

"Spices?"

She nodded. "My extravagance. I also splurge on Farthingale soaps. Your brother's wife is a Farthingale and I believe it is her cousins who own this Oxford soap company."

"So that's your secret."

She looked up from her cooking. "What secret?"

He grinned. "You smell like a delicious fruit. A peach or strawberry."

"Yes, those are the soaps I buy. It is utterly frivolous and an expense we can ill afford, but I think we all need something special in our lives, and soap is a safe enough vice." She gave the ingredients in the pan one last stir. "We'll leave those to simmer now. Next is the pie dough."

She moved about like a whirlwind again, setting out flour, butter, eggs, and water. "The trick to a flaky crust is to keep the butter cool. So we want to get the dough properly kneaded and rolled out before the butter begins to melt. You'll be in charge of the kneading."

"Aye, captain."

He watched her put these ingredients into a large bowl which she then handed to him. "Your turn. You had better take off that fine signet ring. Here, I'll put it in your jacket pocket with your cufflinks and stick pin."

Now that his hands were unfettered, he plunged them into the bowl and began to mix until the ingredients looked like dough. He then removed the dough and began to knead it, trying very hard to think of pie crusts and not Viola's breasts which were what he truly would enjoy getting his hands around.

Gad, he was hopeless.

Viola deserved more from him than this. He was growing to care for her sincerely. She was the last person he would ever use for a casual tumble. Yet, he could not deny his strong physical attraction to her.

She darted from the pan to the long table where he was working, looking quite serious as she watched him work the dough. "That's perfect. Divide it into six equal balls and we'll let them sit for a little while before I roll them out."

He thought she was amazing, loved how she worked with practiced precision.

Since they had a few moments before the next step in their pie baking endeavor, she poured them a cup of tea which they enjoyed while he asked her questions about herself.

"There isn't much to tell," she responded with a shy blush to her cheeks. "I was born and raised right here in Ardley."

"Any beaus? Other than George Haworth, of course."

She laughed. "No. And George is not a beau of mine either."

"He pines for you."

She lowered her gaze. "I know. I just…well, my thoughts are on my father and I cannot think of anyone but him right now."

"Will George ever be in the running for your affections?"

She shrugged. "I honestly don't know. My father wishes he were."

Alexander did not know why he was asking her these questions.

Or why the possibility of George Haworth courting her was upsetting him.

To be a possessive ape about it when he was not courting her, nor had he seriously considered courting her until this moment, seemed ridiculous.

Lord help him, he could now see himself with Viola.

Not just for a day or week or month, but a lifetime.

It was mad, of course. He had yet to meet the three diamonds, not to mention his father would be in an uproar if he chose Viola over a nobleman's daughter. Not that any of it would dissuade him if he fell in love with her. But as she said, she had her father to think about and did not need her life put into further upheaval because he had suddenly taken a fancy to her.

More than a fancy.

She was becoming someone quite serious to him.

"Time for me to roll out the crusts." She set aside her teacup and grabbed a rolling pin to flatten the first three balls and set them each into equal sized baking pans. While rolling out the remaining three that would serve as lids, she began to issue instructions regarding the pie filling that was still simmering in the large frying pan. "That's right," she said in her soft voice, "drain the excess juices and then carefully pour the remaining contents into each baking pan. Drain it well, for too much juice will make the bottom crust soggy and the pie will fall apart when we serve it."

He watched her take a moment to shape the crusts to be used as lids into decorative patterns. She then pierced each one. "This allows the steam to escape so the pies will remain crisp and firm."

"What comes next?" he asked once the three pies were put in the oven. "The clean up?"

She laughed gently and nodded. "I hate this part. But I'll leave the frying pan for later. It has to cool down first."

"We'll do the cleaning up together." He rose from the stool he had been sitting on and helped her gather the scraps to put in a bag for slop for Mrs. Bligh's pigs. The utensils and bowls went into a basin to be filled with hot water which Viola now put on to boil.

Some flour dust billowed as he picked up the bag to put it back in her larder. A little of the dust accidentally landed on Viola's nose.

"Got you," he said with a grin and moistened a clean drying cloth. "Sorry about that."

"No worries, I do it to myself all the time. The flour gets in my hair, on my chin. On my eyelashes."

He turned toward her. "Hold on a moment, Viola. The flour isn't the only thing you're wearing on your face. You've also collected the ingredients of the pie on your chin. A streak of chicken spices right…there. You look good enough to eat."

He was merely jesting, but it suddenly did not feel like a jest as he tucked a finger under her chin and tilted her face upward to meet his gaze.

The girl was so beautiful, staring up at him with her big, trusting eyes and a few silken curls fallen out of place.

To be precise, she looked delicious.

Perhaps it was the fruity Farthingale soap he inhaled as his nose was close to her lightly perspiring neck, or it may have been the enticing aroma wafting about the kitchen as those pies baked that was causing his heart to beat faster.

He tried to calm himself, struggling not to kiss her as he dabbed her nose…then her chin…her cheek, and now her lips that flushed a darker pink under the slight pressure of the cloth.

Lord, he ached to kiss her.

He was going to explode if he did not kiss her.

Never mind that all hell would break loose once he did. "Viola, I–"

She skittered away as someone startled both of them by pounding on the kitchen door. "Oh, heavens. I had better answer it," she said with a nervous titter.

His estate manager rushed in the moment she opened the door.

"My lord–"

"Wilson, there had better be a bloody good reason for the interruption. Miss Ruskin and I are busy here." Well, his mind was busy on something other than baking. He supposed he ought to be grateful for the timely interruption.

Viola was not the sort of girl he could ever kiss unless he was ready to marry her.

Besides, what was he thinking?

She had never been kissed before.

For him to kiss her now would lead to complications. At the very least, he might have frightened her, and then she would have backed out of helping him with his party.

Not that he cared about the damn party.

Wilson cleared his throat. "My lord, your father is here. He is demanding to see you at once."

His blasted father?

Of course, he loved the man.

But he was not going to bow to whatever ridiculous demands he had come to lay upon him.

Viola gave a little sigh of dismay. "Oh, I suppose this means you cannot stay for supper. What shall I do with your pies? Would you like to invite your father to join us?"

Alexander had been looking forward to dining with Viola and her father, especially being in Viola's company. "No, do not invite him here."

"Yes, of course. I see. We would be shabby company for Lord Trent. I–"

"There is nothing wrong with your company or the vicarage or the meal we were planning to share."

"Shall I send two pies up to Ardley Hall once they have cooled?" She began to wring her hands, obviously feeling Wilson's intensely curious gaze on her as well as his own.

"No, we'll have them here. I am staying."

Her eyes rounded in surprise. "But–"

"My father does not get to arrive unannounced and expect me to drop everything I am doing to bow and scrape to him."

She was still giving him that gorgeous, big-eyed stare. "But he is your father."

"I am not a little boy, Miss Ruskin."

The little apple in her throat bobbed up and down.

Lord, this was the first part of her he was going to kiss.

"Wilson, let my father know I shall return in the early evening and that he should not await supper for me."

The man stared at him in disbelief. "But, my lord!"

"You dine with him, Wilson. That is an order."

"I deserve battle pay for this," his estate manager muttered with a groan.

Alexander grinned. "I know. Send word if he is here for something truly serious. But if I know him, he is only here to badger me into doing my duty as earl's heir."

Viola now regarded him in confusion. "Why would he come here to bother you? Surely, he must be aware of your house party. Would your grandmother not tell him? Oh, perhaps not the details, but that you were holding one."

"I'm sure she did, and this is why he jumped on his horse and galloped all the way up here. He wants to be in control of who I invite."

"Well, the invitations have not yet gone out, have they?"

"No." He took Viola gently by the shoulders. "And you are not to say a word to him about the guest list if he asks."

"Why would he ask me? He won't even know I exist." Her eyes widened and she gasped. "You don't expect me to come up to the manor house while he is here?"

"Yes, I do. Did we not agree to have you cook a meal in my kitchen tomorrow? The fish have already been ordered." He had no idea if this was true, but he was not going to have Viola go into hiding as though there was something shameful about her assisting him. "You are to come to my front door, as usual."

He released her and took a moment to stride out with Wilson who also looked ready to admonish him. "You are putting too much strain on the girl, my lord. She has enough worries with her father's failing health. Do not force her to also confront your father when he will assume the worst about your friendship with her."

"I will make it clear to him."

"All he will understand is that you may not have touched her yet, but you sorely want to. I know the sort of man you are and trust you will never do anything to hurt her. But others do not know this, especially your father who may have grown a bit jaded by London society ways. He adores your mother and I am sure he has always been faithful to her, but he is one of the rare ones. How is he to know what you are doing or thinking when you've kept to yourself for so long?"

"I will not have Miss Ruskin demeaned."

"Which is exactly what will happen if you demand she comes to your front door. Let her come to the manor tomorrow but enter through the kitchen since this is where she needs to be for the afternoon. Servants hear everything. You will completely undercut her authority in the kitchen if you and your father are overheard fighting over her."

"All right. Blast it, Wilson. I suppose it is the lesser of two evils. She will be hurt either way."

"No, she will feel completely comfortable in the kitchen and out of sight of your father. You are the one who is dragging her into your Upper Crust world, expecting everyone to accept her as though she has always belonged. But she is quite clear-eyed and sensible. She knows her place exactly."

Alexander wanted to punch a wall with his fist in frustration.

Everyone, even Viola herself regarded her status as beneath him. But she wasn't. This girl was more than worthy to stand by his side.

He returned to the vicarage kitchen in time to see Viola lift the large frying pan and carry it to the sink. "What are you doing? That is too heavy for you."

"I'm going to clean it."

He sighed. "You haven't the muscle for it. That pan is almost as big as you. I'll do it."

She did not look pleased as she handed it over to him. "Mrs. Bligh usually takes care of cleaning up, but I've washed that pan many times before."

"And you may do it again, but not while I am around."

"My lord, may I ask you a question?"

The pies were still baking and the aroma was making him salivate. Why was everyone making a fuss over his simply wanting to help out? Being a viscount did not make him delicate and needing to be pampered. In truth, he hated people bowing and scraping to him or fawning over him as though he were a gift to the world. "Yes, Viola. You may."

She stood beside him, looking up at him as though trying to figure out the mysteries of the universe…or perhaps just trying to figure out what was inside his head.

"My lord, why are you here? Why are you cooking beside me and cleaning up after me? What exactly is going on between us?"

CHAPTER 6

"FRIENDSHIP, THAT IS all there is between us, Viola." Alexander knew it was far from the truth, but what else could he say at the moment? "Perhaps if you were aged and wrinkled no one would be paying any attention to us at all. But good sense and an amiable attitude come wrapped in packages of all shapes and sizes, some of them quite appealing. If you were not pretty, no one would think twice about us."

She nodded and then turned away to pull the pies out of the oven. "These ought to be ready now."

"They look amazing." He inhaled and his senses were immediately surrounded by pleasant scents wafting in the air. Hot pie crust. Game bird. Potatoes and onions. An exotic spice he could not place. "When do we eat?"

She laughed. "As soon as I set the table."

"I'll help." He followed her into the dining room, which was small by Ardley Hall standards, but quite adequate. The furniture was solidly built and of a surprisingly fine mahogany wood. The table, chairs, and buffet were all of good quality. Nothing to match his dining room, of course. Ardley Hall was the finest home in these parts and few could match its elegance.

Viola excused herself to wake her father.

She returned a few moments later, alone and wringing her hands. "With your permission, my lord…"

"What is it, Viola?"

"My father does not feel up to coming down to supper. Will

you be offended if Mrs. Bligh serves him in his bedchamber?"

"Not at all. Is he all right? Should I fetch Dr. Walcott?"

"No, it isn't necessary." She cast him a feeble smile that only made her distress more obvious. "My father is feeling exhausted, as he often does these days. There is nothing any of us can do about it. Believe me, I would already be running to Dr. Walcott's home to fetch him if there was any chance it would help. We've been through this quite often lately."

Alexander raked a hand through his hair. "Is there anything I can do to help?"

She gave a mirthless laugh. "How are you at miraculous healing?"

He winced. "I'm afraid I'm not very good at that."

"Nor am I."

He could not bear to see Viola so forlorn. "Shall I go? You do not appear to be in any humor to entertain me. I would only be in the way."

She shook her head. "No, please stay. I would rather not dine alone. Besides, you have been very patiently awaiting the chance to taste the results of our labor. There's a bottle of wine in the cabinet. Will you pour for us while I bring in one of the game pies?"

"As you wish." He watched her dart off, wondering what thoughts were spinning through her head. Perhaps he ought to have left her, but that did not seem right. She had expressly told him she did not wish to be alone, nor did he wish to go. Besides, he did not need her to be witty and chattering. He just needed to be with her.

Yes, just be with her.

That was a bit of a kick in the head, wasn't it?

The time he spent with her always passed pleasantly and seemed too short.

She soon returned with one of the pies and set it on the table. "Oh, did you not find the bottle of wine?"

He had been thinking about her and forgot to take it out of the cabinet. "Just got distracted." He brought the bottle to the table and poured a glass for each of them. He then settled beside her.

"The moment of truth," she murmured, casting him a gentle smile. "Let's hope you like it."

"Viola, I know I will like it. The only question is how much of it can I devour before I eat you out of house and home?" She set a generous portion on his plate and a smaller portion for herself. Steam rose from the pie when she cut into it and released more of the fragrant aroma. Honey, apricot, raisins, and her aromatic spices wafted upward, mixing with the heavier, savory scents of game meat and potatoes.

He took a bite. "Lord, that's good."

She blushed, looking quite pleased.

He devoured his serving and asked for another. "This is delicious. I've never tasted anything so good in my life."

"I thought it would work well on the party menu."

"Viola, it is a triumph. Make a list of the ingredients you will require and Mrs. Lester will see to it that all is stocked. I'll ride to Oxford myself if we lack anything in Ardley."

She smiled as she watched him eat, her pride in her work obvious. And yet, she was humble as he complimented her with every bite he took.

Was there a sweeter girl in all of England?

He did not think so.

Between them, they polished off the entire pie. Well, he had done most of the polishing off, eating like a ravenous wolf. But he declined when she offered to bring out the second pie. "I came here merely to taste your work, not devour everything in sight. I'll help you clean up and then I had better be on my way before my father sends out a hunting party to haul me back."

"Mrs. Bligh and I will take care of washing these dishes. In truth, there isn't much left to do and she'll tend to it while I look in on my father." She stuck out her hands to show him their delicacy. "See, I do very little of the hard work around here."

He took them in his, running his thumbs in a light swirl along her palms. "They are soft."

He felt her light shiver and understood his touch was affecting her.

The apple in her throat bobbed, a sure sign she was not

immune to him. He understood perfectly what he was doing, the seduction of his touch. He was not a womanizer, but he had learned early on how to arouse a woman's pleasure.

It was not something a man ever forgot.

Yet, how could he do this to Viola?

She was no match for him.

Kiss her.

She cleared her throat. "Shall I pack up one of the pies for you? I'll only need one for my father. He'll hardly eat more than a sliver."

"Yes, I'll take one. My own father will need calming down and I can think of no better way to do it than have him taste your remarkable food."

She glanced down at her hands which he still held in his. "Um, shall I pack it up for you now?"

He chuckled. "Yes, Viola."

He released her hands, knowing it was not well done of him to have taken them in his or held them for so long.

But they felt soft.

They felt so right swallowed in his.

She darted into the kitchen, no doubt to hide the dark pink stains on her cheeks. She'd felt the attraction between them and had no idea what to do about it. Likely, she wanted to suppress it, deny it. Pretend it was all a mistake.

It wasn't.

What each of them felt for the other was real and perhaps dangerous. Their physical attraction to each other was certainly something to be concerned about.

What would happen if they acted upon their feelings?

She returned to the dining room in short order bearing a basket in hand. "I'll retrieve my baking tin and basket when I come up to Ardley Hall tomorrow. Um, that is…should I come up?"

"Yes, I've told you so. We are to taste your fish."

She nodded.

"Viola, you are chewing your lip again."

She looked up at him with anguished eyes. "It is all very confusing. I think you should not keep your father waiting."

"Very well, I'll go." He took the basket from her hands. "But first…close your eyes."

Instead, they widened.

He smiled affectionately. "Do not be afraid of me, Viola. Close your eyes."

She sighed and sealed them shut tight, at the same time holding her breath.

He leaned forward and kissed her softly on the cheek. "Job well done, Miss Ruskin."

His voice sounded strained and husky to his own ears. Not surprising, for he was fighting off a tidal wave of sensations, mostly the urge to kiss her lusciously pursed lips.

He dared not.

She had him on fire.

A kiss on the cheek was safest for now.

Lord, she tasted sweet.

"Until tomorrow, Miss Ruskin."

She opened her eyes and watched him stride out.

He almost turned back to give her the ravenous kiss he ached to give her. But now was not the time. First of all, it was too soon. These feelings he had for her were too new and how could he be certain of them? Second of all, sharing a real kiss between them would overset her, and she was already unsteady because of her father's illness.

But he would kiss her.

Not today, for having to face his angry father was enough to douse anyone's ardor.

As expected, his father was pacing in his study when he returned. "Where have you been, Alexander? Your Mr. Wilson would not tell me. I ought to sack him for his impertinence."

He arched an eyebrow. "You'll do no such thing, Father. If you must know, I was fetching your supper."

"Do not be smart with me."

"I'm not. Come into the dining room with me. I'll wager you've never tasted anything as good as what you are about to eat. Are you hungry?"

"Famished."

That gave Alexander pause. "Did Mrs. Lester or Greaves not see to you?"

His father cast him a wry smile. "I may have barked at them and told them to leave me alone."

Alexander laughed. "Serves you right, you old dog."

He glanced at his father as they walked down the hall to the dining room and waited while his footmen raced about to set the table under Greaves' direction.

Alexander poured his father a drink in the meanwhile.

He resembled his father, was probably a younger version of him. All the men in the Dayne family were big and blond-haired, although his father's hair was a little darker and now turning mostly gray. Their eyes were also a similar shade of blue. Perhaps their temperaments were similar, too. They all had a stubborn streak.

He liked to think that he and Gabriel also had a strong streak of valor, a trait they had probably inherited from their father. It may have been inherited from his mother's side, as well. She had spirit and certainly knew how to deal with his father to keep him in line.

It also helped that his father loved her to pieces.

This is what he wanted for himself.

Gabriel had found this same consuming love for Daisy.

He supposed the entire point of throwing his own house party was to find this sort of love for himself.

If there was a difference among the Dayne men, it was that their father had retained a strong streak of the traditional. This meant he placed far too much weight on his heir marrying a young lady with impeccable bloodlines rather than marrying a young lady who was thoughtful, intelligent, warm, and of good nature. The old man had found the perfect woman in his mother, but it was probably the clever doing of his grandparents that the arranged marriage between his parents had turned into a love match. Left to his own, his father would have botched his wife search.

"The game pie has cooled a little, but I'll wager it is still divine." Alexander settled into a chair beside his father and served the man himself. "Go ahead. Dig in."

His father eyed him warily, but was too hungry to question Alexander. He took a hearty mouthful. Being stubborn, his father said nothing. But Alexander did not need words, for his father's actions said it all. He devoured the first slice and then asked for a second helping.

Alexander grinned. "I told you it is nothing like you've ever tasted before."

"Who is this cook? Will you engage him for your party?"

Alexander nodded. "The cook is a she. And yes, this is what we were doing. Reviewing the menu for my party."

His father sighed and raked a hand through his hair. "I came here to dissuade you from holding it. You ought to be in London with us, going around to all the society affairs. Your grandmother told me of the three young ladies you have selected. I have no quarrel with your choices. They are all from the best families. But why limit yourself to just those three? You are my son and heir. Come to London and you will have a hundred ladies fluttering like butterflies around you."

"This is precisely what I do not want."

His father coughed lightly. "Um, there is also another consideration. Speaking man to man."

"I think I am quite beyond *that* sort of talk. I was married and did father a child, if you will recall."

"All the more reason why you should be somewhere you can satisfy your manly urges without the locals knowing what you are doing and with whom. Why not sow a few wild oats while in Town? No one will question you or care. Enjoy yourself while you seek a wife."

He groaned.

Where was his dear mother to put a muzzle on his father?

"You cannot do such a thing here," his father continued, "and especially not at your house party when the three girls you've chosen will have their parents closely guarding them. If you are caught in a compromising position with one of them–"

"I have no intention of compromising any of them. Nor do I intend to go *whoring* in London. I had that sort of adventure while in university, as most boys do. But I am a grown man now and do not need to prove myself to anyone."

"Son, do you not have these carnal urges?"

"Of course, I do." Viola immediately sprang to mind, images of him taking her in every room in this house, hearing her breathy moans and soft whimpers as he brought her to pleasure. Bloody hell, what was wrong with him?

That sweet girl?

And all he could think of was devouring her.

He drained his wine glass in two gulps. "My private life is my own. I will not have my parents asking me about it. Good grief, what are you thinking?"

"If you must know, your mother and I are very much concerned about you. Come to London with us. Conduct your search there. Take your time. Enjoy life. Let us guide you."

"You as my guide? Dear heaven, no." He rolled his eyes. "Will you come to my party?"

"Alexander, I do not appreciate your insolent attitude." He frowned at his son. "I haven't decided yet about your party."

"Do as you like. The choice is yours."

"I think it is a big mistake. So many things can go wrong. What if you do not like the young ladies you have invited? You've only asked three, and I can tell you, none of them are like your dear Jillian."

"Precisely why I chose them. I do not need an imitation of her."

His father frowned. "But why not? You were very happy in your marriage. Or is it too painful for you? Your mother suggested as much."

He said nothing, for he did not want to get into a further disagreement with this man he loved. But the truth was, he and Jillian had grown up as friends and got along very well. They married because it was the logical next step and had made a very good marriage out of it. They were both happy. All in all, he considered it a love match. But consumed by love? Hungry for each other with a burning passion?

No. This is not what either of them had ever felt for the other.

But these were feelings he was developing for Viola, the

friendship *and* the heat of desire. These feelings were new to him and he had no intention of rushing into anything, especially if he were to end up hurting Viola.

What were the chances this was real and everlasting?

He and his father stayed up late into the night chatting about the running of the Trent estate, about his mother and grandmother, and whatever news his father thought would be of interest to him concerning London. He also listened to his father go on about Gabriel and Daisy, and their children, the old man apparently forgetting he'd lost his own child along with his wife, and perhaps did not wish to harp on the familial joys of others.

It was his own fault, he supposed. He'd brought up Jillian and little Molly in earlier conversation. But his father was now obsessed with the topic, one that would always be raw and painful to him because he had failed to protect them. But how did one defend one's loved ones against a fever that ravaged and ultimately consumed their delicate bodies?

He had no intention of revealing his torment to his father, so he simply listened to him drone on, and tossed in a word here and there.

Finally, his father yawned. "I am done in, Alex. I'll see you in the morning. Perhaps we can get a ride in before midday."

"Yes, easily arranged. I'll make time in my schedule."

He bid his father a good evening and then retired to his own bedchamber. After going through his routine of washing up and settling in with a book to read and a brandy to drink, he finally fell into bed around one o'clock in the morning.

Fatigue did nothing to squelch his dreams of Viola, her naked body soft and lithe atop him, her knees on either side of his hips as he guided her onto him.

He woke up drenched the following morning, the sheets twisted around his taut, tense body. He had only ever kissed Viola's cheek, but one would never know it from the way his body responded to her.

She made his blood run hot.

Molten.

He had to keep that heat subdued.

"Blast," he muttered and rolled out of bed to begin his day.

Alexander had already met with Wilson regarding the day's work, had his breakfast, and finished reading the morning paper by the time his father joined him in the dining room. "How did you sleep, Father?"

"Like a rock."

"Since you wanted us to take a ride, I thought we could visit a few of the local farms along the way. They are your tenants, after all. I merely look after them for you. Are you up to it?"

His father nodded. "It is a good plan. From what I've seen so far, the estate is thriving. You've done an excellent job, Alex."

"I try my best."

"Perhaps after your party, you and I can ride to Trent Hall. I've neglected it a little this past year. It is no surprise, since I am slowing down a bit. Perhaps it is time you took over the running of Trent Hall as well as Ardley."

He nodded. "Suits me."

His father smiled. "You will notice I have given up on talking you into coming to London. Your mother insisted you would never agree, but I had to try. So we shall do it your way and have you get to know those three *ton* diamonds. Hopefully, you'll find one you like and marry her."

"Perhaps, but I'm not making that decision over one weekend."

"But is that not the entire point of your party? Why not choose one and be done with it?"

"Be done with it? Decide in haste and spend the rest of my life regretting it?"

His father sighed. "I do not understand you, son."

"Nor do I," he said quietly.

When his father finished his coffee, they walked down to the stable and had their mounts saddled. The day was filled with sunshine, but there was a stiff breeze and a dampening to the air that boded rain by afternoon. "We'd better get through our ride quickly or we'll be caught in a downpour."

The soft, white billowing clouds he'd awoken to this morning were now darker and beginning to thicken overhead. He and his father managed to visit two farms before Alexander felt a few raindrops and suggested they turn back. "We'll call upon the rest tomorrow if the weather clears. Let's ride back to Ardley Hall."

"You'll have no protest from me, son."

They had just passed through the town of Ardley and were nearing the vicarage when the rain began to fall in earnest. Alexander was about to spur his mount to a gallop when he saw Viola hurrying out of the vicar's residence with her basket of supplies. He watched her glance up, tuck her shawl over her head, and then start running to the manor house.

He called out to her.

She ignored him and kept running.

He rode up to her and cut her off. "What are you doing?" he asked, now dismounting. "You'll be soaked."

Without giving her the chance to protest, he lifted her onto his horse and climbed on behind her. "My lord!"

"Quiet. I'll not have you sopping wet by the time you reach my kitchen. I can assure you, it is most uncomfortable." He wrapped an arm around her waist and held her firmly against his chest as he galloped off.

His father rode beside him, his expression one of utter disapproval.

Well, there would be hell to pay for this.

At least Viola would be dry.

She squirmed in his arms in order to face him.

Her cheeks were in flames and fire shot from her eyes.

Great, she was embarrassed and angry.

He did not care.

Nor could he think straight while she continued to squirm against him.

Fire consumed him every time she wiggled her backside against his thighs.

He could hardly see straight by the time they reached his stable. He dismounted and then reached up to assist her. She looked as though she wanted to smack him in the face rather than thank him for keeping her out of the rain.

She cast him a blistering look, then tore out of the stable with her basket wildly swinging at her side as she ran toward the servants entrance.

He felt a dull ache to his heart.

"Alex! What in bloody blazes was that about?" His father also had fire shooting from his eyes. "Is this why you refuse to go to London? You already have this girl warming your bed?"

"I haven't touched her, nor would I ever take a good girl like Viola outside of marriage. Don't you dare speak of her that way. She's the vicar's daughter." He strode toward the house, hurrying in through the front entry with his father trying to keep up and still tossing questions at him.

"A vicar's daughter? Ruskin's girl? What is she doing here?"

"Who do you think baked that game pie you inhaled last night?"

His father's eyes widened. "That slip of a girl is your cook?"

"Mrs. Stringer is my cook. Miss Ruskin, whose skills are amazing, has only agreed to help out for the party. She's testing out her recipes on me. We'll be trying out her fish courses on the entire staff today." He turned to Greaves who was standing by the front door since it was his post, and listening in on their every word. "I have asked Miss Ruskin to prepare a meal for all of you, Greaves. We'll be taking comments afterward."

His butler smiled. "Thank you, my lord."

Alexander dragged his father into his study and shut the door behind them. "I do not need the entire world overhearing your questions. Care for a drink?"

Rain now pelted the windows.

Viola would have gotten that sweet, little body of hers soaked.

Probably caught a chill.

How was it wrong of him to look after her?

"A port wine for me, son."

Alexander poured the same for himself, even though what he truly needed was something far stronger.

They settled in the large chairs beside the study's hearth.

"Now," his father said, pinning him with a glower, "tell me the truth this time. Who is this girl to you?"

CHAPTER 7

VIOLA'S HEART POUNDED as she hurried into the kitchen to start preparing the fish dishes she had planned for the viscount's party. Mr. Wilson had personally gone to the fishmonger this morning and obtained twenty plump, white fish that now lined the long tables in Ardley Hall's enormous kitchen. Those fish were now waiting to be skinned and boned. "Mrs. Stringer, can your girls handle this work?"

"Yes, Miss Ruskin." She turned to her kitchen staff. "Do as Miss Ruskin tells you, get those fish properly boned."

Viola had known the dear woman all her life and never doubted they would get along well. More important, she felt comfortable speaking openly and addressing her obvious concerns. "Thank you, Mrs. Stringer. Now you and I should have a little talk. Is there somewhere quiet we may speak? It should not take long."

"Yes, Miss Ruskin," she said, her clasped hands giving away her distress. "Although I expect I already know what you wish to say to me. His lordship gave us the orders. We are to take our instruction from you today."

Viola followed the woman into her private quarters. As head cook, she had a pleasant room all to herself just off the kitchen. Viola shut the door to give them privacy. "Mrs. Stringer, has he said anything about my working in the kitchen beyond today?"

She nodded. "He mentioned you would be in charge for his house party. I am to leave and–"

"No! You do not have to leave on my account. But it is important for me to be in charge of the kitchen during the house party. *Only* for the house party. I promise you, my role here is limited to those few days and nothing more. I know he gave you the choice of a paid leave or remaining here. I want you to know you are welcome to stay, if this is what you wish. I will be glad for your help, but you must be willing to take orders from me. You cannot question my authority during those limited days or your girls will take their guidance from you and not listen to me. Can you do this?"

"I'm not sure…well, yes. For you, I would. Most certainly, for you."

"I appreciate your honesty. If you choose not to stay, then I would have us speak to your staff together so they will be comfortable with me and take my orders while you are away."

"Miss Ruskin, will you be truthful with me?"

Viola nodded. "Yes, I would never lie to you."

Mrs. Stringer took a deep breath. "Are you sure his lordship does not intend to replace me?"

"Oh, most certainly not," she rushed to assure her, for the woman looked genuinely stricken. "I give you my word of honor. My duty is to my father first and always. However, you know he is ill. I do not know what the future will hold for me, but it will not be to work in the viscount's household in any capacity."

"Mr. Greaves has seen the way the viscount looks at you. He wants you here."

"All the more reason for me not to stay," Viola admitted.

Dear heaven, even helping out with his party was playing with fire.

"I understand your concern. His lordship is the most honorable man I know, but he is still a man and…if I may speak frankly, you are young and very pretty."

"His party is held for the purpose of finding himself a wife. I do not think his new wife will want me around, nor do I wish to be here once he marries. His family will help me find a position as cook or possibly as companion to an elderly lady in London, or perhaps in a grand home in a Cornwall estate."

"Ah, I see."

"Perhaps I've said too much, but we've known each other for so very long and I would never do anything to hurt you. I'll come here from time to time over the next week to test out recipes and get to know my way around this kitchen. It also helps to have your staff become familiar with me. But they are *your* staff. I promise you. Your position is secure."

Mrs. Stringer gave her a hug. "You are a dear, Miss Ruskin. In that case, if I am given the choice, I would love to take the time to visit my sister. I shall stay if you truly have need of me, but otherwise, I am eager to go."

It was just as the viscount had predicted.

Viola wished she understood the nature of people as well as he did. But for now, she had to prepare the fish and become acquainted with the viscount's kitchen and staff. After a quick tour of the larder, she and Mrs. Stringer inspected the work her girls had done skinning and gutting the fish.

Viola smiled at Mrs. Stringer. "You have trained them well."

She complimented the woman's staff as well, and then began to prepare seasonings that were to go on the fish. Since they were all interested in what she was doing, she held a tutorial for them. "Half this batch will be served hot with crumbles of bread to be seasoned and then baked in the oven." She then showed them which seasonings to use on the breadcrumbs. "Salt, pepper, and a little oil. Next, these fish will go in the oven to bake, but first we must season them with lemon, garlic, olives, and light salt and pepper. I sometimes add garlic to the breadcrumbs, but not if there is already garlic on the fish. It would then overpower the other flavors. The trick is always about balancing the flavors so that each stands out but does not annihilate the others."

The remaining fish were to be served cold and coated in a layer of *moyeunaise* sauce, as the French called it, made from a blend of egg yolks, lemon juice, vinegar, mustard and salt which she mixed together in a bowl. She would add capers as a garnish.

Some of these ingredients were out of her own stock, but she knew the viscount would reimburse her for the expense. While she counted every ha'penny, he was under no such constraint.

To her delight, the kitchen staff was eager to learn more from her, including Mrs. Stringer who proved to be most cooperative. She even suggested making a fish pie as a third recipe, so Viola set aside two of the fish and baked those in a pie crust. All eyes were on her as she explained the nuances of elevating the crust to perfection. "One must keep the butter cool and do not overly knead the dough or roll it out too thin. Every little detail matters."

"But will the crust not be too hard to eat?" one of the kitchen maids asked.

"Not if it is given proper respect and prepared as I indicated. There is no reason for it to be inedible. When mixed right and properly rolled out, it will be as delicious as the filling. Same when you are baking cakes, one never ought to stir the batter too much or you take the air out of it and the cake will never be light and airy."

Finally, the fish courses were ready to be presented to the viscount and his father.

To her dismay, the viscount insisted on her presence in the dining room.

Mrs. Stringer nudged her forward. "You go on, love. Be proud of what you've prepared. I'm sure his lordship wants you to explain the various courses to him and his father. He's proud of your work, too. Let him show you off a bit."

"But what will his father think?"

The woman pinched her cheek and laughed. "He'll think that Lady Trent will never forgive him if he doesn't engage you as head cook for their London household."

But Viola knew the earl would do no such thing. If anything, he would make certain to secure a position for her as far away from his son as possible. She washed her hands, patted her hair to brush back a few stray curls that had fallen over her brow as they'd worked in the hot kitchen, and finally strode into the dining room with her head held high.

The viscount rose and shot his father a warning glance to rise in her presence.

His father reluctantly complied.

"Come join us, Miss Ruskin. You can explain your recipes

while we eat. I've had Greaves set a place for you beside us. You are to dine with us."

She wanted to turn and run.

His father looked as though he was debating which of them to kill first, her or his son. But he said nothing and politely motioned for her to take the seat next to his. No doubt it was to ensure that she did not sit beside his son.

Her cheeks were on fire, but she nodded and cast him a sincere smile. "Thank you, my lord."

The footmen then brought in all three selections of fish.

Viola cleared her throat and quickly explained. "The first is a haddock baked with seasoned breadcrumbs, lemon, olives, garlic, and capers."

The viscount winked at her. "Looks delicious, Miss Ruskin."

She tried to remain professional, but this man always set her heart fluttering and this made her blush. "I hope so," she said, feeling heat creep up her cheeks.

To her relief, his father's dour expression evaporated after several bites. "You made this?"

"Yes, my lord."

"Dear heaven, I've never tasted anything so good in my life. Well, other than the game pie my son brought home for me yesterday."

"I'm glad you are enjoying the fish." She turned to the viscount and smiled at him. "And you, Lord Ardley? How do you find the fish?"

"Delicious. As you can see, I've licked my plate clean. What's next?"

"Your staff suggested I also make a fish pie." She allowed Greaves to cut open the pie and place a healthy slice on each of their plates. "This recipe is basic, but I've also added a little saffron in with the fish, peas, and potatoes."

"Saffron? Is that what was in the game pie, too?"

"Yes." She watched the two men devour everything put before them.

"And what is this third recipe, Miss Ruskin?" the earl now asked, actually smiling at her. However, she did not make too much of it. Liking her food did not mean he would like her as a match for his son.

"This one is hake, baked to flakiness and then cooled. Over it is a *moyeunaise* sauce and also some lightly warmed capers."

"Gad, this is delicious, too," the earl remarked.

"Father, as I've told you, Miss Ruskin is a genuine talent. Do you wonder why I treat her with all the respect she deserves? Nor will I allow anyone to demean her standing."

The earl grunted in dismissal of his son and turned to her. "Will you be including meat courses for this party?"

She nodded. "Yes, my lord. I hope to try those out, but not until after the Midsummer Fair. I've been enlisted to bake for all those in attendance and this is a time consuming undertaking."

"What will you be making for the fair?" the viscount asked.

"Mostly mince tarts, fruit tarts, scones, and bread. Things that can easily be taken in hand and eaten without need of plates or forks and knives."

He frowned. "Are these to be done in the vicarage kitchen? How will you manage it?"

"Most of the ladies in the village will help out. I cannot possibly bake that quantity in my oven. But I prepare the dough for each of them and instruct them on what to add to their fillings. Cinnamon for the apple tarts. Nutmeg, cloves, and cinnamon mixed in with the meat and suet for the mince tarts, although those can also be made without the meat. Not everyone can afford the luxury. Most of the ladies will use the simpler recipe of dried fruit and a splash of brandy for the mince."

"Let my staff help you out, Miss Ruskin," the viscount said. "Before you leave today, let Mrs. Stringer know what you'll need and feel free to use my ovens."

"Thank you for the offer, my lord. But it is not necessary. The village ladies and I have worked out a system and it is quite efficient."

He frowned. "Yes, with you doing all the work, no doubt."

"My only work is making the dough for them to use."

"You? Making all of it? How long does it take you?"

She cleared her throat. "It is manageable."

"How? By your working through the night and then going from house to house to ensure the ladies know what they are doing?"

She cleared her throat again. "There is a little of that...yes. My lord, I have done this without issue for several years running. If I may be so bold as to ask, why are you getting so worked up over it?"

"I am not." He frowned at her. "Fine, I'll say no more about it."

"Do that, son. It is none of your business, as Miss Ruskin has clearly indicated." The earl ran a hand across the nape of his neck. "Miss Ruskin, I believe I owe you an apology. Needless to say, I will no longer browbeat my son into returning to London with me and forgetting about his party. He is even more stubborn than I am and will not be budged from his decision. After tasting your food, I can assure you that my wife and I shall be attending this party of his, which is likely to be a disaster in every way but your meals."

The viscount laughed. "Thank you for that vote of confidence."

He ignored his son and continued to smile at her. "My mother will attend, as well. I think she will be very interested in meeting you."

"I look forward to meeting all the ladies in your family, my lord."

He gave a nod of satisfaction and then turned to his son. "I have no doubt the weekend will be a culinary *tour de force*. However, I'm not certain how the rest of it will turn out since you prefer to hide out like a bear in a cave. You've never had a tolerance for *ton* affairs, including weekend house parties. Let's hope it will not all blow up in your face. You do see how easily it can turn into disaster?"

He stared once more at Viola as he spoke the last.

Why did the earl have such little faith in his son? Hadn't he chosen well in his first wife, Lady Jillian? After the way the man had complimented her on her meals, she knew his reference to disaster had nothing to do with her culinary skills. She could prepare a feast for the entire village in her sleep.

She caught the viscount eyeing her as well.

Oh.

Yes, this was the disaster in the offing. The attraction between her and the viscount. But it would not lead anywhere, nor would she allow it to go beyond a kiss.

Dear heaven, how she wanted this man to kiss her.

But she would not allow a jot more, for she would be no man's mistress.

Just one kiss.

Why did her traitorous body have other ideas?

And why, in heaven's name, could she not feel this way about George Haworth?

CHAPTER 8

ALEXANDER DID NOT see Viola for the next few days, his father having stayed on to ensure they were kept apart. He only complied for Viola's sake. Protecting her honor was the only reason he played along with his father's demands.

Besides, the old man was leaving tomorrow.

At last.

He would have peace in his own home…well, not so much peace as the privacy to ache for Viola without anyone to snoop and comment.

Today was the day of the Midsummer Fair.

As dawn broke on the horizon, Alexander knew Viola had already been up for several hours and furiously preparing her dough. Perhaps she had stayed up all night and not yet gone to bed. He washed and dressed, then saddled his own mount, a seasoned bay he had named Caligula despite the beast's gentle nature.

He had acquired Caligula only a year ago and the name reflected his own vile temperament at the time. "There," he muttered, tightening the cinch. Since the hour was early, he easily attended to the chore himself in order not to waste time rousing the grooms.

He rode off toward the vicarage.

There was a beauty to this early morning hour, the sun glowing behind the hills and a light mist still hovering over the meadows. The air was cool and still damp, and the scents were vivid. Dew-laden grass. Lilac flowering in tumbles over the hedgerows. Mince tarts baking.

He dismounted and strode into the vicarage kitchen which was an utter disaster with bowls strewn everywhere, a mist of flour rising off Viola's work table, and Viola was darting about like a little whirlwind. "I thought you said you only prepared the dough for the ladies of the village. But you are also baking."

She cast him a tired smile, but her eyes were alight and she appeared pleased to see him. "Good morning, my lord. Are you here to criticize or help?"

He grinned as he rolled up his sleeves. "Help, of course."

He hadn't dressed finely, merely tossed on a work shirt and a pair of old, buff trousers. "What shall I do?"

She had flour smudged on her chin, nose, and cheeks. The pins in her hair had loosened and he expected her hair would fall in a glorious, dark tumble if she so much as sneezed. One quick move and it would all come down in a breathtaking cascade about her slender shoulders.

Her sleeves were rolled up and her hands were buried in fat wads of dough. "Take the scones out of the oven and set them on the window ledge to cool."

"I also smell mince pies baking. What am I to do with those?"

She blew a loose curl off her face. "Um, they're only tarts. They have a few more minutes to go. They'll be ready by the time you finish putting the scones out to cool. Then you can help me make another batch, but this time we shall be making strawberry tarts. Once we finish those, then you must go. The ladies will arrive in about an hour to pick up their dough and I do not want them to find you here."

"Why? Is Mrs. Bligh not with you?"

"Actually, she is. She is upstairs assisting my father."

Alexander's expression sobered. "How is he?"

She let out a soft breath. "Not well."

Blast.

"You know you can count on me for anything you need. Do not be too proud to ask for my help, Viola. Your father is adored in the village and so are you."

She said nothing, merely continued to work. "Well, if you insist on making a nuisance of yourself, then take the rhubarb and chop the stalks into small pieces about the size of a fingernail. I'll make half of the tarts with strawberries and rhubarb, and the other half just strawberries."

"Why not some just rhubarb?"

"Requires too much sugar and that is a costly commodity. Now, are you going to help or are you determined to stand there and be a nuisance?"

He did not take offense at her words, merely chuckled. "I am a viscount, therefor it is impossible for me to be a nuisance."

She looked up from her work and cast him a genuine smile. "I do not quite see the logic in that statement."

"No, I don't suppose you would. But it makes perfect sense to any young lady versed in matters of society. A wealthy, dazzlingly handsome – if I do say so myself – viscount is always much desired. One's stature is elevated when in the presence of said viscount."

"Ah, I see. And what is said of a vicar's daughter? Is one honored in any way by her presence?"

He cast her an affectionate smile. "Yes, and if one can cook as well as you, then I would rank her above the daughter of a duke."

Viola laughed and rolled her eyes. "Oh, I think that is a bit of an exaggeration."

"Not at all. You are every bit as worthy as a duke's daughter. Indeed, I would even rank you above a princess."

She paused to regard him. "And this is why your father wants to treat you like a child and put you in leading strings. He wants to hold onto you tightly to make certain you do not botch your wife search. No one but you would ever consider a vicar's daughter as anything more than bordering on genteel. Most would properly rank me as common."

"Not a single thing common about you, Viola. And I am not going to botch my search, no matter what my father thinks. I know exactly what I am doing."

She arched an eyebrow. "We'll see. I would never contradict you in front of him, but I have to agree with his concerns. You ought to be in London where all the eligible young ladies can fuss and coo over you. The last place you should be is in a vicarage kitchen about to slice off your fingers instead of the rhubarb because you are looking at me and not at your task."

He glanced down at his hand, relieved to see he had not actually sliced himself. He wiggled his fingers at her. "All accounted for."

"There is a trick to protecting yourself."

"From those society debutantes or your rhubarb?"

She giggled. "The rhubarb. Tuck your fingers in so that only your knuckles are exposed. Hold the stalks down with your knuckles as you chop. You won't lose any fingers that way."

"Ah, very clever." He quickly chopped up the stalks. "All right, done."

"Excellent. Now put the rhubarb, strawberries, sugar, and a pinch of salt into one bowl. Do the same with the other, only no rhubarb. I put some tapioca on to boil earlier. It is cooling by the oven. Now, you are going to slowly mix the tapioca into each bowl."

He liked following her instructions, felt ridiculously proud of himself for assisting. She also had a naturally kind way of issuing orders, making him feel helpful instead of interfering or slowing her down.

She watched him pour each mixture into the tart molds that already had bottom crusts tucked in them. Then she stepped forward and began to crisscross thin strips of dough across each tart, her fingers working with a feverish speed. "Done." She took another moment to brush a milky looking glaze lightly over each top strip. "Now, set them in the oven."

She had an adorably exhausted smile on her face as she rinsed all the wet dough off her hands, and then sank onto a stool with a sigh of relief. "As soon as the ladies come by to collect their bowls, I shall properly wash up, take a quick nap, and then ready myself for the fair."

He grabbed a clean drying cloth, dipped the end of it into cold water, and sat on the stool beside hers. "Why don't you run up now and tend to yourself? Just tell me what to do and I'll take care of the ladies when they come by."

"Absolutely not! You'll hand the wrong bowl to the wrong lady, and everyone of them will linger and inanely smile at you. Not to mention, they'll wonder what you are doing here, and – dear heaven – wonder whether you spent the entire night here."

"I'll make certain they know I only arrived a few minutes before they did. Send Mrs. Bligh down to hand out the bowls with me. No one will question my presence if she is here." As he spoke, he began to gently wipe the flour and bits of dough off her face and neck.

She was remarkably pretty, especially with the soft blush to her cheeks.

Her nose was also pink.

"Hold out your hands. What is that red spot on the tip of your finger? Blood?"

"No, just strawberries. I guess it was stubborn and did not wash off as I cleaned my hands just now." She held up the finger in question.

Unthinking, he drew it into his mouth and licked his tongue along it.

Viola almost tumbled off her stool.

He caught her about the waist to steady her, which was another mistake because having his arm around her set him on fire.

Lord, how could he be so foolish?

He released her, leaving her to grip the edge of the stool to regain her balance.

"Strawberry and rhubarb," he said, as though nothing out of the ordinary had just happened between them. Oh, sure. Licking her finger was bad enough, but he'd also suckled it between his lips.

She was still staring at him, wide-eyed and ashen.

In the next moment, her face burst into flame.

He groaned, not only because he was sorry…but because he was not really sorry at all. He wanted more of her. All of her. "Viola, I owe you an apology. I did not think. And that mix of strawberry and rhubarb was delicious. I was proud I helped make it and curious to taste it, even if it was on your finger, so I…just hit me with the frying pan and put me out of my misery."

"I had better go upstairs. I'll send Mrs. Bligh down." She knocked over her stool and almost fell over it in her haste to run away.

He caught her again as she was about to go flying onto the hard floor. This time, he drew her up hard against his body. He heard her soft *oof* as her back slammed against his chest. He wrapped both of his arms around her while also contorting in every way possible to avoid placing any part of him in contact with her bosom as she turned to push away from him. Not to mention his immediate contortions to hide the explosion going on in the lower part of his torso the moment her delectable derriere had collided with his male parts.

Mrs. Bligh chose that inopportune moment to walk into the kitchen.

She dropped the ewer she was carrying, frozen in place as it smashed into a thousand pieces on the floor. "Lord, have mercy!"

"Mrs. Bligh," he said in a calm manner, trying to ignore Viola desperately struggling to wriggle out of his arms, "this is not at all what you must think. Miss Ruskin has been working herself to the point of exhaustion. She knocked over her stool and was about to fall over it. I merely caught her before she cracked her head open on the floor. And now I must insist on sweeping up the ewer's shards. Just tell me where I may find the broom and I will take care of it as soon as Miss Ruskin calms down."

His hands now rested gently on her shoulders to keep her facing him. "I have thick boots on. You ladies are wearing house slippers. You will cut your feet if you attempt to move about. You know I am right. Now stop fighting me and let me carry you away from the kitchen."

"Are you mad?"

"Perhaps, but it has nothing to do with that broken ewer. When must I take the tarts out of the oven?"

"What are you talking about? I'll do it. You are not to go near my tarts, my lord. Nor the broom. I'll–"

He emitted a soft growl of frustration. "Do not contradict me. I am sweeping up and that's an end to it. You are to go upstairs and rest before you collapse in a heap on the floor. What good will you be to your father if you are so exhausted you cannot even walk straight? Mrs. Bligh, take her upstairs now. Miss Ruskin, do not fight me on this. That is an order."

Viola pounded her fists on his chest. "I will not have you ordering me about my own kitchen. Those tarts will be ready in five minutes. Only once they are out will I agree to go upstairs and rest. But only if Mrs. Bligh agrees to remain down here and hand off the bowls to the ladies as they come by. As for sweeping, I'll attend to it."

"As you attend to everything? Look at you, Viola. You are so pale, you cannot even stand up on your own. Can you not see yourself wobbling?"

"Who invited you here? Go home." She inhaled deeply. "My tarts!"

She rushed to the oven and stepped on a shard of the busted pottery. "Ow!"

"Blast it, Viola!" He scooped her up in his arms and carried her into the parlor. "Sit here and do not move! I'll take care of your precious tarts. Mrs. Bligh, fetch me a clean cloth and the strongest spirits you can find. Whiskey is best, if you have it. Otherwise, rum or brandy."

Viola was still frowning at him. "You are going to drink?"

"No, I am going to clean your foot so it does not get infected. I'll be right back." He strode to the kitchen to remove her tarts since she would slay him if they wound up burnt because of him. After removing them, he spotted the broom in a corner and quickly swept up, leaving the shards in a neat corner for Mrs. Bligh to dispose of later.

He did not know how to shut off the oven or whether it should be shut off, so he left that chore for Mrs. Bligh as well.

He then returned to Viola, who must have been in pain or else she would have been hopping up and down like a little frog. "Let's tend that foot."

He knelt beside her, removed her slipper, and plucked out the large shard stuck in the sole.

He then placed Viola's foot across his thigh. Since Mrs. Bligh had not yet returned with the requested supplies, he used his handkerchief to wipe away the trickle of blood.

Fortunately, there was not very much of it.

She was blushing again, for he had a hand on her bare calf to hold her foot steady. "I want you to leave once you finish tending to me."

He glanced up from his ministrations. "No."

"No?"

"You heard me. I am going to carry you upstairs once I am done. Mrs. Bligh will escort me to make certain nothing improper goes on between the two of us. Not that there is even a remote possibility of it. You have flour all over your hair and face. Your eyes are bloodshot and your eyelids are so heavy, you can barely hold them open. Not to mention, your foot is still bleeding. You are about as tempting as a rock."

That was an outright lie.

She was insanely adorable and he wanted the world to disappear so he could be alone with her and kiss her senseless.

Now she was crying.

He groaned. "Oh, don't do that."

"I can't help it."

His sigh of relief was audible as Mrs. Bligh hurried back in carrying a clean, damp cloth, a bottle of brandy, and bandages. "Thank you," he muttered, and immediately set about to work on cleansing her foot. "This will sting a bit, Miss Ruskin. But only for a moment. I'll work fast."

Mrs. Bligh watched him. "She takes on too much. Poor thing, I've told her time and again that she must not try to do it all by herself. But does she listen to me?"

Alexander nodded. "She does not listen to me, either."

Viola frowned at him. "I had everything in hand and was doing just fine before you stomped in."

Mrs. Bligh gasped. "Is that any way to talk to his lordship?"

She sniffled. "I suppose not, but I don't care. What can he do to me? Have me drawn and quartered? That will have to wait until after his house party since it will be a complete disaster without my cooking to elevate it."

"Oh, dear. I think you ought to stop talking now, Miss Viola. My lord, she doesn't mean a word of it."

He cast the woman a wry smile. "I'm sure she means every word, but it is all right. Everything she has said is true. I am not angry. I know she is overworked and overset at the moment. I will not have her drawn and quartered just yet."

"Thank you, my lord. That is very good of you. Oh, I hear the ladies starting to arrive. Let me attend to them." Mrs. Bligh lumbered to the kitchen. He heard her conversing with the ladies as she handed them their bowls and dough.

"Where is Viola?" one of them asked.

"She tripped over her stool and hurt her foot. His lordship happened to be passing by and I summoned him over to help. He was in the war, you know. He knows how to tend these sort of injuries."

To his ears, the women seemed genuinely concerned about Viola. Well, everyone liked her. It was little wonder. She was always one of the first to lend assistance. But she looked completely spent now, barely able to keep her eyes open. This had nothing to do with his own stupidity in licking her finger and setting off this chain of events. Working herself to the point of exhaustion was her way of denying anything was wrong with her father or that she was about to lose him.

Had he not been with her, she might have cut one of her fingers while chopping rhubarb. Or burned her hand. Or tripped even if she hadn't been running from him. Such things happened when one was mind-numbingly tired.

She was trying to remain angry with him, but this was not in her nature. She sighed and cast him an apologetic look. "Thank you for tending to my foot."

"I'm sorry I upset you." He wanted to caress her cheek, but he had caused enough damage already. "Truly, I wasn't thinking. I only meant to taste the strawberries." Yes, he was sticking to that lame excuse despite both of them knowing it was a blatantly sexual gesture.

So was the matter of his hand cupping her shapely leg as he

worked on her injury.

And the graze of his fingers along the tender sole of her foot as he bound it.

In truth, was not everything he did concerning Viola fraught with sexual hunger? His every look. His every touch. His dreams of her that filled his nights. "Viola, what time will you be heading to the village green?"

This is where the fair was to be held.

"Around eleven o'clock."

"I'll send my estate manager to you in one of our wagons shortly before then. He'll load everything up for you and drive you down there. He will also stay on to set up your display table. You are not to do any of the heavy work yourself. Leave it all to Wilson. I want your promise on this."

She ground her teeth. "The village men usually do this heavier set up work for me. I expect to be looked after just fine."

"And my estate manager will make certain of it. He will also check on you frequently throughout the day and take you home whenever you are ready. Do you hear me, Viola? You are not to overdo it. If you will not think of yourself, then think of your father. You need to stay strong for him."

Her eyes began to tear again. "That is not fair."

He knew the frail, old man was constantly in her thoughts. It was obvious she was working herself to the ground in a desperate attempt to take her mind off him.

He understood the helplessness of watching a loved one die and aching because there was nothing to be done for them. "I know, my sweet girl. I felt the same when Jillian and Molly got sick. It is the worst feeling in the world. I am here because I do not want you to go through this same agony alone."

Mrs. Bligh lumbered back into the parlor.

He rose. "I am done tending her and will now carry her upstairs. Miss Ruskin, I shall be angry if I hear that you did not rest. Can you manage the kitchen on your own, Mrs. Bligh? I will send one of my men down to assist you, if you wish. As for the fair, I've already told Miss Ruskin that my estate manager will come down here at eleven o'clock to take her and her wares to the village green. He will take care of setting her up. She is to do nothing but point and give orders."

He scooped Viola into his arms.

She felt so good against him.

The scent of her skin had his heart in somersaults again.

She wrapped her arms around his neck and leaned her head against his shoulder. "I suppose it is useless for me to insist on climbing the stairs on my own."

"Utterly useless and your protests will fall upon deaf ears." This girl was so exhausted, he expected her to fall asleep before he reached the top of the stairs.

She felt like a kitten in his arms.

Mrs. Bligh opened the door to Viola's bedchamber. The bed did not look as though it had been slept in at all last night. The room itself was small but tidy and pleasantly appointed. It suited her, for this is what she was, too. Small and neatly buttoned up, but very pleasing.

He set her down atop the counterpane, leaving it to Mrs. Bligh to assist her in changing out of her flour-drenched clothes. "I will see you later at the fair."

He returned home.

Despite all that had happened, the hour was still early and he expected his father would still be asleep. This gave Alexander time to wash up and change out of his work clothes. He allowed his valet to set out an attire befitting his rank because, as viscount, he had a certain dignity to maintain.

Not that he had maintained any dignity at Viola's this morning.

He had done a rather poor job of it.

Hopefully, word of his latest encounter with the girl would not get around the village. Not that he cared, but Viola would, and he did not want her feeling more hurt than she already was.

He sauntered into the dining room just as the clock chimed the nine o'clock hour. In truth, he usually came down to breakfast much earlier. But there would be no work done today in Ardley because of the fair.

His father was already seated at the table, sipping his coffee and reading one of several newspapers that were delivered to Alexander each day. "Good morning, Father."

"Morning." He lowered the newspaper and stared at Alexander.

Oh, drat.

How had the news about this morning's fiasco spread so quickly? And what exactly was the rumor being spread?

Alexander calmly loaded up his plate with eggs, kippers, sausage, and something unappetizingly gray that looked like someone's boiled sock. Well, maybe he would leave that aside.

He then took a seat beside his father. "Is there a reason you are still gawking at me?"

"You know very well my reason."

Alexander arched an eyebrow. "Actually, I have no idea. Would you be so kind as to spell it out?"

"Why were you at the vicarage this morning? And what possible reason did you have for taking Miss Ruskin in your arms?"

CHAPTER 9

"WHO SAID MISS Ruskin was in my arms?" Alexander realized this was going to be a very long day.

"Wasn't she? Do you dare deny it?" His father shot him a castigating scowl. "Alexander, you may be heedless of your own decorum, but think of the poor girl. You will ruin her reputation if you are not careful. Then what will you do? You certainly cannot marry her."

"I can marry whomever I please."

"That is where you are wrong. I am still Earl of Trent and all you have is the courtesy title that I, in my good nature, have given you. I may not be able to stop you from inheriting my title or the entailed properties, but I have full control of the unentailed assets and I am not prohibited from mortgaging the entailed estates to the hilt. I assure you, I will cut you out to the greatest extent possible if you continue with your arrogant attitude."

"Do not threaten me, Father. I have been through war, deprivation, and aching loss. I know what it means to be a proper husband, father, and friend. As the *courtesy* Viscount Ardley, I also know what the villagers under my protection need, and protecting them is what I will do whenever the situation calls for it. As for Miss Ruskin, she was only in my arms because she had worked herself into exhaustion and was about to trip over her kitchen stool. I caught her before she hit her head on the hard floor. That is all. She is a good girl and quite innocent. That should have been obvious to you."

"It was. I have no quarrel with her. But she is a vicar's daughter."

"And an incredibly talented cook."

"That is even worse. You cannot marry a cook."

He leaned forward and met his father's gaze head on. "Let me assure you, if her reputation is besmirched in any way, I shall step up and marry her. So do not think to spread gossip about her, or it will blow up in your face."

"Alexander!"

"You ought to go home, Father. Leave now. Before this argument gets any worse."

"Of all the effrontery!"

"Whose? Yours or mine?" Alexander sighed and shook his head. "We both need to calm down. I am holding my house party. You are still invited, even if you happen to be irksome at the moment. I will meet those three diamonds I have painstakingly selected and intend to spend time getting to know each of them. So why are we arguing?"

He wanted badly to defuse this situation, but neither was he about to stand down from a confrontation if his stubborn father did not let up.

"Fine, no more arguments. Let us just enjoy the day. I will leave tomorrow."

"Does this mean you will join me at the fair instead of sitting here and sulking?"

"Earls do not sulk." He set aside his newspaper and rose. "Shall we walk down there now?"

"As you wish. The villagers are merely setting up. The fair won't start before eleven."

"And Miss Ruskin? Will she be there beforehand?"

"I hope not. I've admonished her to get some rest or she will never make it through the afternoon. No chance she will last into the evening. She stayed up all night preparing her dough mixture for all the ladies in the village to use for their baked treats. On top of that, she made her own tarts."

"I will not deny she appears to be a hard worker."

"She is." He was not going to talk to his father about Viola's fears or vulnerabilities. His grandmother, Lady Eloise, would understand and be someone in whom he might confide. But his father? A good man, but utterly at a loss when it came to true struggles.

They walked down to the village green together, his father in all his glory as people approached him and cheered to see the Earl of Trent among them. They thought he cared enough about them to attend their local fair.

Well, in all fairness, his father was a good man and did care about those in his charge.

The day was glorious, the sky a vivid blue and the weather not too hot. Tufts of white clouds were pushed across the sky by a gentle wind and provided shady relief whenever the sun hid behind them.

The air held the aroma of cinnamon, fruit, and freshly baked pies.

Viola appeared shortly after eleven o'clock, driven by Wilson in one of the Ardley Hall wagons. Alexander breathed a sigh of relief, for her eyes looked bright and she appeared much more refreshed than she had been this morning.

Most of the other food tables and stalls with games had been set up. Space in the center of the fairgrounds had been left for her, and many of the villagers were already lining up to taste her wares.

Several hurried over to assist Wilson set up her table, including the squire's son, George Haworth.

Viola sat in the wagon while they did so, looking every bit the ethereal wood sprite. She had on a simple gown the pine green color of a forest. As usual, she had not a trace of ribbon or lace adornment to embellish it. But she could wear an old grain sack and still look elegant. Her hair was drawn back in a soft chignon that would soon be hidden when she donned the straw bonnet held in her hand.

He frowned.

Why was she still sitting there looking like a lost, elfin princess?

Was her foot hurting her?

He made his way through the crowd, his father at his heels because the old man was going to stick to him like a barnacle to a ship and not permit him a moment alone with Viola. He did not care, for he had already resolved after this morning's finger incident to keep some distance between them.

That resolve fell to the wayside now, but not for any reason other than he was worried about her. This was not like Viola. She should be hopping down from the wagon. When did she ever sit quietly and not take charge?

She did not appear to be in pain, but perhaps she was hiding it very well.

His heart was already thrumming and he could not take his eyes off her now that he had reached her side. "Miss Ruskin, is there a reason you have not yet climbed down off your perch?"

"You made me promise to sit quietly and allow others to help me." She cast him a wry smile. "It is completely against my nature, as you well know. I have been gnashing my teeth and silently cursing you all the while."

He laughed. "I see. Is this why your eyes are shining so brightly? Gleaming as you wickedly think up a thousand tortures for me?"

She grinned back at him. "Quite so. Will you please help me down now?"

He nodded. "How is your foot? Can you stand on it? Or is it too painful?"

"I am perfectly fine. It wasn't a deep cut and the bandage provides sufficient padding to cushion the injury."

"Good." He reached up and took her by the waist to lift her down.

He felt his father's frown at his back.

Not that he cared.

But he released Viola once she stood firmly on the ground. "You are swamped with admirers. The line for your table has been forming for an hour now."

"Oh, dear. I shall sell out within ten minutes," she muttered. "I should have made more tarts. Perhaps I will return to–"

"Perhaps you will simply stay here and enjoy the day. You

need to give the other ladies a chance. No one will pay any attention to their tables while there remains so much as a crumb on yours."

She gave a good natured laugh. "Very well. I fear you are right."

"I am a viscount. I am always right."

Her smile was simply dazzling. Her irritation with him must have evaporated in the glorious sunshine. He watched her a moment longer to make certain she was not hiding the truth from him about her injury, then moved on to greet the other villagers and sample their wares.

Of course, nothing he ate was going to rival Viola's talent.

His father had left his side and now stood beside Viola, assisting her in selling her tarts. She and everyone standing in queue took great delight in this, believing the Earl of Trent was honoring them with his presence and attention.

Alexander knew the old man was doing this to stand like an immovable block of granite between him and Viola.

George Haworth approached him as he stood with his arms crossed over his chest, staring at Viola and his father in the distance. "I understand you have been working closely with Miss Ruskin lately."

"Good day, Haworth." He was not going to be rude to the man, but whatever passed between him and Viola was no one's business.

"Word has it she is organizing a house party for you. Quite a special party, it seems. I hear from your father you are seeking a wife."

Why could his old man not keep his mouth shut?

Well, it was no secret.

His own staff would have whispered the news throughout Ardley days ago.

Viscount emerges from his stupor and prepares to do his duty as heir. Seeking ton diamond to pop out sons.

Gossip was already rife. Did his father have to stoke that fire and blabber about it to everyone at the fair?

George cleared his throat and straightened his shoulders. "So am I."

Alexander now pinned his gaze on the man. "What?"

"I am also seeking a wife, my lord. I wish to marry Miss Ruskin. Her father heartily approves."

Alexander arched an eyebrow and tossed him an intimidating frown.

George paled, for he was more of a scholarly sort than a fighter. He was of average height and average build, and women probably considered him pleasant in looks. His family was wealthy, and he was fairly intelligent. Grudgingly, Alexander had to admit he was a decent fellow. "Why are you telling me this? Are you asking for my permission, too? I can assure you, the choice is Miss Ruskin's alone to make."

"No, my lord. You have the power to take that choice from her."

"Have a care, Haworth. I do not like what you are implying."

"My only wish is to protect her. Rumors get around, if you understand my meaning. It has not escaped anyone's notice how often you are in her company lately, and at all hours."

"Are you mad?"

"Perhaps, but you must have a care about her reputation. I have to think about mine as well. I cannot marry her if she is…tarnished."

"Blessed saints, you think I would ever hurt that girl?" But his father thought the same. How many others were thinking it as well?

"I know your meetings are innocent because I know Miss Ruskin is a good soul and would never do anything untoward. But others may not judge her so kindly. You are the earl's heir, after all. Rich, powerful, and all the ladies consider you quite handsome. For an unmarried young lady to be seen so much in your company…need I say more? Everyone knows she is beneath your station and you will not marry her."

"Is that so?" Alexander began to seethe, for Viola was quality and deserved better than to be talked about like this.

"Scandal is already brewing and it will destroy her father if he learns of it. After all his years of good service to the parish, is he to die knowing there is a stain on his daughter's–"

"Utter another word of that nonsense and I shall lay you low." Alexander felt the blood roar to his head. "How can anyone think she is anything other than sweet and decent? If you claim to know and trust her as you do, then how can you even think to abandon her? Over some unfounded rumors? You've known her all her life. When has she ever behaved as anything less than a lady?"

"She hasn't, not to my knowledge. But people talk and I am not in a position to ignore such chatter. If you admire her as much as you say you do, then put an end to your meetings. It is the only way to protect her reputation. Or do you not care that she will be branded as your mistress? Is this not what men of your rank do? Dally with every pretty girl you see."

"George, do you have a death wish? I suggest you stop talking now."

"I know I should, but I care for her and will not have her hurt by you." He curled his hands into fists and appeared to be building up the courage to toss a punch.

Alexander knew he would never do it, for the repercussions would be too great. Hitting an earl's son? George did not have it in him.

"Miss Ruskin does not understand the rules of these *ton* games," he continued, his tone now pleading. "She is naive enough to believe you sincerely mean to court her. But you and I know that viscounts do not marry vicar's daughters. So, leave her to me. I will be a good husband to her."

Alexander was furious, but held his temper in check. "Haworth, you know me to be a man of honor."

"Yes, my lord. I do."

"Then believe me when I tell you that I will never dishonor Miss Ruskin. You have my oath on it."

This seemed to allay Haworth's fears.

"Thank you," he said, and rushed off to rejoin the festivities.

Alexander was not feeling particularly festive.

As the afternoon wore on and everyone had eaten their fill, the drinking and dancing began in earnest. He wanted to invite Viola to dance, but dared not. He did not care about earning his father's disapproval. But Haworth's words had sunk in. If gossip had gotten around the village about Viola been found in his arms, then he was not going to toss more logs onto that burning flame.

Instead, he danced with George's mother, the wife of the local squire.

He also danced with Mrs. Bligh.

He then shared dances with several of the village girls.

As for Viola, she danced twice with his father…drat the man.

She also danced with the young shepherd lad, Jeremy.

Alexander struggled to suppress his apish jealousy when she danced with George Haworth. Despite their earlier tension, he liked George. The usually mild mannered clot was a decent man and probably would make her a good husband.

Still, Alexander would not hesitate to beat him to a bloody pulp if he dared claim more than a dance from Viola.

He drew a breath of relief when Viola declined a second dance with George, claiming her foot was now a little sore. She then took the opportunity to talk about her mishap and how she would have fallen on her face if he and Mrs. Bligh had not been on hand to catch her.

Gossip dispelled, for the most part.

George was not quite convinced and shot Alexander another troubled glance.

But all in all, Viola had done a thorough job of restoring her reputation, assuming it had ever been in question.

Alexander meant to keep it that way.

He held to his word and did not see Viola again until over a week later when his guests began to arrive for his ill-fated house party. Well, he should stop thinking of it as that. But how could he not?

Despite his wishes, Viola still refused to take that fifteenth guest chamber for herself. Instead, she took over Mrs. Stringer's quarters.

It galled him.

Truly, it did.

Viola deserved better than to be housed in a cook's bedchamber off the kitchen.

But he was not going to pursue the matter since Viola and his entire family would be up in arms if he tried to move her upstairs.

Perhaps George was not wrong to be worried.

He had missed her sorely.

Impatient to see her again, Alexander strode into the kitchen once Greaves had informed him she had settled in. He watched her standing amid the kitchen girls, giving them a speech meant to encourage them for the battle ahead.

He stifled a smile.

She was wearing a chef's apron that must have belonged to Mrs. Stringer since it appeared to be far too big for her. But she'd managed to wrap it securely about her body as well as circle the apron ties twice around her waist. She also wore a mobcap that covered her beautiful curls and made her spectacular eyes look big and bright as sparkling moons.

"Good morning, Miss Ruskin. Are you ready for my guests? Do you have all the supplies you need?"

"Yes, my lord," she said, bobbing a curtsey. "I have come by here every day this past week to review all details with Mrs. Stringer before she departed for her sister's home. Your housekeeper, Mrs. Lester, has also been immensely helpful. As has Mr. Wilson, your estate manager. I am lacking nothing on my list."

"Glad to hear it."

She cast him a pert smile. "Are you prepared, my lord?"

He grinned. "To sample your meals? I have been dreaming of nothing else all week long. What are you serving tonight?"

"That will remain my secret, but I know you will like it."

"I have no doubt." He then took her aside a moment. "Viola, I want to introduce you to my family as soon as possible. I may not have time for it once all the guests arrive and this weekend party is underway. Will you have time for us today? Just tell me honestly. I want to accommodate your schedule, for everyone will hang me if I interfere with your food preparation. Tell me, what is convenient for you?"

"I think we ought to wait a few days before introductions are made. Let them sample my food first. Breakfast, luncheon, and supper. This way they will have a sense of my cooking. But I think the best time for such a meeting is right after breakfast. However, not much beyond it because then I must start on the rest of the daily meal preparations. You have a good staff, but they are not used to my recipes yet, so I must keep a close watch on how they mix the ingredients."

She thought he meant to introduce her as his cook.

Nothing was further from his thoughts.

Well, he was not yet certain what he meant for her to be. "It is only a four day house party, this day counting as day one. Let's plan on introductions tomorrow after breakfast. I'll leave you to it, Viola."

"Good luck to you, my lord."

He arched an eyebrow. "With my wife hunt? Thank you. I'm sure I will need it."

She laughed softly. "You'll do just fine."

"That remains to be seen. By the way, sneak a peek at the three diamonds once they arrive. Try to do this for me. I'll be curious to know your opinion."

Her eyes shone with renewed sparkle as she cast him an indulgent smile. "Ooh, spying. So you still view them as the enemy?"

"No…I…" He groaned. "Blast it, Viola. My family is already giving me a hard time about this. I simply wish to be careful, that is all."

"I know. I should not be teasing you. Forgive me? I'll pop my head out of the kitchen whenever I have the chance."

He dared not tarry any longer, so he left the kitchen and marched to the front door in time to welcome the first of his guests to arrive.

"Gabriel!" He rushed down the steps to greet his brother. "So glad you could make it. I'm in serious need of an ally."

Gabriel laughed. "Oh, I wouldn't miss this for the world. My big brother on the marriage hunt and certain to make an utter mess of it, if our father is to be believed. He hasn't stopped complaining about you. Stubborn. Heedless. Going after the wrong women. That's what he used to say about me before Daisy came along and reformed my rakehell ways."

"You were always the best little brother a man could have. Look at you now, a pillar of society and utterly besotted with your wife."

Gabriel grinned. "Daisy is quite splendid, isn't she? I only hope these diamonds you've chosen to invite have one-tenth her charm."

"Did you bring the children?"

"No, we left them in the care of their maternal grandparents," he said, referring to Daisy's parents, John and Sophie Farthingale. "We thought it more important to be free to concentrate on you. They'll have a smashing time. I can assure you, no shortage of Farthingales to dote on them. Graelem and Laurel are doing the same with their children."

The two of them now turned to the women in the carriage, Daisy and their grandmother, Lady Eloise Dayne. While Gabriel assisted his wife, Alexander helped his grandmother climb down. He tossed aside formality and gave her a big hug. "I'm glad you are here, Grandmama."

"Wouldn't miss it, dear boy." She patted his cheek. "Someone needs to keep a tight rein on your father. He may be the Earl of Trent, but I am still his mother and not above giving him a good spanking."

Alexander laughed. "I hear he has been spouting off about me."

"He is apoplectic over a certain young lady who is your cook. I cannot wait to meet this extraordinary girl. I believe you mentioned her in your letter to me, Viola Ruskin? Is it not so?"

"Oh, lord. What has he said about her? Grandmama, she is a sweet, innocent thing. There is nothing sordid going on between us. You'll adore her. I will have you meet her tomorrow."

She took his offered arm to escort her into the house. "Why not today?"

He shook his head. "You need to try her food first. I'll wager you've never tasted anything so good. She is not my permanent cook, only helping me out for this weekend. Mrs. Stringer is on holiday at the moment."

"I am intrigued. Your father claims she is the vicar's daughter? Have I seen her before? A lovely, little girl with dark hair and big, dark eyes?"

"Yes, that's her." He led his grandmother into the parlor where refreshments were being laid out by Greaves. Tea, lemonade, and sherry for the ladies. Wine and brandy for the gentlemen. Sandwiches, scones, and ginger cake for everyone. There were also miniature tarts filled with ham and cheese, Greaves was proudly explaining to Gabriel and Daisy as he handed one to each. He then repeated the same for his grandmother. "You must try one, Lady Dayne. I vow, you will have tasted nothing like it."

She took one and then smiled up at Alexander. "No wonder your father could not stop talking about the girl. Must I wait until tomorrow to meet her?"

He nodded. "She's too busy preparing tonight's dinner and refuses to be distracted."

"Oh, she sounds quite strident."

"No, she's the sweetest thing. Don't believe anything Father has told you. Where is he and Mother, by the way? I thought you were all coming up together."

"They cannot be far behind us. He might have stopped in Ardley for a reason. By the way, Lady Withnall is riding with them."

He stared at his grandmother, wondering whose bright idea it was to invite London's most feared and influential gossip. It certainly wasn't his. The woman was a little ferret, digging up secrets her poor victims wished to keep hidden in darkness forever.

Not that he had any.

Nor did Viola.

"Was this Father's idea? I did not put her on my list." He was already dreading this weekend and now it was certain to be a disaster.

His grandmother put a calming hand on his arm. "It was my idea. You did invite me with a companion."

He groaned. "I meant some quiet mouse of a helper to assist you because you are old and frail." He shook his head and laughed. "I guess you are not so frail, and you have always been delightfully young at heart. But you and your partner in crime had better not cause trouble here."

"Lady Withnall is completely misunderstood."

Gabriel overheard the remark and burst out laughing. "The tiny termagant is a devil's spawn, Grandmama. Look what she did to poor Ecklesbury only last month, and now Lady Margery's father has called off their betrothal."

"The oaf deserved it and Lady Margery is better off without him."

Alexander frowned. "Perhaps, but is it any of her business? What right does she have to meddle?"

Daisy now cleared her throat. "Alex, she probably saved Lady Margery's life. That fiend, Ecklesbury, was only after her money and had plans to do her in. A honeymoon accident, and he provided with a solid alibi while his accomplices took care of the poor girl."

"It was all the scandal," his grandmother said with a nod. "Perhaps to be society's biggest scandal of the year. Although I am confident some other clot will give Ecklesbury a run for that ignoble title soon enough."

"And you wonder why I want nothing to do with London society?" Alexander muttered, shaking his head. "Well, what can you tell me about these three diamonds I've invited?"

Gabriel winced. "They are all beautiful, witty, and of good families, for certain."

"But?"

Daisy sighed. "Perhaps it is the glamour of it all, and the fact they have each made a spectacular debut. To suddenly be much admired and sought after has made them a little…um, haughty."

"Haughty? As in insufferably vain, inconsiderate, and rude to those they deem unworthy?" Alex groaned.

"Something like that," Gabriel remarked. "You'll find they are used to toadies fawning over them and will likely expect the same of you. Are you ready to give them your constant attention?"

Hell, no. "Please tell me you are in jest."

Daisy frowned at her husband. "But it does not mean this is

truly their character. It is likely they have been swept up in the thrilling whirlwind of routs, musicales, and parties, and will revert to their true selves once the initial rush of excitement passes. This house party may be exactly what they need to regain their senses and appreciate what is set before them."

Alexander poured himself a brandy.

He was going to need the entire bottle.

Gabriel reached for one of those miniature cheese tarts that were not going to last another minute since no one could stop eating them. "Father thinks any one of these charming young ladies will be perfect for you."

"Oh, lord. If he likes them, then I am doomed. Are they really as bad as you claim? As bad as the Fribble sisters he tried to foist on you?" He needed to refill his glass of brandy. Actually, what he needed was a vat of it.

Gabriel could not contain his laughter. "That is for you to decide. I am merely here to watch the disaster…I mean, the game…unfold."

"I count on the three of you to keep him contained. What does Mother think of these young ladies?"

Daisy smiled. "She is exceedingly clever and only wants whatever will make you happy."

Gabriel arched an eyebrow. "Now, it is up to you to figure out exactly what that is."

Alexander was fairly certain he knew what that might be…Viola.

Greaves appeared at the parlor doorway and announced his next guests. "Lord and Lady Trent, and Lady Withnall."

Alexander walked toward them as they entered, and gave his mother a heartfelt hug.

His father spared a moment to pat him on the shoulder before he lunged for the miniature cheese tarts and stuffed two in his mouth. "Who else is here? Oh, lord. These are delicious."

"Only the family just yet." He greeted Lady Withnall, this deceptively canny, tiny woman whose mind was already awhirl as she assessed him.

What was she going to do?

Help him?

Or destroy him?

More important, what was she going to do to Viola?

CHAPTER 10

THE LAST OF the guests arrived by late afternoon, including Alexander's cousin, Graelem, and his spirited wife, Laurel, who happened to be Daisy's sister. Alexander had to admit, these Farthingale ladies were quite extraordinary. His brother and cousin had chosen well.

His father thought the same, for the old man would not stop asking Laurel or Daisy about a spare Farthingale for him. "Are you certain there isn't a cousin hiding out somewhere in England who would be perfect for my son?"

"Father, enough," Alexander said with a groan.

The family and Lady Withnall had gathered in his study for a private meeting a few minutes before the other guests, all of whom had now arrived, came down to supper. Although it was a country house party, they were all dressed formally, the men in black tie and tails and the women in their silks and jewels for this first night.

He had yet to see the three diamonds in their finery and had no idea how their taste in jewelry ran.

Expensive, no doubt.

"What is your strategy?" Graelem asked.

"No strategy, just taking the time to get to know each young lady. Although how anyone can get a proper sense in a matter of days is beyond me. But I am not going to make any special announcements this weekend. One does not fall in love that fast."

Graelem cast his wife an adoring look. "Took me about a

minute."

Laurel laughed. "Liar! You were sprawled in agony on Chipping Way, clutching your broken leg thanks to me, and in so much pain you saw nothing but stars blinding your eyes."

"He didn't need to see you," Gabriel chimed in. "He sensed it by your touch alone. The gentle lilt of your voice. The scent of you."

"I smelled like my horse and I sounded like a Harpy," Laurel insisted.

Alexander chuckled.

So did Graelem. "I loved ye at first sight, lass. Just goes to prove how smart I was."

Lady Withnall pounded her cane on the carpet. "Stop gushing over your wives. It is quite unseemly, although I heartily approve. The point is to have Alexander find a lady suitable to be gushed over. I suggest you start with Lady Aurora."

Alexander was instantly curious. "Why her?"

Lady Withnall cast him a beady look. "Is she not pretty enough for you?"

"They are all diamonds, Lady Withnall. What is so special that I must start with her?"

His mother groaned. "If you are at a loss to see her attributes, then I doubt she will be the one for you. Perhaps Alexander ought to leave her for last."

His grandmother now chimed in. "No, do as Lady Withnall suggests. I think I see the logic in it. Lady Aurora is an earl's daughter. Lady Alicia is the daughter of a marquess. And Lady Charlotte is the daughter of a duke. You are to take them in ascending order, is that not so?"

Lady Withnall nodded. "Indeed, this is precisely the reason. One must always work one's way up."

It sounded completely stupid and trivial to Alexander, but he merely nodded and went along. "Then I shall start with Lady Aurora."

They all made their way to the parlor to await the rest of his guests as they descended for this first night's supper. He could not wait to see what Viola had in store for them. Indeed, the girl was constantly on his mind.

But he had to concentrate on Lady Aurora this evening.

Well, how long did he have to spend talking to her?

Would it not be rude to ignore his other guests on their first night here?

He greeted each one with impeccable courtesy as they entered the parlor.

Now strolling in were Lady Aurora, her parents, and her brother.

"Ardley, I've missed beating you at cards," the brother, Lord Gaston, said in jest and shook his hand.

"Ah, yes. Our notorious card games. But I fear you were the one who always lost, Gaston." He chuckled. "Glad you could make it."

He then turned to the sister, Lady Aurora. The girl was pretty, he had to give her that, but perhaps a little too…glittery. She wore a diamond necklace that could blind a man. She had golden curls and cat-like gray eyes, not to mention a heart-shaped face and pretty lips.

But her smile felt insincere.

He did not know why, it just did. "Welcome to my home, Lady Aurora."

"It is charming," she said without a jot of enthusiasm, looking thoroughly bored as she scanned the room.

Several footmen entered with more appetizing bites prepared by Viola, including those same miniature tarts she had set out for the earlier arrivals. His father had polished that first batch off before the other guests arrived. Greaves must have mentioned it to her, so she had now whipped up some more.

Out of the corner of his eye, he noticed his father attempt to dive on them. But his mother held him back. "None of your trousers will fit you if you keep this up," she chided him.

Alexander squelched a chuckle.

He returned his attention to Lady Aurora and her family. "I hope you found your guest chambers to your liking. We tend to be informal here in the countryside, striving for comfort rather than residing among museum pieces."

"No complaints," her father said cheerfully.

"Nor do I have any," her brother added. "I am heartily enjoying your stock of brandy. I hear Duke Nevins is here with his daughter, Lady Charlotte. I have not seen them yet. Have they arrived?"

Alexander nodded. "They came late. I'm sure they'll be down shortly."

He now turned to the ladies and offered to fetch each a drink.

Lady Gaston tittered like a bird.

The daughter was not the tittering sort. The smile she had given upon meeting him was so brittle, he was surprised her face hadn't cracked.

Nevertheless, he was determined to see this weekend through. "Lady Aurora, may I give you a tour of the Ardley Hall gardens?"

She did not appear impressed, but took his arm. "How delightful."

She sounded about as jolly as a wet sock.

Her mother tossed her a cautionary look.

The girl did not wish to be here and took no pains to hide her irritation.

That was a point in her favor, perhaps. He supposed it depended on the reason for her reluctance to spend the weekend in his company. He led her onto the terrace and then down a few steps leading into his well-maintained garden. "I gather you do not enjoy the countryside. Or is it just me you find hard to digest?"

That caught her attention.

Perhaps he should not have been so blunt.

But there was something about this girl that irked him, and not in any hot-sparks-about-to-be-set-off way. She may appear charming to others, but there was a condescension in her manner that he did not find charming at all.

"You are perfectly acceptable, my lord," she said, now assessing him with an avid eye. "Far handsomer than I expected. Do you never come to London? I haven't seen you around."

"No, I much prefer it here. London holds no temptation for me. It never will, so let me be up front about this."

"I see. That is too bad. I quite enjoy the excitement of Town life. Would you care if your wife spent her time in London while you remained here? Of course, the details can be negotiated. I understand you would expect heirs. But would you hold me here after I had fulfilled my duty?"

"I quite appreciate your candor." In truth, he did. The girl was full of herself, but knew what she wanted and did not want. "It is very helpful. But no, I expect my wife to remain here with me. One can hardly build a married life if one's spouse resides in another city and under another roof."

"I'm glad you appreciate my honesty. I shall return the favor and tell you I have no intention of playing the doting wife to a country squire, no matter how handsome he may be. I have already refused a viscount and the son of a marquess, neither man nearly as handsome as you. But I am within days of receiving an offer of marriage from a duke. One who adores Town life and happens to adore me."

"I see. You are only here in the hope of making him jealous."

She nodded.

"Do your parents know this is what is going on in your mind?"

"No, but they are quite out of touch. My mother, as you may have noticed, is a dithering, fluttery bird. My father is a genial clunch. They hardly have the intellect to devise this strategy. The marriage mart is all out war, you know. At the moment, I hold the advantage. But in a year or two from now? I shall be old news. I am only being frank with you because I wish to be kind and not give you hope that I might marry you. It will make this weekend quite awkward if you are constantly chasing after me."

"That is very generous of you to warn me before I fell in love with you and you broke my tender heart."

She patted her hair. "You are being sarcastic. But be assured, I do have men falling at my feet. Dozens of them daily. It is quite tiresome to be fawned over constantly."

"But you encourage them because you hope the duke will take notice?"

"Yes, and it is working. But I am curious. Why did you bother to invite me? Had you seen me from afar?"

"No, never set eyes on you before today. You were among a list of debutantes I picked out of a hat."

Her condescending smile faltered. "Are you serious?"

He nodded. "Quite."

"I cannot say I like that very much."

He led her deeper into the garden, still careful to remain in full view of everyone in the parlor. "May I give you a word of advice, Lady Aurora?"

She did not look pleased. "I have received enough lectures from my parents."

"I hope you do not take my words as a lecture, but merely as guidance from one who has gained a bit of experience. You are awfully young to be locked in your ways. Marriage is not only about security but also about happiness. If this duke is worthy, you are more likely to gain his proposal through thoughtful gestures and concern for him rather than through attempts to make him jealous."

"Is that so?"

"Yes, it is. Have you thought of your own life after you marry him? It does not simply come to an end. What are you hoping it will be? An endless round of parties and toady friends? Or do you hope to find a man who will always keep you cherished in his thoughts and want to build a life with you? Wish to protect you and make you happy? This duke of yours will find it hard to care for you if you show him no care in return."

She said nothing for the longest while, merely stood with her head bowed and staring down at the rose beds. "May we go back inside now?"

"Yes, of course. The dinner bell will sound at any moment."

"Lord Ardley, are you certain you will not consider taking up residence in London?"

"Quite certain of it, Lady Aurora."

"A pity. You aren't half bad. But a duke is a duke, and I wish to be a duchess. You shall be first on my mind if I have a change of heart."

"I am honored to be second-best. No more than a duke's leavings. It is what every man strives for."

"You are being sarcastic again."

"Yes." He walked her back toward the house. "I like that you have opinions and goals. Convictions, even if quite a bit misguided. Just keep an open mind about what life has to offer you. The path to your happiness may lead you to someone other than this duke."

They were now on the terrace and about to enter the house.

She held him back a moment and smiled prettily. "No, I am quite certain I must have the duke. How else am I ever to become a duchess?"

He arched an eyebrow and watched her as she hurried inside.

Gabriel joined him as he stood on the terrace. "What happened? I cannot tell if you look annoyed or relieved."

"Relief, for certain. She wants a duke."

"Sorry."

"Don't be. If anyone is to be pitied it is the duke she will soon trap. For both their sakes, I hope she grows to like him. But I'm sure they will have beautiful children, even if they never speak to each other again after her breeding days are over."

"Ouch. That sounds harsh."

"Let's go inside. Have Lady Alicia and Lady Charlotte come down yet?"

"Yes, they are in the parlor."

"What do you think of them, Gabriel?"

"Don't ask me. You're the one who has to like them."

Lady Alicia was a tall, stunning brunette with vivid blue eyes and a throaty laugh tinged with sexual awareness. She eyed him up and down, her gaze lingering on his attributes as he approached to greet her. "A pleasure to meet you, my lord."

"The pleasure is all mine," he said, bowing over her hand.

She licked her tongue slowly along her lips and smiled at him.

Bollocks.

He was going to lock his door tonight.

Was he supposed to find her enticing? Perhaps he might have if his brain wasn't already filled with thoughts of Viola.

Lady Charlotte was a petite blonde with emerald green eyes. She could best be described as cute as a button. To his irritation, she played up her little girl looks and squeaky, baby voice that seemed enchanting to the other men gathered in the parlor. Alexander just wanted to stick a finger down his throat and cast up his last meal.

He made a lame excuse in order to step out of the parlor and calm down.

The weekend was going to be a complete waste of time. He already knew he could never fall in love with any of these girls.

He groaned as he heard the *thuck, thuck, thuck* of Lady Withnall's cane behind him.

He turned to face the little crone. "I suppose you and my grandmother knew this would happen."

"What? That you would find all of them lacking?" She shrugged. "Yes, we suspected these diamonds were not right for you. But it was important for you to find this out for yourself. They are among the best of this year's crop. Not a particularly good year, if you want my opinion."

He raked a hand through his hair. "Actually, I would appreciate your opinion. No one knows London society as well as you do."

"No, dear boy. It is not for me to tell you who is right for you. You are a grown man and can make your own decisions."

"Apparently not," he said with a grunting laugh.

The dinner bell rang, so he offered his arm to Lady Withnall and escorted her into the dining room, seating her beside him at the table. His chair was at the head of the table with his father anchoring the other end. The seating was informal, the chart of who was to sit where designed by Viola, but only after obtaining the approval of his mother and grandmother.

This was the sort of thing Viola refused to leave to chance, so he had not put up a fuss when she insisted he include her seating charts in his correspondence. For this reason, he was not surprised to find Lady Charlotte, daughter of Duke Nevins, seated next to him.

She giggled and cooed as she settled in beside him.

He tried not to look pained.

But he had to glance away when she began to bat her eyes at

him and make baby gurgling sounds.

At first, he thought she might be choking.

But no, she was merely flirting with him.

Lady Withnall grinned as she stared at him. *Utter peahen,* she mouthed and then rolled her eyes.

The only bright spot in the evening was Viola's menu which started with a simple onion soup that tasted better than any he'd ever had before. How in the name of heaven did she coax such flavors out of a simple onion? He glanced across the table and grinned at his father who was too busy slurping his soup to look up from his bowl.

He turned to Lady Withnall who seemed lost in her thoughts as she slowly savored each spoonful. "Delicious, isn't it?" he commented.

"Indeed. Quite impressive."

The soup course was followed by a splendid array of main courses, a lamb simmering in its own juices and a honey glazed game fowl that tasted so good, he ate it down to the bone. The vegetables accompanying these meats were fresh from his conservatory garden.

He felt a quiet pride for Viola as the expected compliments began to be muttered, the first coming from Duke Nevins. "You surprise me, Ardley. I did not expect this quality from a simple country cook."

His friends, Lord Hythe and Lord Chesterfield, asked for a second serving of everything. So did Gabriel and Graelem. "Laddie," his cousin, Graelem, said, "I think you will never be rid of us if all the meals are prepared as fine as this."

His grandmother, who no doubt had been privy to his father's constant ranting about his attention to Viola, eyed him curiously.

The desserts were equally glorious, putting everyone in fine spirits for the evening activities. Lady Alicia regaled them with a musical recital, her voice surprisingly pleasant, although he ought to have realized the sultriness in her speaking voice would translate nicely to singing.

His gentlemen guests were enthralled and declared her bewitching.

He ought to have felt the same, but there was a certain smugness to her manner that put him off. However, he cheered and complimented her along with everyone else.

Afterward everyone moved to the card tables Greaves had set out for them and they all settled in for rounds of whist. Alexander partnered his grandmother, the two of them teamed against Gabriel and Daisy.

Each *ton* diamond sat at a different table. Although he did not plan it, each diamond was partnered by an eligible bachelor. He was not surprised to find Lady Aurora's brother, Lord Gaston, teamed with Lady Charlotte and outrageously fawning over her.

Thank the Graces, it wasn't him stuck with her as a partner. However, she was seated immediately behind him, her giggles and baby cooing slowly driving him insane.

Lord Hythe was Lady Alicia's partner for this round.

Lady Aurora was teamed with his friend, Lord Chesterfield.

He was glad there were enough eligible bachelors present to take the pressure off him in paying attention to those *ton* diamonds. Of course, it completely defeated the point of his house party. But it was becoming clear to him that these ladies were not to his taste.

He grimaced as Lady Charlotte burst into giggles and chided Lord Gaston in her baby voice. Gaston immediately apologized despite it obviously being her fault they lost the trick. But how was she to know she ought to have led with a *tensie-wensie* of hearts?

By all the saints in heaven.

Could she not simply have called it a ten of hearts?

He ignored what was going on behind him and tossed in a card to take his trick. "Grandmama, why did you not warn me?"

"Warn you about what, dear boy?"

"These ladies. I sent the list to you and sought your guidance."

"You are a grown man, Alex. Fully capable of making your own choices. However, you went about it like a stubborn idiot."

He cast her a wry smile. "Oh, thank you."

Gabriel and Daisy struggled not to laugh.

"What did you expect me to say? Your father was right in

demanding you come to London to see the young ladies for yourself. I do not say this lightly, for we all know how stupid he can be about such things. One has only to recall his inept attempts to match Gabriel with one of those Fribbles. But you had to do it your own way, staying hidden in your home and relying on gossip rags, of all things, to make your half-hearted choices. You were setting yourself up to fail, and so you have. It is obvious you care not a whit for any of these young ladies."

"I'll choose with more care next time."

His grandmother rolled her eyes. "Will you really go to the bother of throwing another house party? Just come to London with us. It is much simpler and the only right course if you are truly serious about finding yourself a wife."

But this would mean leaving Viola while her father was in dire health.

"I'll think about it. But why can you and Lady Withnall not select a few more hopefuls for me? You are the sharpest ladies I know. I trust your judgment."

"Flattery will get you nowhere, dear boy." She dealt the next round and turned over the last card, the two of spades. "Trump suit is spades."

He had no interest in the card game, his thoughts now on Viola as footmen set out more refreshments for his guests, including a torte drenched in sherry and set aflame with spectacular effect. The desserts were all divine, as expected from this talented girl.

Everyone set aside their card games and moved over to the table which groaned under the weight of these splendid desserts. He supposed this counted as a second round since they'd already had a first round of desserts at the end of their meal.

But no one was complaining.

He happened to glance out the window and spotted Viola peeking in.

His heart soared.

Oh, this was not good.

But he'd sorely missed her company.

She was on the terrace, looking in with eyes wide and a lovely smile as she studied his guests.

He strode out to speak to her.

She realized he had spotted her and darted away.

He saw her run toward the conservatory and chased after her. The conservatory had two doors, one leading to the garden, which is the one he entered through now. The other door led into the kitchen hallway. He could see it was still shut. "Blast it, Viola. I know you are in here." He would have heard that door groan open and then click shut behind her if she had reached it. "Don't hide from me."

He scanned the darkened room, eyeing each shadow and waiting for one to move. One finally did move, and he knew it had to be Viola. He caught her about the waist and hauled her up against him.

Lord, she felt good.

She gasped. "Let me go, my lord. Why did you follow me in here?"

"Why were you sticking your little nose against the window?" He turned her to face him.

"Did you not specifically ask me to study your diamonds? That is all I intended to do. Well, that and see how everyone enjoyed the food."

"It was spectacular. Well done, Viola."

"Thank you. I hope you found your diamonds equally spectacular. The ladies looked exquisite in their fine silks and beautiful jewels, didn't they? Did everyone truly enjoy my cooking?"

"The fact there was not a crumb left over from our supper ought to have told you everything you needed to know. In fact, I am considering posting armed guards around you to prevent anyone from stealing you away."

She laughed as she gave a halfhearted push against his chest in order to squirm out of his arms. But her efforts were lame. He had very light hold of her and she could have broken away if this was truly her desire. Instead, she kept her hands on his chest and sighed. "Lady Withnall came into the kitchen earlier to make a point of complimenting me on the meal."

"You met Lady Withnall?"

"Yes, she was quite kind to me and so very thoughtful."

He emitted a soft growl. "The little snoop. She was checking you out."

"Why would she be interested in me? Oh, that is why you made the comment about someone stealing me from you. You think she wants me to be her cook?"

"No. She has no interest in you as a cook. She's the size of a dormouse and hardly eats, nor does she entertain much. Everyone is afraid of her, so she is always invited everywhere."

Viola laughed. "That makes no sense. Why do people want her around if they don't like her?"

"She knows everyone's secrets. They are all desperate to stay on her good side in the hope she will not tattle on them." She felt so perfect in his arms, as though she naturally belonged there…which she did.

He leaned closer and caught the scent of honey, onions, and ginger spices on her warm skin. No perfume ever smelled finer.

Viola shook her head. "She seemed so nice. I never took her for an extortionist or blackmailer."

"She isn't either of those things. But she does take delight in pricking pompous bubbles or exposing dark secrets when she believes innocents will be harmed. In truth, I like her. But just be wary around her. One never knows what she is up to."

"All right, I'll try to keep on guard. But I am not very good at reading people's motives. It is much easier to be kind and friendly rather than worry about what others are plotting."

"Just be yourself, Viola. I don't mean for you to lie to her. However, you need not spill your heart, either."

She emitted a short, snorting laugh. "Why should she care about my heart? I am nothing to the *ton*."

But she was something to him.

It troubled him that Lady Withnall already knew it. Was he that obvious? She had not even seen him with Viola. Well, his father had been spouting off about the 'unsuitable' girl. Now, the little gossip was sniffing around to see what might turn up.

He did not want to alarm Viola by saying anything to her.

"How was your first day in the kitchen?" he asked, changing

the topic of their conversation. "Any issues?"

"None. It all went very well."

"Everything you made for us today was excellent." He still had his arms around her and had no intention of drawing away. "What was not so excellent were my choices in the diamonds. Lady Aurora is determined to marry a duke and only accepted my invitation in order to make him jealous."

"I'm sorry."

"Don't be. It is a relief for me."

She frowned at him, her face quite beautiful in the silvery moonlight. "You ought to be taking this more seriously."

"I am trying. Lady Charlotte talks like a baby. I think I would hang myself if I were stuck marrying her."

Viola tried not to laugh, but a few chuckles made their way out. "She might stop if you asked her. I'm sure she plays it up because most men seem to like it. What about Lady Alicia? What do you find wrong with her?"

He did not wish to disclose the fact that Alicia was not a virgin. Not that he would condemn the girl for making one mistake, but she appeared to be the sort who enjoyed men and was not shy about giving them her body. She would never be faithful to him, assuming he made the mistake of marrying her. "I haven't had much opportunity to speak to her. Perhaps I will spend a little time with her tomorrow. But not before I introduce you to my family. I will summon you shortly after breakfast, as you suggested."

She nodded. "I had better return to the kitchen. We're just finishing setting up for tomorrow, and then I must go to bed. It has been a long day for me."

"I won't delay you." He gave her cheek a light caress. "Thank you, Viola. You've been the bright spot throughout. Sweet dreams."

"And to you, my lord."

She slipped out of his arms and hurried away.

He watched her leave, following her lithe shadow as she disappeared inside and left him standing alone in the dark of night. As he walked through the garden, he thought he heard someone in the bushes off to his left.

He diverted his course and went to inspect, but whoever had been lurking there was gone and it was too dark to make out any footprints.

He shrugged it off.

Perhaps it was one of the kitchen staff grabbing some air.

Or Lady Withnall snooping again.

Yes, she was the likely culprit.

He would not put it past her, for she was already onto Viola like a bloodhound on the scent.

He took note of his guests when he returned to the parlor, but they were all accounted for. Still, one of them could have run back in here just before he arrived. It mattered little. Even if he had been seen with Viola, who would care if he cavorted with his cook?

But George Haworth's words came back to haunt him.

He had to be more careful for her sake.

What would he do if her reputation was tainted because of him?

CHAPTER 11

AFTER BREAKFAST PREPARATIONS the following morning, Viola hurried to her quarters to wash up and fix her hair. She had been up quite early baking buns, some of which were sprinkled with cinnamon and others contained an apricot filling. These were to go along with the eggs, kippers, sausages, and oatmeal set out on the dining room buffet for the guests to enjoy as they came downstairs in drips and drabs for breakfast.

She tried not to appear on edge about meeting the viscount's family. This was the first time she had been put to the test, having to prove her capabilities to others. As vicar's daughter, the townsfolk of Ardley merely accepted whatever she had to offer. But this was very different, this need to impress members of the Upper Crust so they might recommend her for a position in an elegant household.

But as the minutes ticked by, no one came to fetch her.

Had Lord Ardley forgotten about her?

Well, he had his hands full with three diamonds to court under the watchful eye of his family, not to mention his other guests to entertain. They were now on day two of the party and some guests would start leaving by day four.

He had little time to waste.

She suppressed her disappointment, donned her apron and mobcap once more, and returned to the kitchen to begin preparations for the midday meal. "Miss Ruskin, is something wrong?" one of the girls assisting her in the kitchen asked.

"No, it must be the onions irritating my eyes."

The girl said nothing, merely looked at her askance since no one had started chopping up onions yet. She took a deep breath, afraid she was about to burst into tears. "I'll be right back."

She ran out of the kitchen, making up some excuse about picking herbs in the conservatory. To her relief, she was alone in there. She found herself a shady corner of the sunlit room and allowed her tears to fall. "Viola," she said between ragged breaths, "you are such a ninny."

How could she believe the viscount thought enough of her to drop everything and introduce her to his own family? He must have realized how it would look and decided to put it off for another time…or perhaps not at all.

No, he was a good man and had promised her.

It was a bad case of nerves turning her into a watering pot.

A dark shadow fell over her, one she recognized as the big, muscled frame of the viscount. "Viola, what is the matter? Your kitchen girls said you ran in here to pick herbs."

She nodded. "I guess I had better pick some then."

"Don't bother. They won't care if you come back empty-handed. Tell me what is wrong. Why are you crying?"

She let out a ragged breath. "It is so stupid of me. I thought you were not coming to get me."

He sighed as he knelt beside her. "I would never forget you."

"But it is too late now. I have to prepare your luncheon and don't have time to chat with your family. I am making game pies for today and have yet to roll out the dough or season the filling."

He removed his handkerchief from his breast pocket and dabbed at her tears. "I gave you my promise and I have every intention of holding to it. Never doubt me, Viola."

"All right."

"I will plan better tomorrow morning. You will have your chance to meet my family then. I'm so sorry this morning's meeting was botched. I asked them all to come down to my study, made certain to remind them again last night before they retired to bed. They should have been gathered there half an hour ago."

"You do not owe me explanations."

"Yes, I do. They did not mean to ignore you. My grandmother and mother slept late and have not come down yet. Yesterday's travels must have exhausted them. My father, who has his own agenda concerning my marital welfare, went riding with some of the gentlemen. My brother and cousin and their wives are in the study now if you'd like to join us."

"I would love to, but I cannot."

He nodded. "Yes, too late now. They won't mind meeting you tomorrow with the rest of the family."

"I'm sorry to have put them out."

"You haven't at all. They are here without their children and have more time on their hands than they know what to do with. I'm the one who should be sorry. I should have realized today would not be a good day. Tomorrow will be better." He tucked a finger under her chin and tipped her face upward to dab away more tears. "Ready to return to the kitchen?"

She shook her head.

"Here, keep my handkerchief," he said as they rose together. "You may still need it."

"No." She handed it back to him. "The kitchen staff will make too much of it. I'll grab one of my own."

He held her back when she started to walk away. "Have Greaves or Mrs. Lester summon me if you need anything today."

"I won't. I'm better now. I think being here and not at home with my father has put me too much on edge. It isn't the cooking. I can make these dishes in my sleep."

"Don't worry about your father. He is doing just fine. Mrs. Bligh is with him around the clock and I have Mr. Wilson checking on them several times a day. Mrs. Lester also sent one of her maids to the vicarage to help out Mrs. Bligh. She is Mrs. Bligh's niece, Lila. Your father is in excellent hands."

"I did not realize…"

"I did not want to bother you with every detail while you were so hard at work for my party. I would tell you if there was anything wrong. Truly, I will not hold any news back from you, especially if he happens to take a sudden turn for the worse. I could never hurt you like that. But all is well with him. Wilson told me so not an hour ago."

"Thank you."

"I won't escort you back to the kitchen. Will you be all right now?"

"Yes." She cast him a pathetic smile.

In truth, she did feel better.

She would meet his family tomorrow.

More important, her father was in the best of hands.

She scurried into her room, washed her face again, then stepped back into the kitchen reinvigorated. "Martha, I need the saffron. Dolly, have you peeled the potatoes?"

She had made several extra game pies for herself and the staff. "You have outdone yourself, Miss Ruskin," Greaves said, finishing up his meal before returning to his post by the entry hall.

The others heartily agreed.

She was pleased when the supper menu also met with everyone's approval. The evening servings consisted of fish, a goose baked in a plum juice, and a honey-glazed ham. She mashed her potatoes with cauliflower and sprinkled in a sharp cheese to give it a little punch. The greens were lightly sauteed in butter, bacon, and a hint of garlic.

The dessert course was to be served at midnight, after the viscount's guests had enjoyed a night of dancing. She kept the desserts simple, mostly fruit pies, one or two cakes filled with buttercream, and one centerpiece dessert in the shape of a swan, its wings made of meringue.

She did not think gorging oneself on creamy desserts could be good for the digestion, especially after one's stomach was already shaken up by dancing. But the footmen reported that the guests dug in with gusto. Viola had never indulged in society ways. Obviously, this society set was accustomed to these late night riches.

As for her, she was usually asleep by this hour.

The strains of a lively country reel reached her ears while she finished up in the kitchen. The orchestra played very well and she was eager to hear more. When the crusts and batters for tomorrow's breakfast pies and scones were done, she made her way through the conservatory and into the garden where she could position herself to listen without being seen.

She breathed in the cool, night air.

Oh, it was so lovely out here.

A starry night.

A silver moon.

The divine refrains of a waltz now filled the air.

Since no one was able to see her in this quiet corner of the garden, she removed her mobcap, tucking it in her apron ties, and then quietly began to twirl in time to the music. She closed her eyes and imagined herself in the viscount's arms.

What harm was there in dreaming of a dance with him? It was only a dream. Who better to hold her in the bliss of those muscled arms?

Oh, what perfection.

She spun and spun in time to the music, feeling light as a butterfly.

What was the viscount doing now?

Likely dancing with one of his diamonds.

She wanted to watch him.

But to see him falling in love with one of those pampered pigeons was more than she could endure. It was easier to pretend she was waltzing in his arms, her apron not an apron at all but a cream silk gown, and her boots were satin dancing slippers.

He, of course, looked dashing in his black coattails, the breadth of his shoulders quite magnificent as he stood proudly before her, a figment of her own creation. Powerful. Dangerous. Commanding.

Achingly handsome.

Well, all this was true whether in real life or her fantasy.

Of course, in her fantasy he would be besotted with her and desperate to kiss her.

A splendid first kiss, his lips warm and urgent upon hers.

She was lost in her fanciful dreams and not paying attention to where she was twirling when she suddenly slammed into something solid. "Viola, what are you doing out here at this late hour?"

"Lord Ardley," she said with a gasp.

He wrapped his arms around her to keep her from falling as she bounced off his chest.

She stared up at him. "Why are *you* out here and not dancing with your diamonds?"

"They have been claimed by other bachelors. I strode out here for a breath of air."

"So did I." She was still in his arms and knew she had better push away before she did something quite stupid and asked for a kiss. He was her dream man, after all. And hadn't she just imagined how splendid such a kiss would feel? "I had better go."

"Not a chance. Dance with me."

She gasped again. "What?"

"You heard me," he said with exquisite gentleness. "Dance with me."

"But you are a viscount."

"All the more reason why you must obey." He took her hand in his and then wrapped an arm around her waist. She found herself slowly twirling in his arms. "You look enchanting," he said, his voice once again gentle and quite husky.

She laughed. "Apron and all?"

He grinned. "Yes, I hear aprons are the height of London fashion this year."

"Indeed, all the best cooks have them. Which, by the way, is all I am." She was reminding herself as much as him.

"No, tonight you are an elfin princess. There is magic in you, Viola. In your smile and the starlight of your eyes."

He was going to make her cry.

His words felt so sincere.

He sighed. "You are getting worked up again. Would you rather not dance with me?"

"No…yes…I mean, it is *you*. I should not be here under the moonlight with you. I have never been in a man's arms like this before…well, other than with you. Why am I always tumbling into your arms?"

"Good question. I don't have an answer for it yet. Have you ever been kissed before?"

She gasped a third time. "No."

"Would you like me to kiss you?"

"Yes…no…I mean…"

He chuckled. "Seize the moment, Viola. These nights of enchantment do not come along very often."

She stared up at him. "Do you want to kiss me?"

"Is it not obvious? Yes, I am in agony and there is no cure for me but to kiss you."

He was still twirling her slowly in his arms, but made no move to act on his desire. Was he waiting for her to say something?

Moonlight fell across his golden hair and chiseled features. He was big and muscled and simply magnificent.

The dance was now coming to an end, the opportunity about to pass.

She took a deep breath. "All right. I think I will expire if I do not seize the moment. Although I do not understand why you should want to kiss me when–"

His mouth crushed down on hers.

He wrapped his arms around her and brought her up against his hard body. Yes, quite a firm, solid body, and yet she melted into the length of him as though she were a candle melting against a flame.

His mouth…dear heaven…that mouth so possessively hot and demanding.

Utterly divine.

He did not press his lips to hers so much as conquer her, possess her, plunder her body and soul.

She had never experienced anything like it. The pleasure was almost unbearable…almost. Her heart was racing madly. Her breaths were now coming short and fast. Her legs…did she still have them?

She was not going to pull away from him ever.

She tasted ginger cake and brandy on his lips.

He must be tasting plum pudding on hers.

She held on tightly to his shoulders when she felt her legs completely give way. Her heart had given way long ago and would always be his.

"Viola," he whispered, ending the kiss only to start planting more soft kisses against her neck and throat. "You taste so sweet. Blessed saints, I knew you would."

He drew her deeper into the shadows, leading her to a sturdy oak and gently pressing her back against the trunk of the large tree. He placed his hands on either side of her, and once again crushed his mouth to hers. This kiss was raw and hungry.

Wild and dangerous.

His tongue touched hers.

Her body ignited again.

These sparks of desire ought to have frightened her, for there was no mistaking where they would lead. She did not know unmarried women could feel such things, or should feel this molten ache. Of course, they did. Was this not the fiery path to ruin?

She clutched his shoulders and sobbed against his mouth.

She refused to become his mistress.

He must have sensed a sudden change in her, for he ended the kiss abruptly and drew away with a ragged groan. "Viola."

She took a deep breath, but it did no good, for all she took in was his divine, sandalwood scent and the masculine heat radiating off his body. "Oh, lord…I mean, not you, my lord…just…oh, lord."

She covered her face with her hands.

He drew them away and kissed the palm of each. "I know. Viola, we have to talk about this."

She shook her head furiously. "There is nothing to say to each other. I will never be your mistress."

"No, I…you mistake my meaning."

"Do I? Then what do you have in mind, pray tell? Not even to raise me to the level of mistress?"

"What are you talking about? I have no intention of bedding you outs–"

"Alexander! Release the girl at once!" his grandmother demanded in a harsh whisper, lumbering toward them. But she was not the only one observing them. Her friend, Lady Withnall, walked beside her, thumping her cane on the grass with each labored stride.

Viola's head began to spin.

Oh, no!

What had she done?

Sinned, for certain. She had indulged in a moment of lustful pleasure and been caught by London's most notorious gossip.

She was now ruined, and her father would soon learn of her public shame. It was inevitable. She desperately wished to take the moment back. This humiliation would be the last memory her father would have of her.

Her head would not stop spinning, nor would her heart stop hammering. It was pounding too hard and she thought it was in danger of bursting.

The breath rushed out of her and she could not regain it.

She closed her eyes to steady herself before she fell into a faint.

"Viola," the viscount cried softly and caught her in his arms. Then he growled, a sound low and menacing. "Grandmama. Phoebe," he said, brazenly addressing Lady Withnall by her given name. "Don't you dare breathe a word of this to anyone."

Viola burst into tears.

She had never cried so much in her life as she had over these past few days. "I will never be your mistress, but now none of your friends or family will take me into their home. They think I am soiled and wanton."

He had the temerity to laugh. "Hardly that. Viola, it was your first kiss."

"I know, but no one else knows it. Please, release me. I have to go. I am so ashamed."

He growled again. "Don't ever be ashamed of anything that passes between us."

She sniffled. "Easy for you to say. You're the viscount. I'm the nobody."

"You are not a nobody." He pinned her against him when she tried to wriggle out of his arms. "Do you hear me, Viola?"

"I hear you just fine." She emitted a grunt of frustration because his arms were iron bands around her body and she was never going to break free. "But you are wrong. I am nobody at all.

And now I am a disgraced nobody at all."

"Blast it, you are not."

"Oh, right. Then what am I? The next Queen of England?"

"No," he said with aching softness. "Hopefully, my wife."

She did not know what possessed her, but she managed to extricate her arm from his grasp, haul it back, and punch him in the nose.

He yelped and gaped at her.

She took the opportunity to shove out of his grasp while he stood there looking on in surprise.

"Smoothly done, Alex," she heard his grandmother mutter, and then both she and Lady Withnall began to laugh.

Viola had to leave Ardley Hall.

But first she had to run back to the kitchen to gather her possessions. Perhaps she would just leave everything behind and run straight back to the vicarage. No, she needed her things otherwise she would be forced to return here.

All she wanted now was to be home with her father. Dear heaven, what was she going to say to him? How could she admit to disappointing him when news of her shame would destroy him?

Her eyes were so filled with tears, she could hardly see where she was going. It was after midnight. The vicarage wasn't far, but she had no idea what ruffians might be lurking about at this hour. There was no help for it, she would have to wake one of the grooms and have him drive her home in one of the viscount's wagons.

As for the viscount, he would have to rely on his kitchen staff to prepare the rest of the house party meals.

She was still crying as she stumbled into the conservatory on her way to the kitchen.

"Viola, enough. You need to stop running before you fall and hurt yourself." The viscount caught up to her and grabbed her around the waist. Well, he'd probably been beside her all along and the grass simply muffled his footsteps. Nor was it particularly clever of her to have hit him after he'd said he would marry her.

He didn't mean it.

He couldn't mean it.

"Let me go!"

"No."

"It is bad enough that I kissed you…that I *wanted* to kiss you. And then we were caught in a groping kiss. But did you then have to make an utter jest of it?"

He looked genuinely perplexed. "How did I jest about it?"

She gasped. "*Hopefully, my wife?* That's what you said. Who is ever going to believe that nonsense? Viscounts do not marry cooks."

"How do you know? Have you met any viscounts other than me?"

"No, but that is beside the point."

"It is entirely the point. Did I not promise I would always protect you?"

She shook her head. "No, you promised never to hurt me."

"I'm sure I promised both. No matter, it is the same thing. Marry me, Viola."

She considered punching him in the nose again, but she had gotten away with it once and there was something in his fierce expression that warned she would not get away with it again. "Have you had too much to drink?"

He grinned at her. "If I am intoxicated, it is only because of your beauty."

She rolled her eyes. "That is dreadfully lame, my lord. Truly worthy of a groan."

He raked a hand through his hair. "How do I convince you I am serious?"

"I don't think it is possible." The only thing worse than accepting his proposal was her being stupid enough to believe she would ever exchange vows with him at the altar. Even if he were serious about it, his family would prevent it from ever happening. As nice as they were – and she did like them all, even his blowhard of a father – they would never allow her to marry into their family.

His father was the only one being honest about it.

Lady Withnall and his grandmother now followed them into

the conservatory.

"Great," he said, his sarcasm apparent, "I do not need you two old biddies interfering in my life. I am making a fine mess of it all on my own."

"We are not here to talk to you," his grandmother said. "We wish to speak to Viola."

He put a protective arm around her. "What is it you wish to say to her? I'll toss you both into the cabbage patch if you dare insult her."

Lady Withnall smacked him on the shoulder with her cane. "Behave yourself or I'll tattle on you to your father."

Viola wanted to laugh at the absurdity of the moment, but she was already in so much trouble. She did not need to pile on any more problems.

"My dear girl," his grandmother said, giving her hand a gentle pat. "Neither I nor Lady Withnall is going to hurt you. We happen to think kissing you is the smartest thing my grandson has done in an age. So, the secret of your first kiss is quite safe with us."

"It is?" She glanced at her grandson, this big, gorgeous man who still had his arm protectively around her shoulders.

He nodded. "If my grandmother says it is so, then it is so."

She emitted a ragged breath. "My reputation is not ruined?"

Lady Withnall snorted. "Hardly. If it took you this long to receive your first kiss, then I doubt you are a moral danger in anyone's kitchen."

His grandmother patted her hand again. "Alexander has already arranged for us to talk to you tomorrow morning about your situation. The kiss will not be mentioned. I hope you will not run away. I am looking forward to getting to know you better."

"As am I, my dear," Lady Withnall said with unexpected kindness.

The pair sauntered off, leaving her alone once more with the viscount. "Should I believe them?"

"Yes, Viola. They like you and wish to protect you as I do, so there is no need for you to leave. Let us get through this weekend party and then you and I are going to talk seriously."

She nodded.

Obviously, he was not going to propose to her again.

He had stepped forward to protect her when caught kissing her, but the crisis was now over. "I'm sorry I punched you."

"I'm sure I deserved it." He laughed softly, reaching over to open the door for her. "I'm not sorry I kissed you. Good night, Viola. Are we all right?"

She nodded. "I will remain here and cook for you."

He frowned. "That isn't what I meant."

"Oh." Then what did he mean? She was too tired to care. "Good night, my lord."

She retired to her quarters, undressed and snuggled under her blanket.

But she could not help wondering about tonight's kiss and their being caught.

What might have happened had she accepted his offer of marriage instead of punching him in the nose?

He could not have been serious about it, could he?

CHAPTER 12

ALEXANDER FELT PARTICULARLY proud of Viola. This morning's breakfast was another triumph. He'd had to pry his family from the dining table in order to gather them in his study for their interview of the girl.

He was going through with it because he had promised Viola.

As for him, he wanted Viola as his wife.

He'd kissed her last night and removed all doubt.

She was the woman with whom he needed to share his life. The notion would frighten her, no doubt. However, meeting the rest of his family beyond his father might soften her to the idea.

As for him, he could think of nothing else since that kiss.

She had the softest lips and the sweetest body.

However, he was the densest clot in existence. Why had it taken him so long to realize his perfect match was right in front of him all this time?

Greaves knocked at the study door he had purposely left ajar. "My lord, Miss Ruskin is here." He stepped aside to allow her to enter.

Alexander's heart began to pound the moment she walked in, her eyes big and bright beneath the hideous mobcap that somehow managed to look adorable on her. She had not removed her apron, likely keeping it on to remind him she was no elegant viscountess but a mere cook.

"Come in, Miss Ruskin. Allow me to introduce you to my family." Alexander rose from his chair behind the desk and came around to escort her to the settee. He placed her between his grandmother and Lady Withnall, who was not family, but no one was about to refuse her involvement in today's interview of Viola.

Viola sat with her hands neatly folded on her lap and looking quite uncomfortable. But as his grandmother patted her hand gently, she seemed to ease a little...only a little. The poor girl was scared.

Also present were Gabriel and Daisy, Graelem and Laurel, and his parents.

Alexander now shut the door to afford them privacy.

"A pleasure to meet you all." Viola's eyes were wide as saucers as she took in all of their staring faces.

Perhaps he should have limited the attendance, but he wanted them to meet her and this was the most efficient way to accomplish it. Viola still thought his family was to offer her assistance in securing a respectable position once her father passed. But he had stayed up half the night consumed by thoughts of her and the only position he hoped she would take on was that of his wife.

Since he did not wish to be punched in the nose again, he was going to let the matter of marriage drop for now and simply proceed with the original purpose of this meeting. "Miss Ruskin is the young woman who has cooked the meals you are all enjoying so much."

"Best I've ever tasted," Gabriel said, his smile genuinely kind.

"This little sprite of a girl made them?" Graelem heartily agreed with Gabriel's assessment.

"Would you mind sharing some of your recipes?" Laurel asked with a soft laugh. "My husband would speak of nothing else last night, not even a thought for our children."

Viola had quite a serious look on her face, but it now eased into one of her beautiful smiles. "I would be delighted. I can write them down for you once the party is over. Just let me know which ones you would like. Lord Ardley, would you mind including the recipes in your posts to your cousin?"

He nodded. "With pleasure."

He now turned to the others in his family. "I wanted you to

meet Miss Ruskin because she may need our assistance in securing a respectable position for herself in the months to come."

"Her father is the local vicar here and he is not doing well," his father said, actually speaking with surprising gentleness. Of course, the old man did not know of the kisses he and Viola had shared.

That knowledge would have lit a fuse under him.

He would have swooped down like a bird of prey and shipped Viola out of Ardley as fast as possible, no matter that Vicar Ruskin was ailing and soon to pass on. Of course, Alexander would have brought her right back. Neither of them would have been happy, and Viola would have been in anguished tears, finding herself caught in the middle of their dispute.

Alexander sat back and listened as she responded to everyone's questions, watching with pride as she charmed them all with her sweet nature and unaffected manner. "How did you learn to cook so divinely?" Laurel asked. "Did you have formal training?"

"No, none at all. But I enjoyed making meals for my father and cooking for the various functions we held at the vicarage. There were many when he was younger and more hale."

"What got you started?" Daisy asked. "Your talents are beyond merely home cooking."

"My mother died in childbirth, so it has been me and my father for as long as I can remember. As I grew older, I began to take on household chores usually left to the woman of the house. This included cooking."

"Did you not employ a cook?" Alexander's mother asked.

"Yes, but I quickly realized I enjoyed preparing the meals myself. I tested the recipes out on our guests. The vicarage was quite a gathering spot at the time. But it did not become a passion of mine until I was about fourteen years old. That year, my father took me to Oxford and we came upon a shop that sold spices from around the world. I was fascinated and have returned there at least twice a year ever since."

"For which we are eternally grateful," Gabriel quipped, rubbing his stomach.

She laughed lightly. "The proprietor gave me some recipes he'd brought over from his home in India. After that, I began to collect recipes wherever I could. I experimented with flavors, spices, some quite exotic. It was my way of traveling to the far off places I would never experience otherwise."

"Your breadth of knowledge is astounding," Daisy said. "You ought to put your recipes in a book. I think it would sell quite well. I'm sure among us we have connections to help you get it published."

Viola smiled. "I cook for the love of it. I wouldn't want people to have to pay for the knowledge."

Alexander chuckled. "Do you not have a mercenary bone in your body?"

"Apparently, she doesn't," Graelem said, joining him in a chuckle. "That is quite refreshing, isn't it?"

"If ever such a book were published, it would give you a nice income," Alexander's father interjected. "Wouldn't that appeal to you, Miss Ruskin? An income to allow you to travel the world in comfort and seek new recipes. You might even be invited to cook for royalty. I have no doubt your culinary talents will earn you some renown. You must think of your future."

"I will, my lord. But right now, I am only thinking of Lord Ardley's house party and then getting back to my father. I will consider your suggestion seriously once things quiet down for me."

"We shall talk it over whenever you are ready," Alexander said, knowing he was not letting her go anywhere outside of Ardley unless it was with him. He wasn't looking to stifle her dreams, but he wanted very much to be a part of them. While he loved his life in Ardley, it would be a much sadder place if Viola was not here to share it with him. If she wished to travel, he wanted to accompany her.

But they were getting too far ahead of themselves, so he brought the topic back to the present. "For now, I wanted my family to meet you and you to meet them. Do you have any questions for us?"

"No, my lord. It has been a pleasure getting acquainted with all of you. I had better return to the kitchen or luncheon will not be served on time. May I take your leave?"

Alexander grinned. "I dare not delay you or I shall face the wrath of my own family."

She rose, bid them all a good morning, and then skittered away.

Lady Withnall thumped her cane on the floor. "That went well. She's a lovely girl, isn't she? I believe she will make someone not only an excellent cook but a perfect companion. She is intelligent, polite, and carries herself quite well."

Gabriel and Graelem were grinning at him.

He sighed. "What?"

"She is a gem," Gabriel said. "Don't you dare let her slip away."

He rubbed a hand across the nape of his neck, not wanting to say anything to set his father off while the other guests were still here. "She is special. That's why I've promised to help her once her father passes. In truth, I have been selfishly holding my breath in the hope he hangs on until after this house party, his health is that dire."

"We are indeed sorry to hear this," his mother said.

"I've had the vicar's regular housekeeper sleep in at their home while Viola is here. I've also sent one of my maids there every day to assist the woman. My estate manager checks in on the vicar constantly and reports back to me."

His mother spoke up again. "Oh, dear. The poor girl must be having an awful time of it if what you say is true. Is he truly at death's door?"

"I am no physician, but he has weakened considerably over these past few months. If he continues to worsen at this pace, then yes, he cannot be far from it."

Daisy sighed. "Laurel and I come from a big family and always have plenty of support. I hate to think of her as all alone. Does she have siblings or other family to help her out, Alex?"

"No. Once he passes, she will have no one."

His father cleared his throat. "She has made a good impression on us all, but let us get to the crux of the matter. Alex, you have three beautiful young ladies from wealthy, titled families here to choose as your bride. You cannot disgrace us by marrying Miss Ruskin."

Alexander tensed immediately, clenching his teeth to restrain his temper. In truth, he rarely angered, but Viola was someone special and he had no intention of passing her up because his father was too blindly stuck in his old ways to see her worth. "I will not discuss it, Father."

"Indeed, you will. You have been paying far too much attention to the girl and it is time you understood that men in our position do not marry that sort."

"Just what sort is she? Intelligent? Kind? Thoughtful? I can assure you, if you persist in pressing the matter, I will get on bended knee this very day and propose to her."

His father was fuming again. "I will not have you defy me!"

Alexander was also getting hot under the collar. "And I will not have you threaten me."

"Ah, the joys of family reunions." Gabriel strode over to his wife and took her hand. "Father, need I point out that neither Daisy nor Laurel come from titled families? Nor was I a prize when Daisy fell in love with me. In fact, I had the worst reputation imaginable. Even you believed I was an utter disgrace. But she saw me for the man I truly was. She makes me happier than I ever dreamed possible. I cannot imagine my life without her."

"I can say the same about Laurel," Graelem said. "I was an oaf who trapped her into marrying me for the sake of an inheritance. We Daynes are not so high and mighty as you seem to think we are. But we do marry for love, and I do not see how it is fair to deprive Alex of this same joy we have found with our own wives."

His father appeared more resigned than appalled as he said with little conviction, "But she's a cook."

"Best in all of England, I'll wager," Alexander's grandmother intoned. "Sit down and stop your blustering. You may be Earl of Trent, but I am still your mother and not above putting you over my knee."

Alexander stifled a grin.

He adored his grandmother.

His father now turned to him. "If you are in love with her, then why go through this charade of a house party?"

"Because I am an idiot and did not know I was in love with her at the time. It has been two years since Jillian passed, but I remained too clouded in memories of her to see what was before my very eyes."

His mother emitted a ragged sigh. "My dear, you have had a rough time of it."

"Others have it far worse. But my wife and daughter were an important part of my life and I still feel their loss acutely. However, it is Father who convinced me it is time to move on." Alexander crossed his arms over his chest and now spoke directly to his father. "It is you who made me realize how much I cared for Viola. Had you not pounded into me the need to find myself another wife, I might have remained in my fog for years longer."

"But she is merely a vicar's daughter," he shot back, his anger clearly waning. "And you have beautiful daughters of the highest ranking members of society under your very roof."

"I cannot wait to be rid of them. Nor will I say anything to Viola even after they are all gone. She will never accept to leave her father in his condition. As important, she does not know me well enough to trust that I love her and truly wish to marry her. The girl will take a bit of convincing." He winced. "A lot of convincing. But this is not the time."

"I have nothing against her, Alex. She is everything you say. But do not expect me to be pleased about it. My greatest fear is that you will wake up one day and come to regret your decision. She has not been trained to enter society. These diamonds you've invited here, had they an inkling she was their true competition, would eat her alive."

"All the more reason I would not offer for any of them. I have no desire to be drawn into their petty schemes and squabbles."

"There is more to consider, for she will not only have difficulty making her way in our society, but she will find herself resented by your own staff. How will she gain their respect and that of the townspeople when she is one of them? And now she will put on airs and strut around town as though above them all? They will not stand for it."

"Viola does not strut or put on airs. She will be an asset to me because she understands their needs better than any of us could. As the vicar's daughter, she has been paying calls on the sick and needy in our village for years now. What difference if she makes those same calls as my viscountess instead? Do you think anyone will care? Enough, Father. Let us enjoy the day. These guests are only here for the weekend which is already half over."

He walked out along with his family to join the others who had lingered around the breakfast table and were only now getting up.

He invited the men for a ride while Daisy and Laurel offered to take the ladies into town for a little shopping. The plans were greeted with enthusiasm by all, and everyone went their separate ways to dress for their excursions.

The gentlemen and ladies would only be apart for the morning and regroup in time for luncheon to be served. Alexander had donned his riding clothes and thought he was the first to come downstairs when he noticed Lady Aurora seated on a bench in his garden with her head hung low. She appeared to be on the verge of tears.

Sighing, he walked over to her. "Has something happened to upset you?"

She nodded.

Not wishing to sit beside her and have her throw herself into his arms, which would be taken the wrong way by everyone, he simply placed a foot on the bench and leaned forward. "Care to talk about it?"

"My duke has proposed to someone else."

No wonder she looked as though tragedy had struck. "I'm sorry. Truly, I am."

"It was announced in this morning's paper. Father noticed it and read it to me. The girl is some country mouse from a family of little consequence. Why would he want her?"

"That is an excellent question and one worth pondering if you ever hope to understand what makes for a good marriage. It could be that she truly cares for him."

Lady Aurora huffed.

"A man, any man, wants to know his future wife is interested in him and not his wealth or title. We, too, have hearts that beat. We are not merely objects."

She glanced up at him. "Then why are we not taught to think about such things? Why must it be pounded into our heads to be beautiful and charming when it is all for nothing."

"Lady Aurora, it isn't for nothing. But neither is it all there is to a happy partnership. The problem with the marriage mart is that it is looked upon too much as a means to a marital business arrangement. Some lords are in dire need of salvaging their estates and must set aside their hearts to seek an heiress. But even they hope to find both love and salvation in their bargain. Did you love him?"

"No, I hardly knew him. But I still must have a duke."

"Why? Because you are set on becoming a duchess?" He sighed at her nod. "Duke Nevins has brought along his son and daughter. The son presently holds the courtesy title of marquess, but he will be a duke someday. Have you thought of that?"

"Oh. Well, I did. But it means I would have to wait my turn to become a duchess."

"Is it such a terrible thing? Might I suggest you actually try to be interested in what he is saying, learn his likes and dislikes. You claimed your duke enjoyed Town life but he's obviously chosen the country mouse over you, something you might have realized had you bothered to give a fig about him and not merely his title. You are now given a second chance with Nevins' son. Get to know him. Perhaps the two of you would suit."

"He has been ogling Lady Alicia."

"Likely for reasons other than marriage. He might start looking at you with a serious eye if you paid him any notice."

She cast him a weak smile. "You are now sending me off into another man's arms. Have you no interest in me?"

"No, I'm afraid not. Nor are you interested in me. But I am always available to offer you guidance should you need it. Everyone deserves their happiness, and I truly wish it for you."

"Be careful, Lord Ardley. I may decide you are perfect for me, after all."

He escorted her back inside and was not surprised to find her merrily chatting with Duke Nevins and his son not five minutes later. Well, this was merely a weekend party and Lady Aurora had little time to waste if she was to secure a duke, or in this instance, a duke in waiting.

The men and women parted ways soon after, the men enjoying their bracing ride across the gently rolling hills of his countryside. The women had already returned from town and were showing off their purchases to each other by the time the men returned.

He was pleased to see Duke Nevins' son find his way to Lady Aurora's side immediately upon entering the parlor. "What did you purchase?" Alexander heard the young man ask her.

She smiled prettily. "This brooch. I noticed your cravat pin at breakfast this morning and admired it. It brings out the darker blue of your eyes. Subtle and yet quite attractive. You have a very elegant way about you. When I saw this brooch, I thought about you. I hope the color will look half as nice on me."

"It shall pale in comparison to your beauty." The young marquess offered his arm to her. "Would you care to walk out in the garden with me?"

Alexander stifled a grin.

How easily Lady Aurora had the young man in her thrall. But these young ladies and gentlemen were here for the very purpose of making a match. He expected her to come away from this party with the promise of a happy result.

Lady Charlotte was seated on the settee showing off some fluffy woolen thing she had purchased, a doll of some sort she immediately named *Lambykins*. Ah, because it was a little woolen lamb. *Brilliant.* She then began to make her squeaky, cooing sounds again which the two young lords kneeling beside her seemed to delight in.

Dear heaven.

Alexander went over to the sideboard to pour himself a drink.

Lady Alicia seemed to be holding herself aloof, not looking particularly interested in his friend, Lord Hythe, when the man approached her.

What was going on in her scheming brain?

He turned away and concentrated on pouring himself that drink.

Although he had been away from the marriage game for years, he still knew how to read people and recognized immediately the danger of this particular lady. She needed to be watched carefully. While all three approached the marriage mart with calculation, she was the one most likely to use nefarious means to accomplish her aims.

The other two ladies were easy to read, perhaps because they were both virgins. They used feminine wiles to tempt their young men, but were not offering their bodies. Yes, he could tell they had been kissed a time or two, but nothing more serious. Lady Aurora could very well land her duke in waiting and become a duchess someday. Lady Charlotte would find a titled gentleman who wanted a *cuddly-wuddly* wife. There were such men who enjoyed a helpless female.

But Lady Alicia? That young lady was experienced and devious.

He dismissed thoughts of her when the luncheon bell rang.

He had never seen the elite of society sprint so fast toward the dining table. But this was Viola's skill. By now, they all knew the repast was going to be spectacular. She served a white soup, doing something to the veal stock to enrich the taste, for they were all slurping it down so fast, they did not have time to take breaths in between. Several choruses of "I am going to abduct your cook" were heard from the elder ladies.

"Oh, no," Lady Withnall responded. "She is to come directly to me if she ever decides to leave Lord Ardley. You are all too late. I have already arranged it."

"Your cook is a woman?" Duke Nevins asked.

Alexander immediately tensed.

The men would not leave Viola alone once they saw how beautiful she was.

Fortunately, Lady Withnall was not above dissembling. "Yes, but I urge you never to trespass. She is ruthless in her kitchen and always carries a meat axe in her hand. If you dare to interrupt her while she is at work, she will use that weapon on you without the least compunction. She rules her domain like a tyrant."

"She sounds grim," Lady Aurora said.

"All great artists have volatile temperaments and she is clearly that," his own grandmother replied. "Keep out of her way and she will not chop off any of your body parts."

Duke Nevins harrumphed. "I have no quarrel with the old crone so long as she continues to prepare pleasing meals for us. But you may have her, Ardley. I do not permit anyone on my staff to behave as though they are above me. Such arrogance wreaks havoc on the expectations of the other servants. You shall have a revolt in your own home if you are not careful."

Talk turned to the more pleasant topic of this morning's shopping.

Lady Charlotte mentioned her *Lambykins* again and began to make bleating sounds.

Lord save me.

Alexander had hardly touched his wine and reached for it now.

The luncheon meat was a rump roast flavored with sherry, the meat so tender it melted in one's mouth. This was served along with a savory souffle that he inhaled in two bites the moment it was served on his plate.

After the meal, since the day boasted of spectacular sunshine and gentle breezes, the elder guests took seats on the terrace to watch the younger guests partake of lawn games. Croquet was set up on the side lawn for the ladies and their admirers to play. Since ladies were involved, the game would be lively but more or less sedate.

Meanwhile, Alexander, Gabriel, Graelem, and Lord Chesterfield decided on a doubles match of badminton, which was usually considered a sedate game, but not the way they played it. They treated their sets as more of a blood sport, where one side was determined to demolish the other. Bruises were not uncommon, and the object was to draw blood by striking one's opponent in the nose or lip with the bird that got smacked around mercilessly. Neither was it uncommon for the players to wind up with a black eye. "Bachelors against the married men," Lord Chesterfield called out.

Graelem laughed. "Done. You'll live to regret it, Chesterfield. We married men still have a spring in us, as you weak bachelors shall soon find out."

They were all exhausted and bloodied by the time the last game was called, none of them spared and none of them cared.

They'd had a good time.

Daisy and Laurel came over with moist handkerchiefs to tend to their husbands. "Idiots," Laurel muttered.

"Monumental dolts," Daisy agreed.

Lord Chesterfield enjoyed the attentions of Lady Alicia and Lady Charlotte. The latter referred to his bruises as 'owies' and waved her little lamb doll in his face while Lady Alicia actually did something useful by wiping the blood off the cut above his eye.

Alexander withdrew his own handkerchief and walked over to the nearby conservatory to pour water on it for himself. He caught Viola peeking at him through the glass as he approached, surprised but pleased she had been watching the game.

Of course, he looked like hell and smelled like a sweaty, rotten cabbage.

She grew flustered when she realized he had noticed her and was coming toward her. She tried to hurry back to the kitchen.

"Viola, wait!" He intercepted her just as she reached the door. "Why must you always run from me?"

"I wasn't…I…" She sighed and made no fuss when he took her by the hand. He was not about to take her in his arms, which is what he really wanted to do. But how could he while his shirt was plastered to his body and sweat rolled down his neck? She looked up at him, gracing him with the softest smile. "You look awful, my lord."

He cast her a boyish grin. "I'm sure the others fared worse."

She laughed. "No, I think you got the worst of it. Here, sit down on that overturned bucket and let me dab the blood off you. What were the four of you thinking? Any of you might have lost an eye with the brutal way you were playing."

"It felt good, as though I was alive again," he admitted. "Were you not dazzled by my prowess?"

Her lips turned up at the corners in that glorious smile again. "Oh, yes. Quite impressed each time you took a graceful dive. You looked quite manly as you slammed to the ground, face first…repeatedly," she said with a soft giggle. "But I'm glad you enjoyed yourself. I shudder to think what might have happened had you played a game of croquet and attacked each other with mallets and hard balls. Concussions. Lost teeth. Broken noses."

"One of the wives would have put a stop to it before it ever descended to that." Now that the badminton game was over, he was starting to feel his bruises. He had hit the ground hard a time or two. But he did not care, for he had enjoyed the roughhousing, especially now that it ended with Viola fussing over him.

She tucked her hand under his chin and tilted his head upward so that his gaze met hers. They locked on each other and neither one seemed able to draw away. He was exhausted and yet happier than he'd been in years. Nor could he stop grinning as she delicately began to wipe the blood off his lip.

Gad, this girl was pretty.

"You also have a little blood on your cheek." She wiped that off, too. "I'll have Greaves fetch your brandy. All of you ought to pour it on your cuts to properly treat them."

She stood close, her little body positioned between his legs while she clucked and *tsked* at him. He wanted to put his arms around her and draw her onto his lap. He wanted to kiss her into midnight, but she would dart away like a frightened doe if he ever did.

Instead, he sat quietly and tried to control the fiery spasms sweeping through his body with her every soft touch.

He inhaled her sweet scent. "Strawberries. Cinnamon. Garlic. Lemons."

She moaned and stared down at her hands. "Can you still smell the garlic? I tried to scrub it off with lemon juice, but I can see it did not help."

"Viola, I–"

"Well, well. If it isn't the lord of the manor cavorting with the kitchen help," Lady Alicia said, her smile smug and disdainful as she inspected Viola. "I thought you were the model of sainthood, Lord Ardley. But I see you have deceived us all. Naughty, naughty boy. She is a very pretty kitchen maid. Have you bedded her yet? Or are you still in the early stages of seduction?"

Viola fled the conservatory, darting through the door like a pigeon being chased by hunting dogs. He did not attempt to hold her back, for he did not want Lady Alicia sinking her claws into the innocent girl. Nor did he want Alicia believing Viola was more to him than one of his regular kitchen staff.

Alicia laughed as she approached him. "You needn't worry. I'll keep your little secret. Your mama and dear grandmama need never know what a hound you truly are. Or have you not yet coaxed the little dove into your bed? Keep her, if you like. I would not be one of those wives who demands fidelity in a husband. You and I shall get along well in our marriage, so long as you do not fuss about my own diversions. I would be discreet, of course."

He stepped back when she pressed herself against his body and began to rub herself against him. "Alicia, you are quite mistaken if you think your behavior is in any way tempting me. Nor should I be at all tempting to you in my foul state. I am dirty and sweating."

She licked her tongue along his neck. "Just how I like my men. But I can play sweet and innocent, if this is how you want it."

He groaned. "A word of advice, no man is going to offer for you if you are willing to spread your legs for him so readily…especially when not invited."

"I am quite selective in my bed partners, I assure you," she said, now angry.

"Is that so?"

"I am here because you are someone I want. So why should we not enjoy ourselves?"

He laughed. "You don't know the first thing about me."

"Isn't this entirely the point of your house party? You seem quite tense, my lord. Perhaps a little bed sport will put you in better temperament. I know how to please you. All you have to do is take me into your bed."

He stared at her in disbelief. "That is never going to happen. What are you doing, Alicia? I have no need of you to warm my bed, nor the slightest desire. Did I ever give you that impression? Or is this part of a scheme to lure me into a compromising position? I warn you, it will not work on me."

He took her by the elbow and escorted her back to the guests gathered on the terrace. She had a gloating smile on her face, but he could not make sense of it. He was not particularly gentle as he led her back to the others.

Well, she had made it quite clear she did not prefer tenderness.

Her parents also wore smug smiles.

He expected they were the ones encouraging her to seduce him and had now completely misunderstood the situation. He would make it clear to them later. Right now, he had to tend to his cuts and bruises. He felt a liquid warmth at the edge of his lip and knew he was bleeding again.

He excused himself and hurried upstairs to his bedchamber, calling for his valet. "Marston, get a tub up here. I look a mess and need to clean up before dinner is served."

His valet tried to stifle his amusement. "It was good to see you mixing it up on the badminton court, my lord. I will admit to spying out the window as the four of you tried to maim each other. All in good fun, of course. I'll order the tub and then return to treat the cut on your lip."

"Thank you, Marston." Alexander sighed as he sank into his usual chair beside the hearth. He dared not admit it, but he had behaved like an idiot boy and his muscles were now suffering for it.

But the game had been good fun.

He shed his clothes and wrapped a towel around his hips while awaiting his staff to bring up his bath. He thought it might take a while since Gabriel, Graelem, and Chesterfield were also in need of tending.

There were only two tubs in the house.

He, as host, certainly deserved one. Chesterfield ought to have the other since he was not yet married and needed to look presentable to the diamonds. Graelem and Gabriel already had wives who would help them wash off the sweat and grime. No one would care if they did not look perfect.

He sighed and shook his head.

Lord, he hated this marriage hunt business.

One more day and it would all be over, thank goodness.

He must have been deep in his thoughts, for he hardly noticed the door opening and then quietly clicking shut. "Marston, did you–" He leaped to his feet. "Bloody hell, Alicia! Get out of here now."

"Oh, no. You are not getting rid of me so fast." She started to undo the lacings of her gown.

"Indeed, I am." He grabbed her by the elbow, just as he had done earlier in the conservatory, and led her to the door.

"You will have an audience standing in wait," she said with a triumphant smirk.

His expression turned thunderous. "Is that so? Too bad for you. I will never agree to marry you. So you had better confess all to our audience and admit your trick. If you pretend something happened between us, you will end up ruined."

He yanked the door open and dragged her out.

Sure enough, her parents, Lady Withnall, and his grandmother were in the hall. "I demand satisfaction!" her father intoned.

"Go away, Simmons," Alexander muttered in disgust, then returned to his bedchamber and slammed the door shut.

He was seething.

How could he have let his guard down and not foreseen this obvious ploy? He had known this scheme was coming, just thought she would wait until tonight to set it in motion, something he intended to thwart by simply locking his door.

He had not expected the assault to come so quickly.

"Botheration," he said with a growl, hearing raised voices outside his door.

He could not leave his grandmother and Lady Withnall to fight his battles for him.

He secured the towel around his waist and stepped into the hall again. "I will say this only once, Lord Simmons. Nothing untoward happened between me and your daughter, as you well know, for you are likely the one who pushed her in here only moments ago."

"Are you calling me a liar?"

"Do not think this amateurish trick to discover us in a compromising position will work. I shall never marry her. Do you understand me? *Never* will she be Lady Ardley. So I suggest you pack up and prepare to leave my home first thing in the morning. I give you until the morning out of courtesy, for you deserve to be tossed out on your ear this very moment."

"Now, see here!"

"And if you dare encourage your son to call me out, I warn you now that I shall beat the stuffing out of him. If he dares draw a weapon on me, I shall kill him. Is this your wish? To have a daughter ruined and your heir killed?" He turned to Lady Alicia. "You are a beautiful girl and clever, too. If you can ever stop scheming, you might just find someone who truly cares for you. Stop taking your father's advice. It is bad advice and will only lead you to destruction."

She slapped him and stormed off.

Her mother followed after her, but her father remained. "Lady Withnall, you see how Lord Ardley has abused my daughter. Will you not help me seek justice? He must take responsibility for his behavior and marry her."

The little termagant thumped her cane against the floor. "What I see is an innocent man whose only mistake was to fail to put up barricades against his door. If you dare attempt to shame him into marrying the girl, I shall call you out as a liar. I suggest you and your family take your dinner in your rooms tonight and be gone from here at first light tomorrow."

"We shall see who will win this battle! I'll have the story printed in every newspaper. He'll come crawling to the altar. You'll see. I have royal connections!"

"So have we all, Simmons," Alexander said with a growl. "Don't be a fool. You are hurting no one but your daughter."

The marquess turned to Lady Withnall again, but she had even less patience for him now. "You forget who I am, Lord Simmons. I know all your secrets, and I assure you, every last one of them will come out in the wash if you dare persist with your scheme. As for your daughter, how can you be so vile as to put her reputation in such danger? Lord Ardley is no quaking coward. Nor does he give a fig what the *ton* thinks of him. Admit you picked the wrong mark and just walk away before it is too late."

The man strode off in a huff, shouting for his wife to pack this instant.

"Good riddance," Alexander muttered.

"Put some clothes on, dear boy," his grandmother intoned.

"Marston is bringing up my bath. I'll summon Greaves to keep an eye on the marquess and his family until they are safely off. Bloody hell, what else can go wrong today?"

CHAPTER 13

"WHAT A ROW there was," Sally, one of the upstairs maids, excitedly rushed into the kitchen to report the news to her friends.

Viola tried not to listen in, but the girl was bursting with the gossip and everyone, including herself, was eager to hear it.

"She was caught in his bedchamber and her father was livid. He demanded Lord Ardley marry her, but he refused!"

Viola's heart shot into her throat. "Who are you talking about, Sally?"

"Lady Alicia and Lord Ardley. There he was standing practically naked in the hall and declaring he would never marry her. Not that I was listening closely, for who cares what he was saying when he was standing there with nothing but a towel wrapped around his waist and looking like a magnificent pagan god?"

All work stopped as Viola and her helpers listened to Sally go on. "He's carved of granite stone down to every rippling muscle on that stunning man. I could hardly hear a word of their shouts while the blood was pounding so hard through my ears. Who can blame the lady for allowing him to seduce her? I would have jumped into bed with his lordship myself," she said with a high-pitched giggle.

"Who wouldn't want to be tangled in those sheets with him?" another of the maids said with a similar, irritating giggle.

Viola was going to be ill. "They were found in bed together?"

Sally shrugged. "They must have been. Lord Simmons, Lady

Withnall, and his lordship's own grandmother were all standing in the hall by his door when the lady was discovered leaving his bedchamber. Lord Simmons was going on about finding them in a compromising position and how his lordship had to make it right by marrying his daughter."

Oh, she was definitely feeling ill and clutched her stomach to make it stop lurching. This had to be a mistake. "Are you quite certain?"

"I could not see it all clearly, Miss Ruskin. But her gown was in disarray. No doubt she'd had to hastily put it back on when her angry papa found them. And Lord Ardley was standing there with his arms crossed over his chest, showing his big muscles. Goodness, my knees buckled when I saw them flex."

"And that skimpy towel hastily tucked around his waist," one of the other girls reminded.

"Yes," Sally said with a shake of her head. "But I've never seen his lordship so angry. He's tossed Lord Simmons and his family out this very evening. I suppose they would not want to stay around since the poor girl has been disgraced."

"Still, feels quite harsh of his lordship," another of the maids said. "But how can it be true? He's no scoundrel. In all the years we've worked for him, he's always been a gentleman."

"Perhaps. Perhaps not. How are we to know for certain?" Sally insisted. "He was married all these years, then kept to himself while grieving. Grief can change a man. He might have been noble in the past, but who knows what he is capable of now? A man has needs, doesn't he?"

"But to be so careless as to be caught in his bedchamber with Lady Alicia?" her friend commented. "Come to think of it, he and his wife had become a little distant after the birth of their little girl. Perhaps he has been straying all along and none of us realized it. Just because he never dallied with any of us doesn't mean he didn't dally elsewhere."

Greaves walked into the kitchen just then. "Be quiet, you silly geese. You don't know what you are talking about. All of you, get back to work or I shall report you to Mrs. Lester."

Viola's hands were shaking as she approached the trusted

Ardley butler. "Is it true, Mr. Greaves? Was Lady Alicia found in his lordship's bedchamber?"

His expression turned grim. "We cannot leap to conclusions, Miss Ruskin. He is an honorable man. I have no doubt his name will be cleared."

Then it was true.

She took a moment to steady her breath and then returned to her cooking. After tomorrow, she would be through with her duties here and need not see Lord Ardley ever again. Not that she believed everything Sally had told them. In truth, she could not believe a man could change so drastically in his nature. Like Greaves, she knew there had to be an explanation for the incident.

The viscount was a catch.

These diamonds were here because they hoped he would marry one of them. Perhaps Lady Alicia staged the incident to ensure he would choose her. Or was it possible Lord Ardley, having seen them dance and having chatted with each of them, was now testing them out in bed? Could he be that crass?

"No, he couldn't be," she muttered, sooner believing Lady Alicia and her family had plotted to trap him in a compromising position. These were the sort of games the *ton* played, were they not?

However, even if he was exonerated, she intended to keep her distance. She was a simple vicar's daughter and would be eaten alive by this elite crowd if she did not remain careful. Hadn't George Haworth warned her about this very thing while they danced together at the fair?

And had she not already been dragged into a battle of wills between Lord Ardley and his father? At least his father understood the rules of the game. Viscounts did not marry vicar's daughters.

It was as simple as that.

The man was not being an ogre to her. He just saw things clearly and was being sensible about the futility of her affection for his son.

Viola was so distressed, she could not bring herself to peek into the dining room to find out what the guests thought about her crowning meal that evening. The menu was meant to dazzle them. It had taken all of her effort and knowledge to conceive each dish and carry it out to spectacular effect. She had another spectacular meal planned for tomorrow night, since that was to be the last night of the house party.

She meant to leave them all gasping in delight.

Viola thought she would be calmer by the following day, but it was not to be. Sally would not stop coming into the kitchen to talk to her friends about the viscount and his state of undress during yesterday's incident.

Would they never tire of the topic?

Yes, he was gorgeous.

Rock hard and muscled.

The talk turned bawdy.

The girls on her staff continued to behave like peahens, unable to concentrate for giggling over Sally's comments and making crude comments of their own. Viola did not understand every remark, but she had her suspicions about what each meant.

Her cheeks were aflame.

"Enough!" she finally shouted. "This is the third pudding burned today. Sally, your duties are as upstairs maid, are they not?"

"Yes, Miss Ruskin," she said, lowering her head and demurely clasping her hands in front of her.

"Then I suggest you leave the kitchen and attend to them immediately. Out! Now!"

The girl hurried off.

"As for the rest of you," she said in her sternest schoolmistress voice, surprising even herself by her tone of authority, "next one who burns a pudding will be reported to Mrs. Stringer for reprimand upon her return."

Fortunately, with Sally and her disruptive chatter now gone, the kitchen staff quickly settled down to work. The rest of the day proceeded smoothly. Viola spent the entire morning and into the afternoon hidden in the kitchen. She was about to begin preparations for the supper feast when Horace, one of the young footmen she was friendly with, came in to issue a report on the viscount's activities.

"No one has seen him since early this morning," he said.

Viola paused as she was about to heat sauce in a pan. "Isn't he at the picnic?"

She knew what the viscount was supposed to be doing today since she had helped him work out the schedule of entertainments for the entire weekend.

"No, Miss Ruskin. No sign of him."

"That is odd. Is he in his study? Or his bedchamber?" The mention of his bedchamber had the kitchen girls giggling again.

"Stop it," she ordered, rolling her eyes. "Perhaps he is setting up the archery targets."

Horace shook his head. "No. Not at the archery match either. He rode off after breakfast this morning and no one has seen him since."

Viola's stomach sank into her toes. "Surely, someone must know where he went."

"No, Miss Ruskin. He did not even tell Greaves or Mr. Wilson. I don't think his parents know either."

She wondered whether his disappearance was related to the trouble with Lady Alicia.

She was afraid to ask.

However, she breathed a sigh of relief when Horace rushed in once again shortly before supper to report the viscount had returned. "He's ordered the tub brought up."

Her girls started giggling again.

Several of them offered to carry up his water.

Others offered to wash his body.

"No such luck, ladies." Horace winked. "Marston is guarding him like a hawk and will allow none of you within a mile of him. I'm sure he'll lock his door this time. But I doubt he'll be invaded now. Lady Aurora seems quite taken with Duke Nevins' son and Lady Charlotte is too busy holding off Lord Hythe and Lord Gaston who both appear to be smitten with her."

As preparations for tonight's feast intensified, Viola dismissed thoughts of the viscount and his mysterious absence.

To her delight, and despite her distraction, the supper was a stunning success. She wasn't certain how she had managed to pull it off while her heart was in such upheaval. But she had her pride and was not about to show any weakness to these Upper Crust guests.

Somehow, she had maintained her composure and could now breathe easier as course after course was delivered without a single misstep. The gingerbread chess board and marzipan chess pieces she had spent hours painstakingly shaping and painting with confectioner's paste as the centerpiece of their dessert was a triumph, she was told.

Now, the house party weekend was almost over.

Most guests would depart tomorrow, taking their leave throughout the day. The viscount's family planned to stay on a few more days at the viscount's request, Sally had told her. "I'm sure of it, Miss Ruskin. I heard it from Lady Eloise herself. I don't think Lord Hythe and Lord Chesterfield will stay on although Lord Ardley invited them to do so. Hythe's going to follow Charlotte Nevins back to London, sticking to her like a glove to a hand lest some other bounder gains her attention. Lord Chesterfield needs to return to his estate which is in a sad state of disrepair. He's another one who'll have to marry rich to restore what his father squandered."

Viola silently added herself to those who would leave tomorrow. Her cooking duties were over after tomorrow's breakfast and she intended to return to the vicarage as fast as her legs would carry her.

As soon as the midnight dessert courses were carried out, she left the kitchen for a breath of air while the scullery maids cleaned up. There was little to do to prepare for the upcoming breakfast, so she had the rest of the evening to herself.

She ought to have been exhausted, for this day had been the longest yet. Instead, she felt relieved and also a little saddened that her obligation would soon be over. Would she ever see Lord Ardley after tomorrow? It did not matter, for it was best she keep away from him.

Her resolve not to peek into the music room where this second course of desserts had been set up proved utterly futile. She chided herself for her lack of spine. She had not been on the terrace more than a minute before the merry chatter and bursts of laughter coming from the guests, many of whom were merrily dancing to the strains of a lively reel, overcame her curiosity. Her resolve to have nothing more to do with Lord Ardley collapsed.

She had to see what he was doing.

Was he dancing?

Or off by the long tables set up against the wall and enjoying her desserts?

The marzipan chess set was not her only centerpiece dessert this evening. She had also fashioned a tennis cake baked especially for him and his badminton players. The fragile sugar net had required some finesse to set atop the layers without having it crumble to pieces.

She watched as his cousin, Lord Graelem, helped himself to a second serving of the cake. But all the desserts appeared to be successful, every pie cut into, and many guests digging in with gusto. The extra marzipan chess pieces she had included with this midnight course were all gobbled up, and even the tray of chocolate bakes she had made for this final dessert course was now sitting completely empty atop the buffet.

To her frustration, Lord Ardley had his back to her.

He was casually lounging against the wall, his back to her as he spoke to his brother. She could not see his expression to tell if he was upset or had taken the incident with Lady Alicia in stride and already moved on. Their party was now four members short since Lady Alicia and her family had departed yesterday just before the dinner bell sounded.

The other guests did not seem at all sad to see them go.

Quite the opposite, everyone seemed to be enjoying themselves immensely.

Lady Aurora was engaged in conversation with Duke Nevins and his son. The young marquess was unable to take his eyes off her. Lady Charlotte was also in her glory, batting baby eyes at Lord Hythe and Lord Gaston who were tripping over themselves to attend to her slightest request, just as Horace had earlier reported.

Viola ducked into the shadows when Lord Ardley's brother glanced over. Had he noticed her? Would he say something to Lord Ardley?

Drat.

Since she did not wish to retreat back inside yet, she hurried down the terrace steps into the garden. The night was beautiful and she had worked hard to make this final feast one of her best ever. Did she not deserve a little respite?

She settled on one of the benches in a far corner of the garden, hopefully out of sight of anyone who might stroll by. The night was clear and filled with stars. The scent of lilacs lingered in the cooling air. Sighing, she took off her mobcap and tucked it into the ties of her apron as she absently watched the stars. They seemed quite bright and twinkling, and the moon appeared quite silver tonight.

A perfect night for romance.

Not that she would ever be so fortunate as to be swept in a man's arms on such an evening. Besides, the only man in whose arms she wished to be swept was Lord Ardley, and she was upset with him right now.

Had he taken Lady Alicia to his bedchamber?

"Gabriel thought he saw you sneaking around outside," the villain himself said with irritating cheer as he settled his large, muscled frame beside her.

Well, he wasn't really a villain according to Greaves.

And how could she not notice how beautifully formed his body was after Sally had gone on and on about its magnificence?

"My lord, shouldn't you be with your company?" She was tense and her words came out clipped and sounding quite peckish.

"No, Viola. I should be with you because you are obviously in a snit over what you think happened yesterday."

She tipped her chin into the air. "It is none of my business. Frankly, I do not care what you choose to do with your *ton* ladies."

"For the record, I did nothing. The incident was staged by Lady Alicia and her parents. Do you really believe I would have any interest in her?"

She let out a long breath. "I have no idea what to believe. You didn't have any clothes on and hers were all disheveled."

"Amazing how word gets around." He shook his head and laughed. "She did that to herself, all part of setting me up as the dupe. Mine were off because I had ordered a tub brought up after that badminton game. Speaking of which, thank you for that cake tonight. The four of us had a good chuckle over it. How did you manage to make that net? We all enjoyed it immensely."

"I'm glad you liked it. We call it a tennis cake, but I shaped the rackets to look more like badminton rackets. The netting is made out of sugar." She cleared her throat. "But Lady Alicia..."

"Ah, her. Still not convinced of my innocence? She must have waited for my valet to leave my quarters to arrange for the tub, then crept in. I can only imagine her delight when she caught me undressed."

"So you did not invite her in?"

"Lord, no," he said with a groan that sounded quite agonized. "Upon my word, the entire incident was staged by her and her parents. Rather poorly contrived, I must say. Although it was dumb luck on her part that she caught me in that state of dress...or rather...undressed as I was. I assure you, there is not enough gold in the world her family could have offered to entice me into marrying her. But the incident has upset you."

"I hardly matter. Hasn't it upset you?"

He nodded. "Yes, and I am still seething over it. But I blame myself for letting my guard down. I knew something like this would happen. I should have been prepared."

"What do you think will happen next?"

He leaned forward and rested his arms on his thighs. "Nothing. No one is going to believe them after Lady Withnall steps in to defend me. Not that I want or need her help. But she is a gossip and this is just too juicy for her to pass up, especially since she was there. I can assure you, if I had been guilty of seducing the girl, that little harridan would have been the first to hammer the nails into my coffin. She is feared because she always ferrets out the truth. I don't know what Simmons was thinking to have her and my grandmother present."

"Hoping to shame you in front of them, no doubt."

He shrugged. "Even if all of them believed I had behaved like a fiend, where would it get them? I knew the truth, that I hadn't done anything to her. They had to realize I was never going to marry her no matter how much pressure they applied."

"I see."

"You look at me as though I am an ogre. Why, Viola?"

"I know you are not. Greaves heartily defended you, and the ladies in my kitchen staff all wished they were the ones caught with you."

He groaned again. "I would never dally with any of them. Nor have I ever done so. It was never my style."

"What exactly is your style?"

"I am not a hound. I have never even courted a woman. Jillian and I just fell into marriage naturally out of our years of friendship. I think perhaps I have curmudgeon tendencies, because the social whirl holds no appeal for me and never has, even when I was younger. These ladies, who my grandmother claims are the best of this year's crop of debutantes, are grating on my nerves. I want to stuff that stupid *Lambykins* doll of Lady Charlotte's through my grist mill and grind it to dust."

Viola giggled. "She is a bit much with that helpless little girl act. But men do seem to respond to it."

He gave a mock shudder. "It isn't for me. I'd rather face Napoleon's armies than spend an hour listening to that girl cooing and squealing as she shoves that lamb doll in my face."

She pursed her lips in an attempt to hold back her laughter, but a few chuckles slipped out. "What about Lady Aurora?"

"She isn't so bad, but clearly not for me."

"What makes you think the two of you won't suit?"

He arched an eyebrow. "Many reasons. We have so little in common. She enjoys Town life and the society it offers. She wants the glitter and sparkle, the fancy townhouse, the elegant gowns and jewels, the party life and fine carriages. It is the opposite of how I feel. I'm sure there are many more reasons why we do not suit, but these are the most obvious."

"Would you change your opinion if it turned out she preferred a quieter, country life?"

"First of all, she does not. And, no. Even if it turned out she enjoyed fresh air and quieter living, I would not offer for her."

His comment surprised Viola. "Why not? Don't you find her beautiful?"

He nodded. "I will not deny she has looks that can turn a man's head. All three of them do. The problem is, my heart will not have her."

"What does that mean? Have you even given your heart a chance to get to know her?" Viola did not know why she was asking these questions and seemingly pushing him toward Lady Aurora when it was the last thing she wanted. Anyway, the girl had set her cap for the duke's son. Lord Ardley did not appear in the least disappointed.

Would he now consider holding another weekend house party and inviting another set of debutantes?

What if he decided to spend the rest of the summer in London?

No! He couldn't.

He belonged right here in Ardley.

To her chagrin, she wanted him all to herself.

But the matter was hopeless.

Even if he liked her, it could never lead anywhere but to heartbreak.

She repeated her question when he did not appear in a hurry to respond. "Shouldn't you give your heart the chance to get to know these debutantes?"

"I've come to realize it is useless." He leaned back and stretched his arm across the back of the bench while looking up at the stars. "Love does not work this way for me."

She was eager to pursue this conversation now that he had mentioned love, this very feeling she was struggling so hard to deny. "How does love work, my lord?"

He shifted his gaze from the heavens to regard her, as much as he could see of her beneath the silver moonlight. "For me, the feeling is just…I'm not sure how to describe it. One moment I was in darkness, and in the next, I was in sunlight. Glorious and radiant. I knew I had met the right woman, that she was the one meant for me."

"Did Lady Jillian feel the same way about you?"

He leaned forward and took her hand in his. "I am not talking about her, Viola."

Stared at him, her gaze riveted to his intense, fiery eyes that seemed to capture the stars and make them burn. "You're not?"

"I am talking about you."

She leaped to her feet. "No! You cannot say this to me."

Dear heaven!

Was he suggesting he loved her? Not merely *like* her, but *love*? Or was this the start of a seduction? How could it be anything but seduction?

Her heart began to beat so fast, she could hardly catch her breath. "You failed with Lady Alicia so you are now seeking an easier mark. Well, it won't be me!"

"Blast it, Viola." He rose and grabbed her by the shoulders, turning her to face him. "I never touched her. Why are you still angry over Lady Alicia's stunt? Because that is all it was, a stupid, reckless stunt. I had no part in it. I never invited her into my bedchamber. Nor would I ever do so. What can I say to convince you? Why do you refuse to believe me? When have I ever lied to you?"

Viola shook her head, struggling to hold back tears. "It isn't really about that incident, but some of it is. The problem is, I don't know what to think. This is what you do in the *ton*. Scheme. Manipulate. I am nothing. A nobody to be used and then squashed. Even if I were a somebody like Lady Alicia…I don't know. You put on a facade because the *ton* expects you to comport yourself in a particular way, to maintain a certain style of life, and they destroy those who do not abide by their rules and step on those who are viewed as expendable. Your father understands this."

He took both of her hands in his, his touch gentle and warm. "This is why I rarely go to London. I do not care for their rules. Nor am I ever careless of anyone's feelings. What did I go to war for? Almost lose my life countless times and suffer through unbearable winters and hunger? To come home and kick the poor and weak when they are down?"

She felt ashamed, for he spoke the truth and she was being stubborn out of the simple terror of giving her heart to him. It was ridiculous because he'd always possessed it, whether he knew it or not. What she hadn't expected was to gain his love in return. "I'm so sorry. You are right. It is cruel of me to suggest you would ever stoop so low. It is my fear talking."

"I know, Viola. But you have to trust me."

She nodded. "I'm trying. This is all new to me and I am completely out of my depth."

"Even I feel a little out of my depth just now, despite all my years of experience. But the *ton* cannot destroy me because they have no hold over me. Nor am I a little boy who must obey his father."

"You are his heir."

"That cannot change short of a vote of the House of Lords and he will never put it to the test. Nor can he threaten to cut off my allowance. I have my own independent means."

"If you have all this and are secure in wealth and title, then what do you want with me? Why would you have anything to do with a vicar's daughter?"

"Because you are my sunlight," he said with an ache to his voice that reverberated in the dark of night.

She held her breath, unable to respond.

Afraid to utter a word.

"Simple as that, Viola." The ache was raw in his voice. "You are the one who put the joy back in my life. I should not have said anything to you now. Your head is too muddled with concerns about your father, and it is obvious you have not come around to trusting me yet."

Viola knew it was mostly a lack of trust in herself. She knew so little about life beyond the shelter of this village and had never been romantically involved with any man. To lose her heart to this proud and worldly viscount, to believe he could love her back with equal fervor, was too much to take in all at once.

She was ridiculously naive and impressionable. She knew about food and that was all. How could she trust whatever attraction there was between them to be more than a fleeting interlude?

He was out of a dream.

Rich, titled, handsome. Kind. None of his workers had a cross word to say about him. Yet, he was no weakling to be trod upon.

What could he possibly want with her?

This is what worried her most.

She was no diamond, nor would he ever find a diamond beneath the surface if she were ever polished. "I think you ought to go back to your friends now. They will be wondering where you are, and to be caught with me after your earlier incident with Lady Alicia will raise eyebrows. Perhaps even cast doubt on your veracity."

He frowned. "Only those who don't know me would ever doubt. Besides, it is not the men who are ever ruined in these circumstances. The damage always falls upon the lady."

"All the more reason to end this conversation and let me go. I cannot afford to be seen with you, my lord."

"Alex."

She stared at him blankly. "Good night, my lord."

"Alex," he said more insistently. "I will not have you subservient to me."

"Which begs the point entirely. I am your cook. That is all I am to you. I should never be alone with you like this." She tried to slip her hands out of his grasp, but he would not allow it.

"Answer me this, do you have feelings for me? I want an honest response from you."

Her heart was thumping so loudly, she was surprised its noisy beat was not heard inside the house. "How would you know if I were being honest with you? I could easily lie and tell you all you wish to hear."

He caressed her cheek. "That is where you are wrong. I know the sort of woman you are, Viola. You will always tell me the truth because it is not in your nature to do otherwise. This is at the heart of the matter. Love is built on attraction and trust. It requires both to flourish. This is what separates you from all those other beautiful women, the fact that I trust you with all my heart and soul."

She looked up at him, quite stricken. "What if I do not trust you? No, I've said this badly. I do trust you, but I cannot make sense of these feelings. How can I be your sunlight? It is something so precious and beautiful. It has to be a mistake."

He cast her a wry smile, seeming not at all irritated. "Do you find me attractive?"

She nodded. "All the ladies do."

"And you?"

"Yes, how can you doubt it?"

"What is it you like about me?"

She laughed. "Everything. I cannot breathe whenever I am around you. Is it not obvious?"

He placed his hand on her cheek and lightly ran a thumb along her lower lip, his gentle touch shooting tingles through her. "That eases my mind greatly."

His breath was light and warm beside her ear.

She gasped as his lips grazed her cheek in a feather-soft kiss. He may not be a rogue, but he certainly knew how to make a woman melt. "It does? Why?"

Dear heaven.

He placed another soft kiss along her throat. "Because I know you will open your heart to me once you get over your fears and learn to trust these feelings. You will in time."

She hoped he was right. Even now, she was ablaze.

He'd hardly touched her, those kisses seductively soft and teasing, holding the promise of more.

He left her scorched from head to toe.

She closed her eyes and leaned into him, but in the next moment, he was the one who moaned and drew away.

How was she to tell him she wanted more of him?

It turned out, she did not have to.

She opened her eyes, believing he was about to walk away.

"Viola," he whispered with a groan and wrapped her in his arms instead. "Viola, I want to devour you."

All she could think of were Sally's words, her sighs and swoons over his thick muscles and rippled torso.

His skin was warm and his scent divine.

Devouring was an apt expression of how she felt for him, too. If he were food, she would be gobbling him down, licking off every crumb and dripping of juice. Oh, she was making herself hungry just thinking of it.

He groaned again. "Heaven help me, but I am going to burn to ashes if I do not kiss you now."

"So will I," she admitted, once more closing her eyes and tilting her head upward to meet the crush of his lips on hers, the urgent, plundering fire of his passion. This was everything she craved and everything that frightened her out of her wits.

But it would be their last kiss.

She could not allow this lunacy to proceed any further.

That he should love her?

How was it possible?

She circled her arms around his neck and made not the slightest protest when he lifted her up against him so that her bosom was pressed against his chest and her toes curled in the air. This was how every girl dreamed to be kissed, completely taken in by this all-consuming and shattering craving.

Just this one time.

Just this one memory.

But the nagging worry would not leave her.

What if he truly did love her?

How far did he mean to take it? Marriage between them was unthinkable because of all the obstacles they would face, the most serious being the rift it would cause between him and his family.

She would never forgive herself if this happened.

But if those obstacles were overcome, could they build a life together?

Or would this moment of bliss wash away with tomorrow's rain?

CHAPTER 14

"MRS. STRINGER, YOU'RE back," Alexander said as the noon hour approached the following day, surprised to find her in the kitchen with no sign of Viola. "Welcome. I hope you enjoyed your visit with your sister."

She bobbed a curtsy. "Thank you, m'lord. I did. But I'm pleased to return to familiar surroundings. I hear Miss Ruskin's cooking won raves."

He nodded. "She was the bright spot of the house party."

This was true for more reasons than merely her cooking abilities. He'd seen off the last of the diamonds and their families this morning, and should have been rather pleased with the outcome. If not for his turmoil over Viola, he would have been.

All in all, the house party had been a success. Lady Aurora had caught the eye of the duke's son and Alexander would not be surprised if an announcement of their betrothal appeared in the London papers within a month's time.

Lady Charlotte had captured Lord Hythe's heart, although it was more likely the hefty dowry to be handed over by Duke Nevins upon the silly girl's marriage that tipped the balance in her favor. Hythe's estate was in shambles and he needed that infusion of capital to restore it. But his friend also did not seem to mind Lady Charlotte's baby talk or her childishly coquettish manner. Perhaps it would turn out to be a happy match, especially if she remained in London while he was off in Yorkshire repairing his beloved holdings.

"Are you looking for Miss Ruskin, m'lord?" Mrs. Stringer asked. "She's gone back to the vicarage."

He tried not to appear surprised, for he had expected Viola to send word or stop by his study to advise him of that fact before making her departure. "I see. Of course, she must be eager to return to her father."

Not wishing to appear too eager himself, he spent a few more minutes talking to Mrs. Stringer and the kitchen staff, commending them on a job well done. But he did not like the idea of Viola running off without saying a word to him.

He decided to go after her.

"Greaves, I'll be at the vicarage if anyone asks for me. I shouldn't be long, just want to make certain Miss Ruskin lacks nothing for her father."

"Very good, my lord. What shall I say to Lord Trent if he asks for you?"

His family and Lady Withnall were to stay on for another few days, and he was looking forward to at least one or two relaxing afternoons and evenings with them. Of course, the food would be a step down after Viola's amazing meals, but Mrs. Stringer was a good soul and her food was quite palatable. "You can tell him where I've gone and that I will return within the hour."

He ordered his horse saddled and rode off toward the vicarage.

It did not take him long to spot Viola, for she was toting a bag of her clothes in one hand and a basket of her herbs, spices, and baking utensils in the other. They were obviously too heavy for the slight girl to manage on her own. But she was too stubborn to admit defeat and appeared determined to struggle home without anyone's assistance. She was walking so slowly, it took him no time to catch up to her even though his horse was moving at a casual lope.

He frowned as he dismounted beside her. "Why did you not ask Wilson to bring you home in one of the wagons?"

She blushed, or perhaps her cheeks were red from exertion.

She looked tired, quite delicate and vulnerable.

What was she thinking to attempt to manage this all on her

own?

"I did not realize it would be quite the burden to carry my belongings home. But I am halfway there and will muddle on my own the rest of the way without your interference."

"Don't be ridiculous." He took the bag and basket from her hands. "Do you wish to ride? You look exhausted, Viola. Truly, no jest. But I see you would rather collapse on the side of the road than be in my company. Shall we talk about last night?"

"No," she said with a vehement shake of her head.

"Ah, I see. You wish to pretend nothing of what we are feeling for each other is real. Is that it?"

"There is nothing we can say to each other that will change anything. Last night's kiss was a fanciful dream."

"And our garden waltz? Your first kiss? All of it a fanciful dream?"

She nodded. "One of us has to be practical about it."

"Practical? Is this what you think your running away from me is? I beg to differ. It is the most painful and impractical thing you can ever do. As you will come to realize, you cannot run from your heart."

"Perhaps not, but I can do my best to rein it in."

He shook his head and laughed softly. "You think you can rein in your feelings? Not you, Viola. Of all people, not you. Have you been crying?"

She frowned at him.

He caressed her cheek. "You look as though you have been."

"I am fine. Perhaps I did not sleep as well as I might have last night."

He set down the bags a moment to lift her onto Caligula because he had no intention of allowing her to walk the rest of the way home. Nor did he intend to mount behind her, something that would only set her off because she was a little powder keg of turmoil, afraid of her own feelings and wishing to blow him up to get him out of her life.

Too bad, because he meant to marry her. "You look like you were up all night crying. Why are you so overset at the prospect of a match between us? You would make an excellent viscountess.

You were born for it."

She shot daggers at him. "I haven't been trained to take on this role and would humiliate both of us within an hour of our marriage. Why do you refuse to see this?"

"Why do you refuse to acknowledge your strengths? Your caring. Your grace of bearing. Your intelligence and compassion. Need I even mention your outrageous talent? I have never seen anything more splendid than the feasts you prepared, not even in the royal court."

"Precisely. I may be an excellent cook, but this is all I will ever be to your friends and family."

"Blessed saints, you are thickheaded. You would make Ardley Hall a happy place again and put all our guests at ease because you are kindness and warmth personified. There is no malice in your nature. We will be inundated with guests because they will all adore the food churned out of the Ardley Hall kitchen under your supervision, and they will equally enjoy your hospitality. No one will ever want to leave. They will accept you as my viscountess more readily than they accepted me as viscount."

"But there are so many little things I do not know. Who is to be seated next to whom at the dinner table? Who is to be avoided and who must I invite? What about my clothes? I haven't a single silk gown."

"That tears it, how can I possibly marry you then? If only there was such a thing as a dressmaker's shop where such a gown could be made," he said with gentle sarcasm.

"You are mocking me."

"Never, Viola. I am merely pointing out that your concerns are trivial and easily remedied."

"They are not trivial to me."

"Yes, they are. You called them *little* concerns and this is precisely what they are. Inconsequential. Overcome with minimal effort." Even Caligula whinnied and nodded his head as they ambled down the familiar road between Ardley Hall and the vicarage. "See, even my horse agrees."

He glanced back at her and saw her lips curve in the hint of a smile.

Ah, progress.

"You mustn't give up on happiness because you are afraid to embarrass me or yourself," he said, trying to keep the frustration out of his voice. "I have been raised in society and am fully aware of the games played. Yet, I still fell for Lady Alicia's ambush. If it can happen to me, experienced as I am, then anyone can falter. None of us is perfect. We all make mistakes at one time or another. The point is to acknowledge them, deal with them, and move on. And another thing–"

"There's more? You are suddenly very talkative, my lord."

"Because you are hard to persuade. As for your concerns about fitting in, you will see that for every arrogant diamond who looks down her nose at you, there are a dozen frightened debutantes who will adore you because of your kind heart."

She appeared to be taking in his words, but he could not tell if she was persuaded or still irritated with him. "Stop fidgeting in the saddle or you'll fall, Viola."

"But I want to walk beside you."

"Why? Because you are ready to admit you love me? Or merely because of appearances?"

She sighed. "You are holding the reins and my bundles while I am seated upon your horse. This sight will have tongues wagging."

"That may be so, assuming anyone sees us. But if this is your only reason, then I am not letting you off Caligula. I'll fix any gossip if it proves to be a problem."

"You are quite highhanded."

"I know."

"As for fixing gossip, you may be able to frighten people into keeping quiet, but you cannot stop them from thinking the worst."

"This is where you are wrong. It is an easy fix."

"How?"

"You'll kick me in the head if I tell you what I would do."

"No, I won't. Why must you be so irritating about it? Just tell me how you will arrange it."

"I have already told you and got punched in the nose for it. My intention is to make you my viscountess. Marriage is the remedy.

How's that for being clear?"

She dismounted and came to stand in front of him with her hands on her hips. "Do not say another word about that foolish proposal. You are the reason my sleep was so troubled last night. Every time you open your mouth, you make it worse."

He grinned. "Not quite the words of love I hoped to hear."

She rolled her eyes. "Nor will you ever hear them from me. I am your cook, not some fine lady. One of us has to be logical about this situation."

"I do not see a situation."

"You *kissed* me last night."

He cast her an affectionate smile. "You kissed me back."

"This is what has upset me most. I responded *passionately,*" she said with a whispered emphasis on the last word as though it was something sinful. "Dear heaven, what you must think of me."

She was obviously distressing herself.

He had found her response delightful.

Did she not understand he was completely in love with her?

Irrevocably and eternally.

"Yes, Viola. You are the most sinful, wanton creature I have ever encountered," he said in obvious jest, but when he glanced at her, she looked to be in agony. "I was merely being sarcastic. I've told you before, you are the sweetest thing imaginable. Liking my kisses does not change that."

"But now, you think you can come to me whenever you want to be kissed. This is not what I am or ever want to be. I will not be your *chippie.*"

"My what?" He would have laughed out loud had he not been aware of how much his attentions were upsetting her. "You are my angel, Viola. A rather deaf angel because you refuse to acknowledge what it is I am really offering you. I would not hurt you for the world. How many ways must I say this? I intend to marry you, if you'll have me."

"Dear heaven, stop saying this. Can you not see it–"

"I am in love with you."

There.

He'd admitted it.

Perhaps not with finesse, but she had to know his feelings were sincere.

To his dismay, his words had the opposite effect.

She burst into tears. "Why are you making it so difficult when I am trying to do the right thing?"

"The right thing? For whom? Certainly not for me. Nor for you." Indeed, this was not at all the response he'd hoped for. "The offer of marriage remains open," he said with a heavy sigh. "You just let me know whenever you are ready and I shall propose to you properly…or you may simply respond with a *yes* at any time, be it tomorrow, a month from now, or a year."

"I will not hold you to those words."

"Because you think I do not mean them?"

She cast him a guilty look.

"I have never meant anything more in my life." He set her back on his horse and said nothing more until they reached the vicarage gate. "I'm coming in with you. Go up and see your father. I'll wait for you to come back downstairs."

"Why would you wait for me?"

"I want to know your father is all right. I would also like you to take inventory of your supplies. We'll make a list and Wilson can send one of the footmen into town to gather whatever items you lack and deliver them to you. Don't be frugal, everything is to be charged to my account."

She inhaled lightly. "Yours?"

"Yes. I owe you that and more. Why did you not come to me to collect your wages? I pay my debts and we had a bargain that you more than met."

Her cheeks turned a bright pink. "I'll come by tomorrow or the day after to collect what I am owed. Is that all right?"

"Come by any time, Viola. You are always welcome in my home."

"A little too welcome, I think."

He laughed, but it did not contain much humor. She was fretting again, worrying about feelings that neither of them could deny and terrified of what accepting to become his viscountess would demand, especially if it took her away from her father.

There was also the matter of trust. He did not like to see her overset, but after the Lady Alicia incident, he knew he had a long way to go to regain it.

He hadn't done anything wrong.

He'd said as much repeatedly, not only to her but to his parents. Even if she believed him this time, there still remained the smallest doubt. How long before he grew unhappy in the marriage and sought his 'sunlight' elsewhere?

He knew this fear was foremost on her mind.

Even his parents had their doubts. If his own parents could not trust him wholly and completely, then how was Viola ever to manage it? Of course, since she had not an ounce of venal greed in her, she would never accept to marry him until she felt confident enough in herself and in him to make their union work.

Any other girl would have leapt at the chance to be his wife, not caring a whit about love or faithfulness, just wanting the prestige and wealth attached to his name.

He helped her down when they got to her door.

She excused herself to run inside while Mrs. Bligh took the basket containing her spices and the bag containing her clothes from his hands. Viola scooted upstairs while her housekeeper lumbered to the kitchen.

He suddenly found himself standing alone in the hall.

Was this not a representation of what his life had been these past two years?

Alone.

Adrift.

It wasn't long before Mrs. Bligh returned. "My lord, would you care for some tea while you wait? Do make yourself comfortable in the parlor. I'm sure Miss Ruskin won't be long. Her father…well, he may not even be awake to speak to her. I did not want to say anything seeing as she was so busy at Ardley Hall, but he's taken a turn for the worse."

He frowned. "Tell me, Mrs. Bligh."

She gave a curt nod. "He must have had a bad spell during the night because this morning, I could not get him out of bed. Even though he seemed to recover somewhat, he had to cancel today's service. I did not have the heart to send word to Miss Viola seeing as the lass was coming home in a matter of hours anyway and he truly did appear to be on the mend."

"I see. Then I had better wait. I think his daughter will require my assistance."

She nodded. "I plan to sleep in a few nights longer. She ought not be left alone overnight. I do fear the end is near for her father."

Alexander's heart tugged, for he'd been through this personal hell himself and understood how the loss tore one's heart to pieces. "When it happens, you are to come directly to me. Will you do this, Mrs. Bligh?"

"Yes, m'lord."

"Good. My family is still here so there will be no eyebrows raised if I take her into my home should the worst happen. My mother and grandmother will look after her and act as her chaperones."

He was about to start Mrs. Bligh on a list of supplies they might need when Viola came rushing back down, her face ashen and her breath coming in short spurts. "Lord Ardley, please…my father is protesting, but I think I must summon Dr. Walcott. Will you talk sense into him while I am gone?"

"Stay here, love," Mrs. Bligh said. "I'll fetch him. Won't take me but a moment."

The Ruskin housekeeper grabbed her shawl and hurried off.

"Let me have a look at your father," Alexander said, now following Viola upstairs and fearing the worst.

Her father, although looking quite ghastly, was sitting up in bed and had a stubborn scowl on his face. "My lord, I did not realize you were here."

He started to struggle out of bed but Alexander stopped him. "Please, do not get up on my account. Your daughter is worried about you. Just rest while Mrs. Bligh summons the doctor to look at you."

"I don't need–"

"Yes, you do. He is not only summoned for you, but for the sake of your daughter. Can you not see how much she is suffering over your condition? So be quiet and let us get you the best care possible."

"But tomorrow's sermon–"

"You can prepare it from your bed. Your daughter is home now and will fetch you whatever you need. I'm sure she'll also make you something delicious to eat. Ask her about my house party. Her cooking was spectacular. She was the success of the party."

The vicar cast him a wan smile. "I knew my little girl could do it."

"I am not a little girl, Papa," she said, her voice shaking lightly as she stood beside Alexander.

Her father's expression softened. "You will always be my little girl. Even when you are married to–"

"Do not tell me again to marry George!" Viola emitted a sob and ran out of his bedchamber.

"Oh, dear. I've upset her," her father bemoaned. "Botheration. She thinks I am still talking about George Haworth. My lord, have you gotten the license?"

He patted the pocket of his jacket. "Yes. Taken care of yesterday. But your daughter is reluctant. As you can see, she cries at the mere mention of marriage, whether it is to George or me."

"This is my fault. I should have realized and warned you about it. She is overset not only because of my health. I have been pounding it into her head that George is the right man for her. The reason I was so adamant about him is…oh, what a fool I am. Viola loves you. She always has. I was so worried she would remain a spinster and struggle for the rest of her life because you could not possibly love her in return. She is guileless and her heart is so innocent. She would never accept to marry someone else while she still loved you. I was determined to work on her and wear her down. For her own good, of course."

"And now, you've convinced her a little too well," Alexander said, suppressing a groan. "She thinks she will betray you if she accepts to marry me. No wonder she has been giving me such a hard time. I think we must talk to her together…if I can ever get her back in here." But his heart eased now that he fully understood the reason for her distress.

To accept him meant betraying her father's wishes, or so she thought.

She would come around once she realized her father approved of their union.

The vicar sighed. "I think everything that has happened this past week has put her on edge. Cooking for your guests, being away from me, and then returning to find me so ill. But this is precisely why you must move ahead with your wedding plans. I would like to be around to see my little girl happily settled."

Alexander winced. "I think I had an easier time convincing you."

"Viola is very sentimental. She wants everything to be just as it has always been for us. But things change. These attacks of mine are coming on more frequently now. I had a bad one this morning, but I am feeling better now."

"Dr. Walcott will look you over anyway. Let me see to Viola." He had heard a door slam shut down the hall, so he strode toward what he knew was her bedchamber and knocked. "May I come in?"

"Go away!"

He opened the door and strode into the small but nicely appointed room. "I'm sure I heard you tell me to enter."

She sniffled and dabbed at her tears while seated atop her bed. "I'm sorry. It is all too much for me."

He knelt at the foot of her bed within arm's reach of her, but made no attempt to take her in his arms or upset her further by sitting beside her. "I know. Your father does seem steadier. He is comfortably resting against his pillows and his breathing is only mildly labored. I won't deny he is weakening, but he has got time left in him yet. Your father has agreed not to make a fuss when the doctor arrives. He would like to talk to you."

She shook her head. "I cannot yet. I am too overset."

"All right. Why don't you go downstairs and prepare him one of your excellent meals?"

"Mrs. Bligh just fed him."

Alexander arched an eyebrow. "Nothing compares to your cooking, Viola."

She groaned. "Very well. In truth, it will keep my mind off his worsening condition. I'll spend the afternoon crying if I am not doing something useful to take my mind off him."

"Make enough for me, too."

She had been looking down at her hands while speaking to him, but now glanced at him in surprise. "What about your family? Are they not here still?"

"Yes, but they'll get along just fine without me. I'll return to them once Dr. Walcott has seen to your father and I've made certain both of you manage to put something in your bellies."

"You shouldn't be so nice to me. I haven't been very nice to you."

He took one of her hands in his. "You have been splendid. Perhaps one day you will see yourself for the treasure you are. But for the record, you don't owe me a thing. I expect nothing in return from you. I am here because I want to be."

He nudged her off the bed and was escorting her downstairs to the kitchen when he heard Mrs. Bligh returning with Dr. Walcott. "Let him see to your father. The three of us will talk afterward."

Fussing about the kitchen appeared to put Viola in better spirits.

"What are you going to make?" he asked, taking a seat on a stool beside her work table.

"Just a broth. I don't think my father can hold down anything else just now. Nor can I." Her eyes widened suddenly as she stared at him. "Oh, but you'll need something heartier. I'll–"

"Broth is fine for me. I'll be eating again as soon as I return to Ardley Hall."

They were alone in the kitchen since Mrs. Bligh had immediately gone outside to hang up the laundry. "I should not say this after the trouble I've given you, but I am going to miss you, my lord. I enjoyed my time at Ardley Hall…and my time with you."

He smiled. "I haven't even left you yet and I am already missing you. But to be clear on my feelings, I will not accept any half measures or compromises on this point. I want you as my wife."

"You must stop thinking like this!"

Blast, he'd upset her again. "What? Honorably?"

She stirred the broth.

He let the matter drop, for Viola was in too much turmoil, not yet settled in her home, and desperately worried about her father. As for him, after spending two years in his fog of grief, he was ready to move on with his life. Perhaps he was ready because he had found the woman with whom he wished to share his future and his dreams.

This was Viola.

But he had already said too much and she was not ready to hear any of it until she realized her father had given his blessing. To pursue the matter now would be the same as banging his head against a wall. She loved him. It was obvious in the way she'd responded to his kisses.

The rest of it would eventually fall into place.

The marriage license was good for thirty days. If she needed longer, he would simply obtain another one. Her father intended to assuage her concerns, but it might take her a little time to absorb his sudden change of heart. He had obviously done a thorough job of convincing Viola that she would be betraying his wishes if she did not marry George.

Ah, the complications of love.

Once assured by the doctor that Vicar Ruskin's condition was stable, he and Viola went upstairs to share a meal with him in his bedchamber.

They ate quietly, engaging mostly in small talk. But Alexander saw the vicar tiring and did not want to put off their discussion any longer. "Viola, I have something to ask you."

Her spoon clattered into her bowl. "No."

"Dearest," her father said. "You do not even know what his lordship is going to say."

"I have a strong suspicion, and I do not want to hear it."

"Enough, child. I will not have you giving up your dream because you think I will disapprove. All I ever wanted was for you to be safe and happy."

She nodded. "With George."

"No, it has never been about him. I wanted to see you settled with a good man who would love you and make a good life for you when I was no longer around. My lord, I think it is time you showed her what you were doing for much of yesterday."

Alexander withdrew the license from his pocket. "Viola, your father and I have been talking these past few days. We both think it is a good idea."

"What is? What are you holding in your hand?"

Her father emitted a sigh of exasperation. "A marriage license, obtained with my hearty consent and approval. Lord Ardley came to speak to me yesterday. I do not think any man will treat you better. He loves you. Is it not obvious? Why are you now frowning at us?"

Viola appeared stunned. "But, Papa. I–"

"Don't 'but, Papa' me. I know what I am talking about. I have been a vicar long enough to recognize love when I see it. I blame myself for not realizing his lordship felt the same about you. This changes everything, Viola. He loves you and you love him. Do not be afraid to admit your feelings. My greatest regret will not be in dying, for we all must reach an end someday, and I have had a full and rewarding life. But I will never forgive myself if you deprive yourself of happiness because of something I've foolishly led you to believe."

"Papa..."

"You deserve every happiness, my beautiful child. I shall never rest easy knowing I have been the obstacle to it. Forget George, poor fellow. All I ever wanted was for you to find a good man to love. Open your eyes, Viola. He is there beside you."

She gazed at Alexander for the longest time, her expression softening as her father's words sank in. "I suppose you expect me to say it to you now?"

He laughed softly and tossed her a cautious smile. "Only if this is how you truly feel. I hope it is."

"Dear heaven, how can you think it is otherwise? Have I not made a complete idiot of myself over you?" She leaned forward and kissed him lightly on the lips. "I love you with all my heart. Never a moment's doubt. Just overwhelmed with fear. Panic.

Worry. But never a doubt of my feelings for you."

"That is a relief. For a while there, I thought George Haworth might win out."

Her father groaned. "The poor blighter. He never stood a chance."

Viola nodded. "My heart has always been yours, my lord. I could never marry another man."

"Nor will any other woman claim my heart. I love you, Viola. I will tell you so every day of our lives together."

She threw herself into his arms and hugged him fiercely. "Don't ever wake me from this dream."

"Wouldn't think of it, love."

The vicar rang the small bell he kept beside his plate to ring for assistance. "Mrs. Bligh, come in here quick!"

Their housekeeper lumbered in, her expression one of alarm. "Vicar Ruskin, what is it?"

"Sit down and join us. We are about to toast my daughter and Lord Ardley. They are getting married."

Her shriek could be heard into the village.

In the next moment, Alexander was swallowed up in her enormous bosom. "I knew it had to be love. I'm so happy!"

She tore out of the vicarage toward town.

"Blessed saints," Alexander said with a laughing groan, "I have never seen that woman move so fast in my life. The entire village will know within minutes. I had better get back to Ardley Hall before my family hears the news from someone other than myself." He turned to the vicar. "Will you be all right while Viola and I return to Ardley Hall to tell my family?"

Viola gasped. "I should not have let Mrs. Bligh run off. I cannot leave my father on his own."

"Nonsense." The vicar waved them away. "She'll be back in a few minutes, child. Get on with you. His lordship is right to want you by his side. You must tell his family together."

"No, no. Look at me." She patted her hair and glanced down at her serviceable work gown. "I cannot meet them looking like this. I will not."

Alexander realized she had her pride and would not come to

them looking like the kitchen help…which is what she had been for purposes of his house party. "Viola's right. I will come around to fetch her later."

He took her hand in his. "Have supper with me and my family tonight. You will look beautiful no matter what you choose to wear or how you decide to style your hair. Just be yourself. I do not need you putting on airs. I fell in love with *you,* not what others think you ought to be."

He then rode back to Ardley Hall, knowing he had work to do not only to calm Viola but his father as well. He would not put it past the old man to undermine his plans.

"There you are, Alex," his father said, coming toward him as he strode in. "I was wondering where you were hiding."

"Not in hiding, just at the vicarage making certain all was well."

"You were with that Ruskin girl again."

"Her father is in very bad health, as I've told you. We had to summon the doctor, for he was unable to get out of bed this morning. But he is much steadier now. Still too weak to leave his bed. Viola's cooking perked him up."

They walked out onto the terrace to join the other family members who were enjoying lemonade and a poppy cake Viola had made for them before leaving this morning. She had also made a platter of those little cheese tarts his father adored.

So typical of the thoughtful girl.

He wanted her back here.

She belonged with him at Ardley Hall.

His sunlight.

Indeed, the sun would always shine for him no matter the storms raging overhead so long as she was by his side as his viscountess.

"Alex," his father said, regaining his attention as they settled in with the rest of the family, "I've been giving your situation some thought."

He arched an eyebrow. "I don't need anyone meddling in my business. In fact, I would like to speak to you about Viola."

"What you do about her is my business. You are my heir, and

for the sake of the family and the earldom, I must be certain you are not about to make a decision you will come to regret."

"I won't. And by the way, it is too late. I have made my decision and already asked Viola to marry me."

His father leaped out of his seat. "Are you mad? You are intoxicated with this girl and need to clear your head of her. This must end now! Come to London with us for the month. Wilson can take care of whatever needs to be done here while you are away. Have him look after the vicar and his daughter, if you must. We'll settle a tidy sum on her to keep her quiet and end this misbegotten affair."

Alexander rose, steam pouring out of his ears. "Not another word, Father. She will not be bought off. She will be my wife. And you had better get used to it."

Gabriel rose to stand beside him. "Father, be reasonable. Can you not see she is good for Alex?"

Graelem and his grandmother also voiced their agreement.

To his relief, he seemed to have the support of everyone else in the family. Even Lady Withnall was thumping her cane and declaring Viola to be a gem. "Trent, that girl is quality. Why do you refuse to see it?"

Alex turned to her. "Thank you, Lady Withnall. I am sincerely grateful for your approval."

"She is good for you, dear boy. Your grandmother and I quickly saw it."

His grandmother smiled at him as she nodded. "Indeed."

But all Dayne men were stubborn and his father was no exception. "No, no." He shook his head, looking genuinely overset. "What do any of us know of this girl? Am I to accept your cook into the family? You are asking too much of me, Alex."

"She is not my cook. She only agreed to help out this weekend as a favor to me."

"For a fee, I'm sure," his father retorted.

"Yes, but only because I insisted on it. She has not bothered to collect it yet."

"Why should she when she knows you are about to give her all you have?"

Alex was at the end of his rope and moments away from throttling his father. "She has asked nothing from me. But I am now asking you to stop your objections and just be happy for me."

"I love you dearly, my son. But this is a mistake and I will do all in my power to prevent it." Having said that, he stormed off.

"Oh, hell," Gabriel muttered.

Alex meant to go after him, but his mother held him back. "Leave him, Alex. He will work it through on his own."

"Work it through? Or ride straight down to the vicarage and attempt to buy her off? I will not have it."

His mother still had a hand on his shoulder. "No, for all his bluster, he would never be so crass as to do such a thing."

Alex wasn't so sure.

What was his father going to do?

CHAPTER 15

VIOLA HAD JUST washed up and donned her prettiest gown to wear for tonight's supper at Ardley Hall when Mrs. Bligh hurried into her bedchamber. "Miss Viola," she said, her eyes wide and concern etched on her face. "Lord Trent is here to see you and he does not look at all pleased."

She sighed. "Thank you, Mrs. Bligh. I shall attend to him."

All she wanted to do was run away, but she would not allow the earl to intimidate her. She hurried downstairs, glad she was as presentable as she could possibly be, and glided into the parlor to greet him. "Lord Trent, what a pleasant surprise. Do sit down."

He refused and continued to pace across the carpet which had once been elegant, but was now fraying at the edges. The parlor itself was far smaller than the grand one at Ardley Hall. Still, it was certainly acceptable to receive callers. "May I offer you tea? Refreshments?"

"No." He paused to stand in front of her. "You cannot marry my son."

"Cannot? Or is it merely you hoping to prevent it?"

"He is a catch, a good and decent man. A war hero. He can have any woman in England he wants."

Viola arched an eyebrow. "And yet, he chose me. Believe me, my lord, I struggled even harder than you to figure out why he would ever look twice at me."

He paused in front of her, his manner quite belligerent. "Whatever you did to seduce him, it will not work. I shall put a stop to it."

She frowned at him. "Shame on you for thinking only of yourself and not giving any thought to how badly you are hurting your son. First of all, I did not seduce him. Nor has he seduced me. He is too honorable and holds me in too much regard ever to treat me that way. If you have come here to insult me, then you may leave right now."

"I will not leave. You cannot marry my son."

"The only one who will ever stop me is Lord Ardley himself. If he does not love me and wishes to put an end to our betrothal, he has only to say the word and I will oblige."

Doubt clouded his father's eyes. "At what price?"

"What do you mean?" They were still standing in the parlor facing off like two rams about to butt heads.

"Everyone has a price, Miss Ruskin. What is yours?"

"To even ask such an insulting question shows how little you know me. I would never stand in the way of his happiness. If he wishes to back out, then let him do so. It is his heart I cherish, not his wealth. He may keep every last shilling."

"Will you put that in writing?"

"No, she will not," Alexander said, striding toward them.

Viola had not heard him come in, so fixed was she on his father. "Lord Ardley, I did not realize…how long have you been standing there?"

"Long enough to hear everything. And the name is Alex. You are my equal, Viola. Stop insisting that you are not. Why are you here, Father?"

"To talk sense into Miss Ruskin, of course. Keep out of this, Alex. Let me do what needs to be done."

"Not on your life." He extended an arm to Viola. "I'm here to escort you to Ardley Hall for supper. You will be received warmly by the other members of my family who have retained full control of their faculties and are ready to welcome you into the fold. I promise you, Viola. My father is the only one with his head stuck up his–"

"Now, see here! Don't you dare to talk about me that way."

"And don't you dare insult Viola."

"Alex," she said with an ache to her voice, the sound of his name so foreign on her lips. "Do you not see? It is happening already."

He looked at her as though she had stabbed him through the heart.

But he had to be made to consider the damage done by an unwanted union. "I am already destroying your family. How can you ever be happy if you and your father will never speak to each other again? Nor is it fair to make your family take sides. It will split you all apart."

She now turned to his father. "Do you think I have not tormented myself trying to figure out what your son sees in me? I am no more than a vicar's daughter who helped him out with his house party. But I am proud of who I am and make no apology for it."

She walked out of the parlor and moved to the front door to show them both out. "I do not apologize for loving your son. I doubt he will apologize to you for loving me. If we marry, I shall be the best wife to him I can possibly be. I will treasure every moment with him and work tirelessly to heal any rift between the two of you because he loves you so much."

Alex was now frowning. "*If* we marry?"

She nodded. "Let us put the wedding plans aside for now. I cannot leave my father anyway. It would destroy me if he passed and I was not by his side."

He folded his arms across his chest and cast her a stubborn look. "No, this is exactly what your father does not want. He needs to know you are well settled and protected. He will not be at peace if you put off our wedding. Stay here after we are married, if you must. I'll join you, if this is what it takes. It doesn't matter where we are so long as we are together."

"You would do this for me?" Viola had accepted his marriage proposal, but it was far from a thing certain when or if they would ever wed. Her father's health was precarious and she dared not leave him to move into Ardley Hall. Nor would her stubborn father leave his familiar surroundings for Ardley Hall. This had yet to be worked out between them, or so she thought.

Apparently, this viscount she loved was willing to give her everything she asked.

She melted into his arms. "Thank you."

His father stormed off.

"My lord…I mean…Alex. Goodness, that sounds so odd."

"No, love. It sounds perfect."

She cast him a worried smile. "Should we go after him? He's so angry and it is agitating his horse. What if he hurts himself?"

"He's been riding since he was a child. He'll be fine and can make his own way back to the manor whenever he decides to cool down."

But the beast was now bucking and kicking as his father tugged hard on the reins, further riling the horse as he impatiently attempted to climb onto the saddle. "Oh, Alex. He is going to get kicked."

She had no sooner uttered the words than the beast landed a blow to his father's shin. His father yelped in pain, hopped backward, and promptly lost his balance. He fell hard in the most awkward position. She and Alex raced to help him. "Father!"

Viola grabbed the horse's reins and tried to soothe the big steed while Alex carried his father back into the house. "Get away from him Viola or he'll kick you, too."

She released the reins and the horse galloped off to find his own way back to the Ardley Hall stables.

Could anything else go wrong?

"How is he, Alex?" She hurried into the parlor behind him and watched as he carefully set his father down on the settee. His father yelped again as Alex removed his boot and then cut his trouser leg which was already torn and stained with blood. "Is his leg broken? Shall I fetch the doctor?"

Alex nodded. "Bloody, stubborn fool. I don't think there's a break, Viola. Just a bad gash, and I think he's now thrown out his back. Stay with him. I'll get Dr. Walcott."

"Me, stay? Shouldn't you be–" But he was already running out the door.

Viola sighed. "Here, Lord Trent. Just lie back and let me elevate your leg. That's it. Lie still and I'll return in a moment with clean cloths and some brandy."

She hurried to gather supplies as fast as she could, calling for Mrs. Bligh's assistance. But the woman was upstairs tending to her own father. "Good grief. Dealing with one father is bad enough. But two?" she muttered before calling back up to Mrs. Bligh. "Never mind. I'll attend to Lord Trent myself."

There was little she could do but apply pressure to the gash to stop the flow of blood.

Alex's father was moaning and blaspheming all the while she tried to keep him comfortable. Applying brandy to the injured shin had him shouting curses again. Fortunately, she did not think the kick had broken his leg. There was no bone protruding. But the diagnosis would be left to Dr. Walcott who may as well set up his infirmary in the vicarage since he seemed to be here more than anywhere else, lately.

She breathed a sigh of relief when Alex hurried back with the doctor within a matter of minutes.

As she moved away, she realized her gown was stained with blood. Well, it mattered little since she could not possible go up to the manor house for supper now.

Alex seemed to read her thoughts. "If necessary, I'll have Mrs. Stringer send down supper for us all. But I still hope you and I will dine at Ardley Hall tonight. Dr. Walcott, when can my father be moved?

"I do not think it is wise to attempt it today. His leg is fine, just a nasty cut. His leather boot absorbed enough of the blow to keep the bone from breaking. But your father has thrown his back out and will be in agony for that. He shouldn't be moved just yet. Leave him here overnight. Viola, do you mind having him sleep on your settee? He'll also need a hot compress applied to his lower back."

"All right," she said with a nod.

"Good. I'll come by first thing in the morning to look in on both gentlemen."

Lord Trent was not at all pleased. "I will not stay under this roof! I demand to be taken to Ardley Hall."

Alex turned to Dr. Walcott, his expression fuming. "Will his back be damaged if I summon a wagon to pick him up now? If he wants to be an idiot about it, who am I to stop him? I'll make certain the wagon is well padded to minimize jostling."

"I think it should be all right, my lord. He will ache like bloody blazes, but Miss Ruskin has enough on her hands with her father and does not need more burdens piled on her."

"Thank you. Viola, can you put up with my father for a little while longer while I ride home?"

She nodded.

"Good. You have my permission to gag him if he is rude to you in any way."

She grinned. "I will not hesitate to do so."

Alex rode off and the doctor left soon afterward.

His father had not stopped scowling at her even though he was the reckless fool who had brought this misery upon himself. "Well, Miss Ruskin. You must be gloating."

"To see you hurt? Never, my lord." She applied a cool compress to his forehead and left a moment to boil some water for a hot compress for his back. She soon returned with the hot towel but made certain it was not so hot that it burned him. "This might ease the twinges. Just relax. Close your eyes, if it will help."

"You do not have to do this for me," he grumbled.

"I would do this for anyone who came to the vicarage in need of assistance, whether a prince or a pauper."

He winced as she helped him take off his jacket and then lifted his shirt to apply the heat directly onto his skin. "Your gown is ruined, Miss Ruskin. My blood is all over it."

"I know. Mrs. Bligh will do her best to boil out the stains."

He grunted. "I'll pay for a replacement if they do not come out."

"Thank you for offering, but it isn't necessary. Despite what you think, I am not penniless nor am I a fortune hunter. I do not need your money or your son's. Nor do I want it."

"Is that so?"

"Yes, it is." She kept the cloth pressed to his back. "I argued just as strongly with your son about his marriage proposal. I refused to consider it at first because I did not think I would make a good viscountess. It may be that I never will. But I have come to realize I will make your son a very good wife. He said I was his sunlight. Can you believe it? I cannot think of a lovelier compliment. To put lightness in his heart after his years of grief is something quite special, don't you think?"

His father grunted again.

"I have no idea what he sees in me, but it must be something. Your son is no fool. In fact, he is one of the wisest, most thoughtful men I know. I suppose I don't know very many, but I have seen enough fools pass through the vicarage to understand the difference."

"I suppose you think I am among one of the biggest fools to pass through your door."

"No, my lord. You love your son and think you are protecting him. But all you are doing is hurting him by questioning his intelligence and foisting society's standards on him when he has never cared for, nor abided, by their rules. He is also your heir and you are no doubt concerned that my common blood will now taint your noble bloodline."

"Do I not have the right to be concerned?"

"You do. But answer me this, how am I worse than any of those debutantes who attended the house party? One of them maliciously tried to trap your son in a compromising position. Another one walked around with her Lambykins doll and spoke like a baby the entire weekend. The third attempted to use your son to make a duke jealous. And you expect your son to prefer one of those ladies who will never make him happy in a million years?"

"They would have brought powerful alliances. Increased our wealth and holdings."

"You are right. Alex would have had all that and been miserable every day of his life. You of all people should understand this. What would your life have been without a woman as wonderful as your wife by your side? Thirty-five happy years together is a blessing. Why would you want to deprive Alex of this same joy?"

"I do want him to have this."

"Then start listening to his heart instead of your wrongheaded rules for him."

She said no more to his father and was disappointed when he did not seem to warm to her in the least. Well, she would leave him to Alex now. But she was so disappointed that she hadn't budged him off his position at all. Not for her sake, but for that of his son.

It did not take Alex long to return with the wagon and several footmen to assist him in carrying his father onto the mattress stuffed atop the wagon bed. He issued instructions to the footmen, but surprised Viola by remaining behind with her. "Should you not return with your father?"

"No, my mother will see to him. I'm sorry I had to leave him alone with you. Was he awful to you?"

"I endured. Besides, he was in too much pain to say very much. I did most of the talking, but I doubt he was persuaded to like me any better."

Alex put his arms around her. "Well, I like you. I hope that counts for something."

She smiled up at him. "Yes, it is everything."

He kissed her on the lips, an encompassing sort of kiss that expressed desire along with something deeper and everlasting. It was not so much a lover's kiss as that of two souls bonding for life.

She kissed him back with all her heart, realizing something quite miraculous in this moment. This is what marriage to him would be like, the two of them sharing trials and joys that would strengthen their bond until it was unbreakable.

Even now, it was stronger than she had realized.

Alex had known this is how it would be between them.

He wanted her.

She no longer questioned the reasons.

She wanted him so badly, too.

A fiery ache spread through her as he deepened the kiss. She felt the strength and passion behind it, and could not wait to experience their union on their wedding night.

She thought of Sally and the kitchen maids chattering and

giggling over him.

Rippling muscles.

Hot, taut body.

She wanted to touch his skin and feel the weight of him on her as he claimed her.

She hadn't known anything about what men and women did together, certainly not the intimate details, until Sally had run into the kitchen in a dither over Alex's body. From that moment on, the talk had turned quite bawdy.

Sometimes, explicitly so.

Her mind had absorbed every scandalous detail like a sponge.

Alex tore his lips off hers with a wrenching groan. "Viola, I am in agony. Let's set a wedding date. My family is here and so is your father. The villagers need no more than an hour's notice to show up at the church. Even less if they hear there'll be food and drink offered afterward. As for me, I don't need to invite anyone else. We can hold a proper celebration later in the year for anyone we've left out. What do you say? Will the day after tomorrow do?"

She nodded. "It is mad and utterly impractical, but yes."

"Thank you, love. The wait will still seem endless for me."

"For me as well," she admitted. "I'll need to borrow your kitchen staff again. This is not negotiable. If we're to have a proper wedding breakfast, then I will need to give Mrs. Stringer and her girls instructions on the menu."

He grinned and held up his hands in surrender. "Instruct away. I am not messing with your food."

"Will you see to the musicians?"

"Yes, love. I'll take care of that and summon the vicar from the neighboring parish to conduct the service. What about your gown?"

She glanced down at herself. Her finest gown was now stained and probably could not be salvaged. "I..."

"Never mind. Laurel and Daisy will figure it out for us." He gave her another quick kiss and then turned her toward the stairs. "I'll wait down here while you run up and change. I still intend to have you join us for supper."

"Are you certain? There could be a battle."

"No battle. My father will be writhing and moaning in his bed. Everyone else will be enjoying a meal at the dining table and delighted to get to know you."

She quickly changed out of her finest, now ruined, gown and sighed as she looked for another suitable one to wear. Well, none of her clothes were fancy. She considered them to be simple but elegant. Another of her Sunday best would have to suffice.

Besides, she did not think any of the ladies would pass a remark.

She finally decided on a blue gown, a very pretty blue the color of a May sky, that had a little satin trim around the collar. Digging through her small jewelry box, she added an opal necklace to go with it.

She hurried into her father's chamber to kiss him goodnight since he would soon be fast asleep. "Sweet dreams, Papa. We've set the wedding date for the day after tomorrow. It will be a mad rush to get everything done in time. But we'll figure it out."

"All that matters is your happiness, my beautiful child. I will be ready, no matter the day or the hour." He kissed her cheek. "Enjoy your evening. Be yourself and they will love you. Even Lord Ardley's father will come around soon. You'll see."

"If you say so. Goodnight, Papa." Any doubts about her appearance were erased as she walked downstairs and saw the enraptured look in Alex's eyes.

"You look beautiful, Viola."

"It is a pretty gown, don't you think?"

"I was looking at the girl inside it," he said with a grin. "Yes, the color looks very pretty on you. You ought to have a similar one made of silk for my parents' anniversary party. I shall be the envy of every man there."

She paused as he was leading her out the door. "Will your father allow me to attend?"

He laughed. "I have no idea. I hope he will come to his senses by then. But my mother will and that's an end to it. My father hasn't won an argument with her that I can ever recall. In truth, she has always been the tougher of the two. It may not appear so just now, but my father is the most softhearted of us all."

"But he loathes me."

"No, he doesn't. I promise you."

Viola was not certain of the reception she would receive from any of the others, but with the Earl of Trent laid up in bed, she was met with nothing but warmth. It struck her then how much she would gain from marrying Alex. It had nothing to do with his wealth or title, but all to do with him and the family she was about to marry into.

"I never knew my mother," she told the ladies when they retired to the parlor for sherry while the men remained behind in the dining room after supper to speak among themselves. "She died giving birth to me. She was an only child and so was my father. My grandparents, all of them, passed on while I was still a child. But they never resided close by, so I don't think I saw them above once or twice in my life. There has been no one for me but my father in all these years."

"Poor thing," Lady Withnall said.

"Oh, no. I have had a good life and do not complain." She now turned to Lady Trent who was seated beside her on the sofa. "In marrying your son, I am also gaining an entire family I never had before. A grandmother. Parents. Brothers and sisters," she said, smiling at each lady in turn. "This is the true fortune, I think."

They heard a roar of laughter emanating from the dining room where Alex was holding forth with Gabriel and Graelem. The three of them marched in a moment later, Alex carrying a tray of the tiny cheese tarts Viola had taught his kitchen staff to make. She had asked Greaves upon arrival to send word to Mrs. Stringer to prepare them for the earl, seeing as he liked them so much and he was in dire need of cheering up. "Pardon us, ladies, but we must abduct Viola for a few minutes."

His mother eyed him warily. "What are you boys up to?"

"Teaching Father a lesson," Gabriel said with a smirk. He walked over and kissed his mother's cheek. "Don't worry. We will do him no physical harm."

Of course, the ladies were not to be left behind.

They all barged in on his father who was propped on his side with pillows under his back and looking quite miserable. Alex held out the tray of cheese tarts. "Viola had these made for you, Father. What do you think about that?"

"Blatant bribery," he grumbled, looking quite hapless as he held a hot towel to his back. "But it won't work."

Alex shook his head. "I thought that would be your response. You are right, it is a low thing to do. How dare she be considerate of your feelings and seek to provide you something so thoughtful. I assure you, I would not have done so."

"I am in no humor for your sarcasm, Alex. Hand me the platter and begone with all of you."

"What? And have you take a single bribe? Not on your life." He began to pass around the tray. "Grandmama, would you care for one?"

"Thank you, Alex. How delightful." She popped a tart into her mouth.

He then proceeded to offer one to each lady except Viola, and then to Gabriel and Graelem.

Laurel swallowed hers and then chuckled. "You are diabolical, Alex. I heartily approve. This is exactly the sort of thing I would do."

Viola did enjoy his father's send up, but did not have the heart to deprive him beyond this little jest. Alex offered the last one to her. "What do you say, Viola?"

"I know how they taste. It is my recipe, after all. I think your father should have it."

"No, he is not one to be bribed. We all heard him quite clearly. I think you must have it."

She shook her head. "Please, has he not suffered enough?"

"Not nearly enough," Alex said with a grin. "He's piled this misery on himself."

His father erupted. "Blast you, Alex! I shall call a special meeting of the House of Lords and have you not only cut out of the family line but see you hung, drawn, and quartered as well! Ow! My aching back! I'll have the lot of you–ow! Bloody impertinent whelp!"

Viola took the last tart off the tray and handed it to the Earl of Trent. "Calm down before you rupture your spleen in addition to your other miseries. Here, this is for you. Do not stuff it all in your mouth at once or you will choke on it."

He eyed her warily. "Why would you offer me this after the way I've treated you?"

"Because you love your son and he loves you. I would never deprive anyone, no matter how cross or unreasonable, of something they loved."

"It is just food," he grumbled.

"One would think it was the breath of life to you the way you are going on about it," Alexander muttered.

His father took the tart and ate it in two bites. "Almost as good as yours. Thank you, Viola."

"You are most welcome, my lord."

He scowled at the others. "Alex, come here. The others…get out of here. I need to talk to my son and his future wife."

Lady Trent scurried over to her husband and kissed his cheek. "I knew you could not be this insufferably dense for long."

He grumbled and lovingly shooed his wife away.

Once the three of them were left alone, the earl regarded her and Alex for a long moment. "Viola, will your father be in sufficient health to stand by you?"

"No, my lord." She emitted a ragged breath to steady herself. "I am not even certain he will have the strength to attend. Has your son told you? We plan to marry on the day after tomorrow for my father's sake. He is in a very bad way."

"And therefore the urgency of a wedding," the earl said with a nod. "He wants to know his little girl is secure."

"Yes, my lord. It is his greatest worry. I think he will have to be carried in for the ceremony and then carried back to bed as soon as it is over."

"How thoughtless of me to upset him with my howling at his daughter."

"He is all right. He knows I am not spineless nor easily intimidated. It will take more than mere howls frighten me. I understood your concern. You only meant to protect your son."

"No, I was vain and selfish, just as you accused." He glanced down at himself as he lay on his back with a compress against his spine and a bandaged leg from where his horse had kicked him. "This is what I got for it."

"Punishment enough, my lord," Viola said.

"Self-inflicted," Alex said, arching an eyebrow and folding his arms over his chest as he met his father's gaze.

"Stop rubbing it in," he said with a grunt. "Viola, I will stand up for you at the ceremony if your father cannot. It is the least I can do to make it up to you and my son."

Alex let out a breath. "Thank you, Father. I hoped you would come around. But I fear both fathers may need to be carried in."

"No, son. I will do it, even if I have to hobble down the church aisle using a cane."

Viola put a hand over her heart. "Thank you, my lord. That is extremely generous of you."

"Did I not tell you my father was wonderful, Viola?" Alex murmured, relief and joy evident in his expression.

Viola's insides melted at the love both men held for each other.

Stubborn, prideful, and also deeply protective and adoring.

There was a wealth of sentiment in the smiles exchanged between them.

She was relieved this crisis had passed so quickly.

Alex must have known it would, for he knew his father very well and seemed as capable of managing him as his mother was.

"Gabriel and Graelem will hold you up if the cane is not enough. And now I will have Greaves deliver the second tray of tarts made just for you. Rest up now, and thank you again." Alex leaned over and planted a kiss on his father's forehead.

"And you, Viola? Do I not get a kiss from my daughter-to-be?"

"Will you allow it, my lord?"

He nodded. "If you can bear to kiss an old fool."

She kissed him on the cheek. "Thank you, from the bottom of my heart. I will not disappoint you."

Viola was ecstatic but completely exhausted by the time Alex excused himself to escort her home. Greaves opened the front door for them. "Your carriage awaits, my lord."

It was a well built curricle drawn by a pair of matched bays.

Alex put his hands around her waist to boost her into the seat and then quickly climbed up beside her. "Thank you for being so gentle with my father when he was nothing but an ogre to you."

"As you told me just today, we all make mistakes. Best to deal with them and move on. This is what your father has done."

"And you've forgiven him?"

"Yes, it is much too difficult to hold onto anger. Don't you think?"

He chuckled. "Remember that whenever we have our first fight. Although I'm not sure we will ever do more than occasionally bicker. You are too sweet and I am too much in love with you. Hurting your feelings would hurt me more."

"Goodness, I had no idea you were so softhearted."

"Only for you," said with a wink and a roguish smile.

She rested her head against his shoulder as he drove the curricle down the lane toward the vicarage. She could feel the power of his muscles and could not wait for the moment she was wrapped in them. "There's not much of a moon tonight. The clouds are covering it up. Good thing the horses know their way," she remarked, now wishing they had set their wedding for tomorrow even though it was the most impractical thing to do.

"Viola, I don't know what you are talking about." He wrapped an arm around her shoulder and leaned in to give her a possessive and utterly divine kiss. "From where I sit, it is all sunlight."

CHAPTER 16

ALEX COULD NOT wait to pick up Viola from the vicarage the following morning. She was to spend the day with the ladies in his family and Lady Withnall, all of them doing the thousand things necessary for tomorrow's wedding, while he and the men had almost nothing to do but keep out of the way.

He had already sent word to the musicians who were more than eager to return to Ardley Hall to play at their celebration breakfast. He had also made public the announcement of tomorrow's wedding and the breakfast to follow, inviting all the villagers to attend.

Marston had seen to his clothes for the ceremony.

Alex had already sent a carriage to bring the vicar from the neighboring parish to the vicarage today in order to perform the marriage rites first thing in the morning.

Indeed, he was taking no chances.

He did not even need to obtain a bride token since his grandmother had insisted on giving him one of the Trent family heirloom pieces given to her when she had married his grandfather. It was a small but beautiful ring set with diamonds and sapphires that would look perfect upon Viola's small hand.

All that was left for him to do was retire to his study while his staff scurried about polishing the silver, dusting every nook and cranny, and moving furniture. Mrs. Lester was in her element, overseeing all these details. He also needed to stay away from the kitchen where Viola intended to take charge. No one, not even

Mrs. Stringer, was going to get in the way of her delicious food. In truth, Mrs. Stringer did not seem at all put out. Quite the opposite, she looked forward to taking direction from Viola.

Well, Viola certainly had that loveable way about her.

She opened the door to him as he climbed down from the curricle and strode toward the vicar's residence.

Her smile was indeed like sunshine.

"Are you ready, love?"

She blushed profusely, for Mrs. Bligh was right behind her and had overheard the endearment. "Yes…I…good morning, my lord."

He scooped her up in his arms and kissed her thoroughly. "Do not be angry with me, Viola. I am the happiest I have been in years." He winked at Mrs. Bligh who was giggling beside her. "Give me your cheek, Mrs. Bligh, for I must kiss you, too."

The woman did not hesitate. "Oh, my lord. You are a handsome, wicked one."

She darted off after he had placed a chaste kiss on her cheek and returned a moment later with a large box in her hands. "Do not forget this, Miss Ruskin."

"Oh, I wouldn't ever." Viola took the box from the woman and then turned to Alexander. "It is my mother's wedding gown. It will require alteration, of course. But I thought it would serve nicely considering I have no time to sew a new gown for myself."

He took the box from her hands. "Daisy and Laurel will help you. I think they are quite adept at these tasks, even though Laurel can also handle a whip or sword better than any man I know." He laughed. "Keeps my cousin in line. Graelem can be quite the stubborn Scot once he gets something in his mind."

Viola was surprisingly organized, although it should not have surprised him since she had years of training in planning large events as vicar's daughter. He left her to the ladies, but kept an eye on her activities because he knew she would not rest until all was done, even if it meant exhausting herself. But she was to be the center of everyone's attention tomorrow and she deserved to sparkle.

First on her list was the wedding gown alterations.

The ladies kicked him out of the spare bedchamber they were using as their sewing room. "Go away, Alex," his mother said. "We'll take care of Viola."

Less than an hour later, he noticed Viola scurrying past his study door which he had left open to observe the comings and goings. "Where are you–"

"No time to chat," she said breathlessly. "Wedding breakfast menu next."

He grinned and let her dash off to the kitchen.

His mother, grandmother, and Lady Withnall were only minutes behind her.

Gabriel and Graelem were seated in his study, the three of them watching the activities. "We ought to go for a ride," Gabriel suggested. "We're only in the way here."

Graelem agreed. "Laurel warned me not to interrupt her while she's sewing Viola's gown. She'll use me as her pin cushion if I dare interfere."

Alexander sighed. "All right, but I'll be putting a stop to Viola's work by four o'clock this afternoon. I won't have her fretting over every detail or preparing the entire wedding breakfast herself. I have a staff for this."

Gabriel patted him on the back. "Good luck with that. Daisy is as sweet natured as Viola, but even I know better than to get underfoot when she's planning a party. You needn't worry. The ladies will handle her. They all know tomorrow is her special day."

"Are ye ready for it, Alex?" Graelem asked. "It has all come on quite fast."

Alexander shook his head. "Not that fast, for it was two years in the making. I am more than ready now."

As they rode across the countryside, Alex thought back to when he first began to notice Viola. She was born and raised in Ardley, a sweet child always helping out her father. He had liked her, but never looked closely at her while she grew into a young woman because he was married and not one to break his wedding vows.

However, by the age of fourteen, Viola was already considered the village beauty. She grew lovelier each passing year, and any man would have to be dead not to notice her charms. She was often surrounded by hopeful young men who sought to court her, but she never gave any of them encouragement.

As for him, the first year after the deaths of Jillian and Molly was a dark hole. He did nothing but work the Ardley properties and retreat to his study or bedchamber afterward. It was in the second year that he began to rejoin the living, attend church services on Sundays, and lend his presence to the various fairs and other events held throughout the year. Viola was always there, growing lovelier by the day, her smile always genuine and warm.

He found her occasional touch soothing, her food incredible, and her conversation always interesting. Her laughter was as sweet as a gentle summer breeze and somehow always lightened his heart.

And yet, she was shy.

She would never have revealed her feelings had he not taken to drinking himself into a stupor and passing out drunk in front of the vicarage. Was it only last month? Of course, he could have remained sober and simply walked down from Ardley Hall to begin courting her.

But he would not have taken that leap while sober.

Breaking from the past was the hardest thing he'd ever had to do.

The older ladies were having tea in the parlor when they returned from their ride. Knowing the household would be a turbulent hive of activity, he, Gabriel, and Graelem had stopped by one of the local taverns for sausage rolls and a pint of ale before riding back home.

His mother waved him in. "Ah, there you are. Where did you boys go?"

Alex shrugged as he responded for them. "Just tearing along the hills and valleys. Our horses needed the exercise anyway. Then we stopped to eat at the Wild Boar Inn. How are you ladies managing?"

"All is well in hand. The furniture has been moved out of the main rooms. Silver is polished. Viola's gown alterations are done.

Laurel and Daisy are upstairs attending to the last touches right now. They were going to join Viola in the kitchen once they finished. Perhaps they are there already. Viola, of course, is busy issuing instructions to Mrs. Stringer and her staff."

"Instructions, my arse." He shook his head and laughed. "I'm sure she is elbow deep in dough and preparing most of the dishes herself. I'll see you later."

"Where are you going?" his mother called after him.

"To the kitchen, of course."

Gabriel and Graelem followed him. So did the ladies.

Alex strode into the kitchen and came to a sudden stop. The others piled up behind him, knocking into him as they also took notice of the scene before them.

"I don't believe this," Gabriel burst into laughter.

The long tables were piled high with mixing bowls, baking tins, eggs, flour, herbs, fish, fowl, figs and plums. The ovens were going at full blast. Mrs. Stringer and her staff were chopping, boning, mixing, and the scullery maids were scrubbing out massive pans and handing them off to be reused. In the middle of all the commotion were Viola, Laurel, and Daisy, all three of them with their hands dug into large mixing bowls filled with dough.

"Blessed saints, that smells divine," Graelem muttered, also breaking into laughter.

Pies were cooling all around them and more were baking in the ovens.

But what stunned them all was the presence of his father seated on a stool beside Viola as though it was a throne, chattering away as he pointed and nodded and tasted ingredients.

"What in blazes are you doing down here?" Alexander asked him. "Shouldn't you be in bed? You are still nursing a sore back and an injured leg."

His father looked up. "I'm helping, of course. Viola needed my advice. Besides, I am feeling much better today. Hardly a twinge to report."

"Oh, lord." He shook his head and laughed. Was this not the very man who had threatened to put an end to their wedding plans only yesterday?

Viola smiled up at him. "Care to help?"

Sunshine spilled into his heart.

This girl was magic.

He glanced around.

Everyone was smiling, even his father who had to be in pain no matter how vehemently he denied it. But one would never know it from the joy in his expression. The man had never been in a kitchen in his life, and here he was holding court as though it was the most natural thing for him to do. He sampled one of the apple pie fillings. "A little more cinnamon." Then sampled a fish sauce. "Needs more lemon."

Alexander could not stop laughing. "Miss Ruskin, are you almost finished down here?"

She nodded. "As soon as I roll out this last batch of dough."

He marched toward her. "Leave it to Mrs. Stringer."

The maids giggled and scurried out of his way as he slowly made a path toward Viola.

Her mouth formed a delectable 'O' as she noticed the wicked smolder in his eyes. "But, I'm almost done."

"It is four o'clock."

Daisy and Laurel grabbed their bowls and scooted out of the way as he reached Viola's side.

Viola's eyes were now wide and beautiful as she hastily set her bowl aside and wiped the dough off her hands. "Um, is there a significance to the hour?"

"You are getting married tomorrow," he said with a soft growl.

Her smile was a sunburst as she shook her head and laughed. "I do recall that was the plan."

She squealed when he suddenly lifted her into his arms. "Oh, my!"

Lord, she truly was meant for him. He loved the softness of her body and the way it fit perfectly against him. "Mrs. Stringer, can you manage without Miss Ruskin?"

"Yes, my lord," she said, unable to quell her own laughter. Her maids were tittering and grinning, all thought of work set aside for the moment as they watched him and wondered what he planned to do next. "All is well in hand. We have her instructions."

"Good."

Viola started to protest. "But I–"

He kissed her on the mouth.

A deep, commanding kiss, albeit too short for his liking. But the point was to stop her talking and it did the trick. However, it also caused an uproar in the kitchen…in a good way, he hoped. Mrs. Stringer and her maids clapped and cheered, banging pots together and whistling as he kissed her again, this one more prolonged.

His father groaned, but did not really look overset. "Alex, put her down before you destroy all discipline within your household."

"Not on your life." After two years of a moribund home, he wanted a little joyful chaos. "She is mine and I aim to hold onto her."

"I'm not going anywhere," Viola whispered in his ear as the howls and whistles continued. "I love you, Alex."

"Thank you, love."

His family and Lady Withnall were all looking on, trying to look indignant and appalled, for he was misbehaving and completely unrepentant about it. But they relented and grinned as he strode past them with Viola in his arms.

"I think Laurel and I must have a closer look at our kitchen when we get home," Graelem teased. "Seems there is some fun to be had."

"Where are you taking her?" his mother asked, obviously worried about what he intended to do next.

"Back to the vicarage. She is done with work for today." He was never one for social conventions, but he did have sense enough to know the boundaries of behavior and he had already crossed over the line by behaving like an ape just now.

Viola was a traditional girl. Kissing her and carrying her in his arms was about all the scandal she could manage. Betrothed couples were allowed more intimacies, but he was not about to take her into his bed before they had exchanged their wedding vows.

He could wait a day for this.

After all, he had been waiting all his life to find Viola.

"Greaves! Greaves!" He strode into the hall, still holding her in his arms. "I need the curricle brought around."

"At once, my lord."

Viola sighed. "I had more to do in the kitchen. You shouldn't have carried me away."

"You are not going back into the kitchen. Have you gone over the menu and recipes with Mrs. Stringer?"

She nodded.

"Then it is time for you to take a breath, love."

"Oh, you are wicked."

He arched an eyebrow. "Why?"

"You called me 'love' and now I can never be angry with you."

"This is what you are to me. Lovely. Loveable. And I am deeply in love with you."

She sighed again. "I love you, too. Are you going to put me down?"

"No. I like having you in my arms."

"You are embarrassing Mr. Greaves."

He turned to his butler and grinned. "Greaves, are you embarrassed?"

"No, my lord. I think you are showing extraordinarily good judgement."

"See, he does not mind my making a fool of myself over you." It took another few minutes for the conveyance to be brought around and the box with her gown then safely stowed in it.

Viola had not stopped blushing in all that time, but she would have made more of a fuss if she were truly overset by his behavior. He helped her onto the curricle's bench seat and climbed in beside her. "Ready?"

She nodded. "Will you merely drop me off or stay and visit?"

"I am at your service. I'll do whatever you wish."

She thought on it a moment, pursing her kissable lips. "You have your entire family here. Go home to them."

"Are you sure, Viola?"

"Yes. I need to spend time alone with my father, assuming he is awake and can talk to me. I'll sit beside him and read if he isn't."

They rode the rest of the way to the vicarage in silence.

One more day and they would be married.

Could her father hold on that long?

CHAPTER 17

VIOLA STARED AT her reflection in the mirror, wondering whether her mother had looked like her all those years ago when she had wed her father. Did she and her mother have the same eyes? The same color hair? How proud her father would have been to stand beside the two women he loved most in his life. In all these years, Viola did not think a single day passed when he did not miss her mother.

But he had never held her death in childbirth against her.

"Children are innocent," he always told her and would say the same to his parishioners in similar situations.

She ran her hands along the pale blue silk, feeling her mother's spirit within the gown and within herself. Her father had given her the gown and insisted she wear it for her own wedding day. "It was your mother's wish," he'd said.

Viola was not certain how he would react to seeing her in it now.

Mrs. Bligh bustled in. "The Earl of Trent's carriage has just turned in the gate. I'm sure the rest will follow soon. You look so lovely, Miss Viola. Not a soul will be able to take their eyes off you. What else do you need?"

"Nothing, Mrs. Bligh. I am all set."

The woman's niece, Lila, who worked at Ardley Hall as a maid, had been sent to assist her this morning. The girl was familiar with the vicarage since she had been here assisting her aunt while Viola was at Ardley Hall for the house party.

"Doesn't she look marvelous, Auntie?" Lila said. "Do you like the flowers in Miss Viola's hair?"

Mrs. Bligh nodded. "Yes, indeed. You did a fine job."

"My heart is in a flutter," Viola admitted. "I cannot believe the hour is at hand. Is my father ready?"

"I helped him downstairs and he is waiting for you in the parlor."

"How does he look?" she asked, wringing her hands in worry.

Mrs. Bligh patted her cheek. "Like a new man. His little girl is getting married and there is not a thing in the world that ails him or will ever stop him from participating in your special day."

"Well, let's hope he does not overdo it." Viola hurried downstairs to find him. "Don't get up, Papa. The Earl of Trent's carriage just pulled up. I'll ask his footmen to assist you into the church. They'll seat you in the front pew. Will you be all right? I hope you don't mind that Vicar Ainsley will conduct the wedding ceremony and not you. Your role today is father of the bride."

"Stop fretting, Viola. All will be fine. Ainsley is a good man. I do not mind his officiating since I will be crying too hard throughout it anyway."

"Oh, Papa."

"Don't you start crying now. And do stop fussing over me. Let me get a proper look at you. Twirl around and let me see how pretty you look in your mother's gown."

She slowly turned. "What do you think?"

He withdrew his handkerchief and quickly blotted the sudden well of tears. "Best day of my life. You look beautiful, my child. Your mother would be immensely proud."

She bussed his cheek. "The gown is perfect. She is with us today."

Their courtyard soon filled with carriages, carts, and horses as Alex's family and villagers began to arrive. Many were on foot since the vicarage was on the outskirts of Ardley and an easy walk on this fine day.

The sun shone, and Viola felt it was her mother smiling down on her.

Gabriel and Graelem walked in with several footmen. "We've

come to collect you and your father. Alex is impatient for the ceremony to commence. Any second thoughts, Viola?" Gabriel said with a grin. "My brother can be a cantankerous bear."

"I will feed him whenever he gets unruly," she joked.

He laughed. "That tactic worked brilliantly on my father. Just keep those cheese tarts flowing and he will be forever in your thrall."

"Laurel has not stopped talking about your recipes," Graelem remarked as they left the manse and walked across the courtyard to the church. The footmen had gone ahead with her father, carrying him in a seat made of their arms. "She and Daisy enjoyed helping out in the kitchen. They used to prepare meals in their own home with their cook, Mrs. Mayhew. Fair warning, those Farthingales are going to abduct you the moment you step foot on Chipping Way."

Gabriel nodded. "This is where their parents reside. A lovely street in elegant Mayfair. Our grandmother lives next door to Daisy and Laurel's parents, John and Sophie Farthingale. You'll like the entire family. I've never seen so many aunts, uncles, or cousins in my life. I doubt you'll mind if they take you hostage for the week you are in town."

Viola smiled. "I think I shall like that very much."

"They can be a bit overwhelming," Gabriel continued, "but they're also generous and kind. They travel in hordes, and I cannot keep up with all the children. They are like little crabs popping their heads out of the sand. A dozen more show up every time you turn around. I have a hard enough time keeping track of my own."

"You'll like Gabriel's children. They are as sweet as Daisy," Graelem said. "Mine are beasts, especially the eldest. His name is Ragnar and he thinks he is a marauding Viking. His little sister is just as bad."

Viola could not stop smiling.

This was everything her father had hoped for her, not only a husband but an entire family to call her own.

Lord Trent stood by the church doors looking quite dapper. "Go find your wives, lads. I'll take over from here. Take my arm,

Viola. Are you ready? Here we go."

Viola had to admit the earl knew how to make a grand entrance.

She would have just walked in, but he held her back at the threshold until everyone packed in the pews and standing along the edges had quieted and all eyes were on them. Then he marched her slowly down the aisle toward his son, managing a regal stride despite his limp and reliance on his cane for support.

She noticed her father seated not in the first pew but at the lectern where he always gave his sermons. He intoned a blessing as she and the earl walked toward the altar. To hear him speak had her tears flowing.

"Alexander insisted on it," the earl whispered. "He did not want your father left out of the ceremony."

"Your son is most thoughtful. You raised him well." It was the loveliest gesture possible. She could hear the pride and happiness in her father's voice. What better gift could Alex have given her?

"I wish I could take credit. Alex has always been this way, a thoughtful child and very much his own man. Both sons have made me proud, showing wisdom where I have not. But everything is as it should be now."

Her heart melted when Alex stepped forward with a confident stride to lead her to the altar. All the Dayne men were handsome, but Alex stole her breath away. His features, usually stoic and indecipherable, were completely relaxed and expressive.

He was happy.

She hoped to make him feel this way every day of their marriage.

The ceremony was shorter than expected, but this had to be Alex's doing as well. Her father would never make it through a long ceremony, so he must have requested Vicar Ainsley to trim it down. Suddenly, they were at the exchange of vows. "Do you, Viola Ruskin, take this man…"

"I do."

"Do you, Alexander Farnum Dayne, Viscount Ardley, Knight of the Garter, Knight of the Order of…" The vicar recited a string of his impressive titles, which made her wonder how this accomplished man had come to choose her. She now understood his father's initial reluctance to approve their betrothal, for she had nothing behind her name.

Only herself.

Only her heart.

"I do," Alex responded, his voice ringing clear.

With the blessing of the Church, the vicar pronounced them husband and wife.

The kiss they shared to seal their marriage was quite prim compared to the one he'd given her in the Ardley Hall kitchen yesterday. However, there was a mischievous glint in his eyes that promised their private kisses would be quite the opposite of prim and proper.

He maintained a dignified air throughout the day's entertainments, responding with grace and cordiality to their well wishers. After sharing several dances with her, he then danced with his mother while she danced with his father who hobbled his way through a reel, mostly standing and holding her hand while she twirled and hopped around him. Still, he made it through with only a few grimaces and never once howling in pain. The poor man might feel the results of his exertion when he retired to bed tonight.

As for her father, he had made it to the wedding breakfast but was in no condition to join in the revelry. He sat in a comfortable chair in a shady spot beside Alex's grandmother and Lady Withnall, the three of them chatting away and not seeming to run out of conversation.

The dances had been lively reels until now, but the musicians slowed the pace and played a waltz.

Alex came up to claim her for this dance. "May we speak about tonight's arrangements?"

She nodded. "Of course."

He drew in a breath and then let it out slowly before beginning. "This will be our first night married. Do you wish to spend it here or at the vicarage?"

"I'm glad you asked, Alex. I would like to spend it here."

"Truly?"

She nodded, knowing her answer had surprised him. "Yes. Besides, my father would not hear of my staying with him tonight. I received quite the stern lecture last night. He blistered my ears."

Alex grinned. "He did?"

She nodded again. "He insisted my place was beside you from this day forward. He said you had arranged for Mrs. Bligh and her niece, Lila, to watch over him so there will always be two people at the vicarage to look after him, day and night."

"I thought it was necessary. Mrs. Bligh cannot manage him all on her own."

"That is very thoughtful of you. It eases my mind tremendously. I'll visit him daily. He insists it is more than enough."

"How do you feel about making this our permanent arrangement?" he asked, his expression remaining one of concern.

"In truth, I still feel unsteady about it. But I know it is the right thing to do. I cannot stop whatever is going to happen to him even if I watch over him like a hawk. And you deserve better, too. Ardley Hall is close by and I can be summoned at a moment's notice if the need arises."

He spun her around in time to the music. "I thought you would require more convincing."

"It is hard on me, but my father made me understand the right of it." She shook her head. "This…seeing us together…means more to him than anything else I could ever do for him. He and I have always been close. We share our thoughts and he listens patiently to all my dreams. There is nothing left unsaid between us. Nothing left unresolved. No angry words we wish to take back. I do not think my father and I have ever had angry words between us."

He said nothing, but she noticed shadows suddenly clouding his eyes.

Did he have regrets about words left unsaid between him and Jillian?

Perhaps this was something for them to talk about in the future. Not tonight or even a week from now.

Someday he would open up to her.

Tonight, they belonged to each other and no one else.

Nightfall descended late in the summer, and no one was in a hurry to leave while the food and drink were flowing. Her father had been taken home in the earl's carriage much earlier in the afternoon along with Mrs. Bligh and her niece, but it was nearing midnight by the time the last celebrants departed and the family retired to their rooms.

Finally, she and Alex were alone in his bedchamber.

She had never seen a room so large. It was the size of the entire upstairs at the vicarage. In addition to the enormous canopied bed and exquisitely carved wardrobe, the room also contained a seating area by the hearth and a mahogany wood desk beneath one of the rows of windows. A magnificent carpet of oriental design covered the floor, and drapes in a dark emerald velvet hung on the walls and the bed canopy.

This was just his bedchamber.

Attached to it was a dressing room and another door led to the bedchamber used by the viscountess. *Hers.* Did he intend for them to sleep apart? She peered into the room and then back at him in question.

"Jillian slept there," he said quietly, and she sensed the agony in his words. "We did not share quarters after Molly was born. I…but it no longer matters. You are my wife now."

"Is it expected for me to sleep in there?" The room was decorated in feminine florals and quite pretty, but she knew her parents, during their brief marriage, had always slept together. She assumed this is how it would be for her, as well. However, rules were different for the upper class. What was she supposed to do?

"Only if you wish it."

She glanced at his bed. "Am I permitted to stay with you?"

"Yes." He cast her a wry smile. "It is preferred."

She nodded. "Then if it is all right with you, I would like to stay with you."

There had been a palpable tension in the air a moment ago.

It now disappeared.

Alex cupped her face in his hands and gave her a gentle kiss.

"It is more than all right, love. Excellent choice."

She watched him as he began to disrobe by softest candlelight, his gaze fixed on her and a small smile tugging at the corners of his lips. He removed his jacket, waistcoat, and cravat with a casual ease, then started undoing the buttons of his shirt.

One at a time.

Teasingly slow.

Her heart began to pound louder with each button undone, each time revealing a bit more of his chest and the light spray of gold hair across it. His skin looked golden by the candle's light, and there was no hiding the firmness of his glorious torso. She gripped the small side table beside her when he removed his shirt to reveal all that rugged muscle.

Dear heaven.

Sally had not been exaggerating when she waxed poetic about his body.

Her blood heated and a thousand butterflies now fluttered within her belly. He had to know the effect he was having on her, for his gaze was still on her and he was grinning. "You next, love."

Oh, she adored the way he spoke to her in that deep, gentle growl. "Um…" She licked her lips. "I'll need help."

Most of her gowns were easy to slip on and off, but this one required assistance because the intricate buttons and lacing were all on the back.

"I see," he said, the deep timbre of his voice resonating through her and making her tingle. He turned her so that her back was to him and then began to unlace the ties. Once again, he took his sweet time, pausing to trail light kisses along her neck with each lace untied and each button undone. She was mindless by the time he had the gown off her.

She closed her eyes, wanting to feel the sensation of his hands on her body as he turned her to face him and began to nudge the chemise off her shoulders. He kissed her bare shoulders, then slid his hand inside the loosened chemise and ran his thumb in a slow swirl along the bud of her breast.

Bursts of heat shot through her body.

She clutched his shoulders, holding firm to those massive

muscles as he lowered his head to her breast and put his mouth to it. Fire raged through her, for his lips scorched her to the core, and his tongue…*dear heaven,* the things he did to her with it.

Then they were on the bed, her clothes off and her hair unpinned so that it tumbled down her back and over her shoulders in dark, cascading waves. She did not know what to do or what to expect, but he took command and led her ever forward to exquisite heights, teasing her with every bit of his body so that she was a ball of fire by the time he was ready to claim her.

Not merely claim her, but conquer her.

Plunder her.

Take possession of her heart and soul.

She could not get enough of him, adored the weight of him atop her, and loved the way he held her with aching need and urgency. He ignited her blood and had her pulses wildly throbbing by the time he finally entered her and moved inside her. Their hips rubbed together and their hearts beat as one.

"Are you all right, love?" he asked with typical consideration, for there was no one more thoughtful than this wonderful man she could now truly call husband.

"Yes…oh, dear heaven…yes." He had her so mindless, she was surprised to get a single word out. She wanted him deep inside of her and sighed when he obliged, then groaned when he kissed her with a primal heat and quickened his thrusts with delicious urgency.

His hands were all over her.

His lips, too.

He kissed her breasts, flicking and swirling his tongue over their taut peaks. All the while, their bodies remained in intimate contact, his sleek and powerful as he buried himself inside her, and hers completely molten as she soared to the stars…and kept her soaring until he also joined her on that climactic journey.

"Blessed saints, you are sweet," he said with a growl when they were both spent and breathing hard in delight. He slowly rolled off her, but kept her close and wrapped her in his embracing arms so that she now lay atop him with her hair tumbling over his chest. He ran his fingers through her hair, smiling as he gently brushed the longs strands back. "You are mine, Viola. And I am yours forever."

"I was always yours," she whispered and nestled in his arms.

He claimed her again in the middle of the night, taking her with that same mix of exquisite tenderness and savage heat. He brought out the wanton in her, too. She had never known her body could respond in this way to a man's touch. Well, it was to his touch alone.

She ached with desire for him, her own need shockingly wild and unrestrained. But he did not seem to mind, purposely encouraging her soft gasps and purring moans. His smug grin as they soared again and slowly came back to their senses said it all. He liked this power he had over her body, liked stirring her to passion and knowing she was helpless to resist. "You do the same for me, love. I cannot get enough of you. But I had better behave myself or your body will be sore in the morning."

He shifted her so that she was once again nestled in his arms.

This is how this vicar's daughter fell asleep, delightfully snuggled in the viscount's arms. "I love you, Alex."

CHAPTER 18

London, England
August 1823

"LET ME INTRODUCE you to Lord Fenhaven and his daughter, Lady Felicity Rose," Alexander's father said to him and Viola as they stood on the family reception line in the elegant Trent townhouse to greet the crush of guests invited to the gala celebration of his parents' thirty-fifth wedding anniversary.

Alexander exchanged a knowing glance with Viola, for the young woman now before them had been on their list of diamonds under consideration for his house party last month. "A pleasure to make your acquaintance, Lady Felicity Rose."

She tossed Alexander a smile, although it was more a curl of the lips than anything sweet or charming. "I understand you are newly married." She now turned to Viola with an arrogant tip of her chin. "And you are the vicar's daughter who caught him in the parson's trap. Our society must quite overwhelm you. Poor thing, I'm sure you are worried about making a *faux pas*."

"Not at all. We entertained often at the vicarage." Viola smiled at the girl. "I hope you enjoy the party. It is a pleasure to meet Lord and Lady Trent's friends under such happy circumstances."

Lord Fenhaven managed a polite word to Viola before hastening after his daughter.

Alexander gave the pair no more thought before turning to

meet the next guests in the queue. Many were delighted to hear of his new marriage, but quite a few were not. Alexander bridled at their subtle contempt of Viola's lowborn status. His grandmother was standing to the left of him and gave him a nudge whenever she sensed he was getting irate over the petty barbs.

Viola was not oblivious, either. But to her credit, she maintained her poise and responded with grace and charm despite the overt snubs.

This is why he loved her, Alexander decided.

She had the kindest heart and gentlest instincts.

He'd called her his sunlight, and she was just that. One could not help but be warmed and happy in her company. This is what it took to be a true viscountess, this natural grace and poise Viola showed to all.

He glanced at his brother who was standing alongside Daisy to Viola's immediate right.

Gabriel cast him a grin and leaned over to whisper in his ear. "You and I would be hiding in the card room by now if it weren't for our wives to keep us in line. Bollocks, here comes the dowager Duchess Merriweather. She's going to invite us to her musicale."

Alexander laughed. "Lord, spare us."

Viola heard their whispered remarks. "What is wrong with that? Your father told me she has a lovely home in Belgravia and usually engages professional singers and musicians as well as featuring the accomplished daughters of the elite who are out to snare husbands. Does this not make for a lovely evening?"

"No," Gabriel said with a mock shudder. "I will never understand how insipid screeching is supposed to entice a man."

That remark earned him a poke in the ribs from Daisy. "Behave yourself. I can attest to the fact that no *accomplished* daughter wishes to be thrust in front of a crowd of leering knaves, most of whom are in their cups before the ill-conceived recital ever starts. You gentlemen are not the only ones wincing and grimacing at these affairs."

"I shall be sure to applaud the young ladies, no matter how good or bad they are," Viola said, her soft heart once again revealing itself.

Alexander leaned toward her and whispered in her ear. "I like the way your body sings for me, love. Perhaps you will give me a private recital tonight."

She blushed to her roots.

His grandmother slapped him across the back of his head. "Behave yourself, Alex. I did not hear what you said to your wife, but her face is as red as beets, so it must have been something completely inappropriate. Viola, ignore your husband. He is a naughty lout."

They all moved off the receiving line a short while later. He and Gabriel joined their father in opening the anniversary ball by dancing with their wives. In truth, it felt good to be here with his parents and brother, even if his father was still behaving like a bit of a dunce. The old man adored Viola, of this Alex had no doubt. But he still insisted on pointing out all the young ladies Alex could have courted had he bothered to come to London before falling in love with Viola.

Each time he did this, Alex merely sighed and raked a hand through his hair. "Yes, Father. But I'm happy with the wife I have."

That was an understatement.

He had been floating on air since marrying Viola.

None of these young ladies came close to her warmth or intelligence, not to mention they did not have her beautiful, trusting eyes. Perhaps it was these elegant surroundings and the dazzling display of wealth and power that brought out the mercenary qualities in so many of them.

Well, they were under pressure to secure their fortunes in order to maintain a pampered style of living, and yet had been given no useful training in developing character or strength of purpose. Added to this was his father's horrendous taste in suitable young ladies. Clearly, his grandmother had guided his father's choice in a wife. The man would have made a terrible match for himself if left to his own judgment.

Alexander may have been off the marriage mart for years, but he quickly took stock of the supposed diamonds like Lady Felicity Rose who was another in a string of fortune hunting schemers. Of course, such ladies were all sweetness and smiles when speaking to a gentleman they considered a catch. But they were quite disdainful of those they considered lesser. To a one, they considered the footmen serving champagne to be unfeeling cattle to be ordered about.

It was such a small thing to be polite and show a little patience as these harried servants rushed to fulfill the demands of their guests. But servants were too low, like the scrapings on one's boot, and would never be looked upon kindly by these ladies.

He gave Viola's hand a light squeeze. "I love you."

She smiled up at him. "Why so sentimental all of a sudden?"

"Just glad I married you. They're playing another waltz. Come dance with me, I need to hold you in my arms for a while."

"I am ever your obliging wife." She glided into his outstretched arms. "What are you seeing that has riled you?"

"Fashionable society. It is everything I have always hated." He began to twirl her in time to the music, moving with an easy grace along with the many other couples on the crowded dance floor. But it was almost impossible to avoid being bumped into or, in turn, bumping into others.

Suddenly, a young lady stumbled when another couple collided with her and the gentleman who was her partner. She could not regain her footing and fell to the floor.

Viola gasped and immediately reached out to help the poor girl. "Oh, dear. Are you all right. It is a frightful crush out here, isn't it?"

Lady Felicity Rose and her dance partner were the ones who had spun into the girl. Unlike Viola, the *ton* diamond stood there with a triumphant smirk on her face.

Alexander knelt beside the girl to help her up.

What did the diamond think she was gaining by demeaning the fallen girl?

Alexander assisted the embarrassed young lady to her feet since her partner seemed to have disappeared in the crush. As he and Viola guided her out of the line of dancers, he noticed the girl was limping. "You've twisted your foot."

She shook her head. "I'll be all right in a moment. Thank you for your kindness. I'm such an awkward thing. I wish I could hide somewhere until this party was over."

Viola cast Alexander an imploring look before returning her attention to the girl. "Do you have a partner for the supper dance?"

She shook her head. "No, not that it matters since I cannot dance now anyway."

"Then sit with us until you recover your strength. My husband will not mind." She glanced at him again, her eyes still pleading.

"Yes, do join us when the bell rings for supper. I am Lord Ardley and this is my wife, Lady Ardley."

She nodded. "I know. You greeted me on the receiving line, but I doubt I made the slightest impression on you. I never do. I am eminently forgettable."

Viola inhaled sharply. "Don't ever say that. I remember you. Miss Adela Swift, is it not?"

The girl's eyes widened in obvious surprise. "Yes, it is. Thank you, Lady Ardley."

"Call me Viola, please."

"Oh, I couldn't do that. You are a viscountess."

Alexander winked at Viola. "A brand new one. She was a vicar's daughter until a month ago. Apparently, that is a crime to some people's way of thinking. But I found her quite irresistible and had to make her mine."

The young woman seemed astounded by their friendliness.

"I suppose you've been having a difficult time of it in London," Viola said with a sympathetic smile.

Adela nodded. "I don't fit in. I have made a few misfit friends, but they are not here tonight."

"Ah, you consider yourself a misfit? Then my wife and I are bound to like you," Alexander said, making a light jest since the girl seemed about to burst into tears. "Here, Miss Swift. Take my arm and I shall escort you to the dining room. No reason for us to wait and battle the horde once the supper bell rings. Is that all right with you, Viola?"

"Yes, an excellent idea. This will also allow us to talk quietly and get to know you, Adela."

"Thank you, I would be honored."

He seated Viola and Adela, and then left their side a moment to let his father know what had happened.

Lady Felicity Rose stopped him as he was about to return to the dining hall. "Why are you wasting your time with that country cow? Her father is a lowly knight. She is no one of consequence and her dowry is small."

"What do I care about her dowry? The young lady was in distress and it seemed the right thing to do."

She pursed her lips in disdain. "Is this what you war heroes do? Come to the rescue of every pathetic thing?"

"Kindness toward others is not heroic, it is simply common decency. Something you have obviously neglected to learn. What have you done lately to recommend yourself to anyone?" he admonished this diamond who was too caught up in her own importance. "I can assure you, your looks will soon fade and no man of quality will look twice at you, if this is all you have to offer."

Well, now he'd done it. Offended her and would likely get himself slapped for it, which would certainly be reported in tomorrow's gossip rags.

Fortunately, she merely sneered at him, even though slapping him had clearly crossed her mind. However, a quick calculation on her part brought her to the conclusion that striking him would bring the wrong sort of attention upon herself as well.

"What did that horrid young woman say to you, Alex?" Viola asked when he returned and settled with a grunt in the chair beside hers.

"Nothing important. She is a haughty piece of goods. Completely unsuitable to be anyone's viscountess." Indeed, young ladies like Lady Felicity Rose were scary. Not an ounce of compassion in them. He would rather face the French army, for death would come swiftly when lined up against a wall to be shot.

But marriage to one such as that diamond?

An excruciatingly slow death.

Viola lightly kicked his foot to nudge him out of his darkening thoughts. "Tell Alex what you told me about your cave explorations, Adela. What sort of fossils did you find in Devonshire?"

Adela Swift turned out to be someone very much like Viola, modest and intelligent. A pretty girl, but not nearly as beautiful. No one could hold a candle to Viola's strikingly good looks as far as Alexander was concerned.

Their supper conversation afterward was surprisingly interesting, and the sumptuous fare comprising of game fowl, fish, and various meats was good, but also nothing to compare to Viola's cooking. "Have you found anything of significance in these caves that might appeal to the Royal Society, Miss Swift?" he asked.

"I think so. Plant fossils mostly, my lord. A few shards of pottery which indicates these cave dwellers had some sophistication. I've also come upon drawings on the cave walls of unusual beasts I have yet to identify. I have friends at home who join me in my explorations. We are hoping to find a bone or two belonging to these extinct creatures, but no luck so far. As for the Royal Society, they have rejected all my ideas to date."

She laughed softly and shook her head. "They have experienced archeologists, but not one of them is inclined to work with me. If I could get the attention of the British Museum, I would drop those righteous windbags at the Royal Society. But the museum staff has already allocated its budget for their own projects and do not appear all that interested in what they consider amateur digs."

Alexander listened with interest. "This must be quite frustrating for you."

She nodded. "It is, but at least they are not rude in rejecting me. The pompous oafs in the Royal Society demean all my work for no reason other than I am a woman. Yet, I have no doubt at least one of them will later claim my discoveries for his own, and not one of their Fellows will condemn him as a plagiarist. It is indeed infuriating and quite frustrating."

"Can you not publish your work independently?" Viola asked.

"No." Adela took a bite of her food and shook her head. "No one will accept my submissions without the backing of a reputable society." She took a sip of her wine and then set her glass down while regarding them thoughtfully. "May I ask an impertinent question?"

Alexander nodded. "Yes, as long as it is not too impertinent."

"Why are you paying attention to me? I am not nearly as pretty as someone like Lady Felicity Rose, nor am I wealthy. The marriage mart is excruciating torture for me and every party I am forced to attend simply proves how out of my depth I am. So how do I attract the kind attention of ones such as you? Forgive me for another impertinent comment, Lord Ardley. But were you not married to your lovely wife, every debutante in this room would be stabbing me in the back to push me out of the way so they could share supper with you."

Alexander winced. "These parties hold little enjoyment for me. Viola is new to this, too. But I daresay, she handles these affairs much better than I do. We would much rather be home in the company of those we know and trust. Just because a girl is beautiful, does not mean a man should be swept away by her. Most of these diamonds quickly lose their sparkle because they are intolerant, mercenary, and sometimes downright cruel."

She smiled. "This is why you had me join you for supper. You pitied me."

"I would not call it pity so much as common courtesy and consideration. I was angry when I noticed several other young ladies sneer at you. Lady Felicity Rose was not the only one showing you discourtesy."

"I try to ignore them as much as possible. Still, it hurts."

He nodded. "Any man of quality would have a far more pleasant time with you than any of them. Dazzling looks count for something, but you would be surprised how quickly that brilliance fades once one's true nature is revealed…or how beautiful one can become when one is as loving and compassionate as my wife."

Viola blushed at the compliment. "Thank you, Alex."

"When we are through with supper, Adela," he said, "I will introduce you to my sister-in-law. Daisy is a Farthingale and quite well connected. Her sister is Lily Farthingale. Perhaps you have heard of her."

Adela's eyes rounded in surprise. "Yes, I've heard of Lily Farthingale. What scholar hasn't? I wish I had one-tenth her brilliance. I would love an introduction. Does she have any sway with the Duke of Lotheil? He is chairman of the Royal Society and I believe Lily is married to his grandson."

"She is." Alexander grinned, enjoying the chance to do something productive while in London. "She and the duke got off to a bad start, but he adores her now. However, she and her husband spend most of their time in Scotland."

"Oh."

"You will have your chance to meet the duke. He adores all of Lily's sisters. His other grandchildren are also married to Farthingales. He cannot escape that family connection, nor will they allow him to avoid you."

She laughed. "Thank you, my lord. Seems my stumbling on the dance floor was the best thing that could have happened to me tonight."

After introducing Adela to Daisy and Gabriel, he took Viola back onto the dance floor for the last waltz of the evening. "I love you, Viola. You grow more beautiful in my eyes with each passing day. I think my heart is going to burst, you fill it with such joy."

"I feel the same way about you, Alex. I'm so proud of how kind you were to Adela."

"It wasn't a chore. These diamonds…I never acquired a taste for their shallow brilliance. They are just lumps of coal with a thin layer of shine on the surface. Dig deeper and there is nothing there but coal dust. No heart. No compassion. No sunlight."

"I hope Adela meets a nice gentleman who will appreciate her for her strengths. She may not have stunning looks, but she is quite pretty in a quieter way."

"I agree. She will find someone. Her perfect match is out there, and he will be no idiot popinjay." He spun her onto the terrace where the air was cooler and the pleasant scent of roses filled the starry night. "I'm going to tell you again how much I love you."

She laughed. "I won't complain."

"I love you, Viola. And you look beautiful in blue silk. The gown suits you to perfection. But I am going to take it off you the moment we retire to our bedchamber. In fact, I am suddenly feeling exhausted. You had better take me up to bed right away or I might faint."

She laughed again. "Hold strong, my love. The party will be over very soon, and then I will undress you and tuck you into bed so you may sleep off your exhaustion. I had no idea I had married such a delicate man. Should I sleep on the sofa tonight so as not to disturb you?" she teased.

"Cruel woman, don't you dare. I will not get a moment's rest without your soft curves to cushion me or your pointed elbows jabbing my side."

"Oh, no! Do I really do that to you?"

He grinned. "No, love. I am merely teasing you. I love the way you fit against me. You are perfect, Viola."

She kissed him on the cheek. "Then nestled against you is where this vicar's daughter shall always be."

"Thank you, love. Are you tired yet?"

She laughed softly. "Yes, it so happens I am suddenly exhausted. Apparently, I am quite delicate, too. Astonishing how this fatigue can suddenly come upon a person. You had better take me up to bed."

"Ever your dutiful servant, Lady Ardley." To avoid the crowded ballroom, he took her hand and led her across the terrace to the double doors leading into his mother's private parlor. From there, they made their way up the back stairs to their bedchamber. "I've heard there is a cure for exhaustion," he said once they were inside their room and he had locked the door.

"Oh, really?" She arched an eyebrow, dubious in the face of his wicked grin. "What is this miracle remedy?"

"One must remove all of one's clothes and leap into bed with one's spouse."

She groaned. "Could you not come up with something more original than that remark?"

"No, but I am eager to show you how it works." He emitted a soft growl as he came up behind her and kissed the slender curve of her neck. "Let me help you out of those encumbering clothes,

Lady Ardley."

"That is most kind of you, my lord." She sighed as he wrapped his arms around her. "Then I will help you out of yours, for I am ever your dutiful wife."

"Just how dutiful?"

"What do you mean?" she asked, turning to study the wicked gleam in his eyes with much amusement.

He whispered in her ear, then gave her lobe a sensual nibble. "Well, love? Are you up for it?"

She laughed and led him eagerly to their bed. "Yes, for I fear you have utterly corrupted this once innocent vicar's daughter."

They tumbled atop the counterpane, laughing and kissing each other as they struggled out of the last of their clothes, and wrapped themselves in each other.

Afterward, Alexander took Viola into the circle of his arms and stroked her arm lightly as they lay together in the darkness now that their candle had gutted out. But he did not mind the blackness of the night, nor would he ever again, for Viola was beside him.

And Viola was his sunlight.

EPILOGUE

Chipping Way, London
December 1823

ALEXANDER WAS PLEASED he and Viola had made the journey from Ardley Hall to London at Christmastide. Viola needed the distraction after the death several months ago of her father, and he needed to properly restore the familial bonds he had neglected over the years. They had arrived yesterday in the early evening and were now settled in for the next few weeks in the townhouse belonging to his parents.

However, their first duty after having a late breakfast this morning was to head to Chipping Way to call upon his grandmother, Lady Eloise. She resided next door to Daisy's parents, John and Sophie Farthingale.

He and Viola were to dine with them and the entire Farthingale brood tomorrow night.

But today, they were at his grandmother's door and eager to see the old dowager.

Her butler broke into a smile when he opened the door and saw who was standing on the other side of it. "My lord, it has been such a long time. A pleasure to see you."

"Good to see you looking hale as ever, Watling. This is my wife, Lady Ardley."

"I have heard nothing but raves about you, my lady. Seems

you are a family favorite."

Viola cast him a genuinely warm smile. "Why, thank you. That is very kind of you to say. I have heard nothing but wonderful things about you, too. It is a pleasure to meet you, Watling."

The old butler's smile was quite doting as he said, "The pleasure is all mine, my lady." He then turned to Alexander. "Your grandmother hoped you would come by today. She is in the parlor with Lady Withnall."

"Ah, I might have known. Those two are thick as thieves. What would a visit to London be without seeing that little termagant?" he jested loudly enough for Lady Withnall to hear him.

"Impertinent whelp," she called back, thumping her cane. "You know I have the ears of a bat. Get in here so your grandmother and I can properly box your ears."

His heart softened at Viola's trill of laughter.

She had been devastated upon her father's passing, and although she had tried to hold strong, he knew there was a vast emptiness in her heart over it. But she adored his grandmother and her companion in crime, and he knew these two old dowagers would help take away some of Viola's sadness.

He knew the way to the parlor, having spent many happy childhood days here whenever his parents traveled. He and Gabriel were little devils, but his grandmother somehow managed to survive their mayhem. "Grandmama," he said with affection, kissing her lightly wrinkled cheek.

In turn, she greeted him effusively, her eyes as bright as ever and twinkling. "Come have tea with us, dear boy. I've missed you so much."

"I'm hardly a boy, although I have not behaved like a responsible adult lately. With Viola's help, I am here to amend that oversight." London wasn't far from Ardley, and yet he had made the trip only once for his parents' anniversary ball this past summer. Prior to that, he had visited not above twice in the last five years.

His grandmother was not at all put out by his neglect, and instead showed him nothing but kindness. "Nonsense. We all struggle, at times. You are here now and this is all that matters.

Viola, how are you, my dear?"

She cast the two ladies another of her genuine smiles that made the room glow brighter. "I am well, I promise. Your grandson is the best husband. Being back here with his family and dear friends is doing me a world of good."

"We are glad to hear it, my dear," Lady Withnall said with a kindness she reserved for very few people. "What are your plans while you are in Town?"

"We are having an early supper tomorrow night with a horde of Farthingale relatives," Alexander said, accepting a cup of tea from his grandmother. "I suppose you have been invited, as well."

The two dowagers nodded.

"Miss Swift has been invited, too," his grandmother said.

"I'm glad to hear it. Viola and I arranged for them to meet Adela on our last visit this past summer, and it seems they are making some headway with the British Museum regarding her fossil finds."

"I've heard a little about it," his grandmother said. "It is slow going. The Duke of Lotheil has also been trying to help her. He was invited to dine with us tomorrow, but had a prior engagement and cannot get out of it. However, he has been quite helpful to Adela in making introductions to the museum and the Explorer's Club. Unfortunately, the Fellows in the Royal Society remain firm in their refusal to accept a woman in their ranks. Lotheil is for it, but he is in the minority. Even as their chairman, he can do nothing to persuade the others."

Lady Withnall nodded. "If Lily Farthingale could not move them, then I doubt any young lady will be able to crack those hard nuts. Well, perhaps it will happen years from now when we are all long gone."

"I hope it happens sooner," Viola said. "Adela is a nice girl and clever, too. But her family does not have the wherewithal to support her for another London season. She will be going back home after the holidays, and I expect that will be an end to her scientific dreams."

"Not to mention her matrimonial aspirations," Lady Withnall intoned.

Alexander's grandmother regarded her partner in crime. "You know, Phoebe…we could take her on and sponsor her next season."

Alexander groaned. "Grandmama, should you be meddling in the girl's affairs?"

"Who is to help her if we do not, Alex?" She took a sip of her tea and then set her cup down. "Besides, now that you and Gabriel are well settled, what is there for us to do? Phoebe, we must make a list of suitable gentlemen for the girl to meet."

Viola clapped her hands. "Yes, it is a wonderful idea."

Alexander shook his head and groaned. "Oh, lord. I hope you have better luck with your lists than I had with mine."

Viola laughed. "We did make some pretty bad choices for you, didn't we? But I hear Lady Aurora is now married to Duke Nevins' son, and Lady Charlotte will soon be wed to Lord Hythe, so the summer house party turned out to be quite successful for them."

Lady Withnall nodded. "Even Lady Alicia is now married to a dolt of a man almost twenty years her senior. But they will suit quite well because neither wants anything to do with the other."

Viola shook her head. "Then why bother to marry if they don't like each other?"

"The husband is a commoner but rich as Croesus," she said, thumping her cane. "Your eyeballs will pop when I tell you how rich he is. He wanted to marry into an established, titled family. She wanted everything his money could buy…and he can buy everything."

Viola laughed heartily as she turned to Alexander. "I would not trade you in for all the riches in the world. I think I made the best bargain of all."

"We know," his grandmother said, casting Viola a doting smile. "We were just worried Alex would never get out of his own way to admit how much he loved you. We knew we had to attend your summer party, if only to give him a nudge in the right direction if he remained too dense."

"Wait, are you saying you knew I was in love with Viola before you ever met her?"

His grandmother nodded. "Yes, it was obvious the moment you wrote to me regarding your list of diamonds."

"What do you mean? How was it obvious? And how can you take credit for knowing Viola was the one for me when you approved of our selection of those three *ton* diamonds?"

His grandmother rolled her eyes. "Dear boy, I called them *astounding* choices because this is what they were. Astonishing in how wrong they were for you. It was clear from your very first letter that the right girl was beside you all along, only your fogged brain would not allow you to see it."

Lady Withnall thumped her cane again. "We knew we would adore Viola before we ever met her. Anyone with the ability to pull you out of your darkness had to be someone worthy of your love. Besides, every word you wrote about her proved you had lost your heart to her already. She was helping you out. You relied on her judgment. She was talented. Amazing. Incredible. You mentioned her in every sentence."

He cleared his throat and chuckled. "You exaggerate. I'm sure I did not."

"Yes, dear boy. You did." His grandmother smiled at him. "So leave Adela to us. We will find the perfect young man for her."

Viola turned to him with a broad smile on her face. "You mentioned me in every sentence?"

He arched an eyebrow. "Apparently. I will concede that you two old biddies were quite insightful in this instance. But I am not always so dense. In fact, I pride myself on being quite alert."

Viola grinned at him. "Is that so?"

He nodded. "Yes, love. Alert enough to realize…" He glanced at the two dowagers and then back at his wife. "Never mind. We'll talk about it later."

Her smile faded into a frown of concern. "Talk about what? Is something wrong?"

"No, love. I think it is very right."

She still appeared perplexed.

His grandmother cleared her throat. "What my grandson is trying to tell you is…he believes you are with child."

Viola's eyes rounded in surprise. "I…oh, Alex! I wasn't sure yet. How could you know? I promise, I wasn't trying to withhold anything from you."

He took her hand and gave it a comforting squeeze. "I know. It is all quite new, isn't it?"

She nodded.

"I've suspected for about a week now." He, insatiable hound that he was when it came to her body, had recognized she was off her cycle, and Viola was the precise sort of girl who was always punctual. Also, he'd noticed her breasts increasing in size. He could not miss such an obvious clue when he had explored those exquisite mounds thoroughly and knew exactly how they fit in the cup of his hands.

She stared at him. "A baby? Our baby? Do you think so? Are you sure?"

He nodded. "Yes, love."

"Dear heaven. Now I am the dense one." She laughed as she placed a hand on her stomach.

He reached over and covered it with his own. "A new life, Viola. Although it is still early days." He looked to the older ladies. "I hope you will say nothing just yet. We'll let my parents and Gabriel know in due course. But, Lady Withnall…"

The little harridan rolled her eyes. "Give me some credit for common sense, Alex. Besides, I have scandals to spread that must take precedence."

Viola's eyes widened. "Really? Anything juicy?"

"Viola!" When had his wife turned into a gossip?

She grinned at him. "Sorry, my love. But my father and I did get used to reading those scandal sheets and it is one of the things I miss most about our mornings together. He loved to pore over each line of gossip and was happiest when coming upon a thoroughly sordid, biblical sin. It is awful of me to miss this morning routine of ours, I know. We never reveled in the misfortune of others, but hoped his parishioners might learn from these mistakes and avoid them. I promise you, I could never take pleasure in another's misfortune."

"I know." He kissed her on the forehead. "You are perfect."

And she was, Alex was certain of it.

More than perfect for him.

He stared at her…just stared with pride at his radiant wife.

There was something to be said for marrying a vicar's daughter.

He would recommend it to every viscount who asked.

THE END

Dear Reader

Thank you for reading *The Viscount and the Vicar's Daughter*. When Alexander Dayne, third Viscount Ardley, is pressured to remarry and get about the business of siring heirs, his search takes him far afield to find the right woman. Yet, vicar's daughter, Viola Ruskin, has been in front of him the whole time. It is not until he is ready to move on that Alexander realizes she is the only one for him. I hope you enjoyed seeing familiar characters from the Farthingale series, especially Daisy Farthingale and Gabriel Dayne (from *Rules For Reforming A Rake*), not to mention Lady Eloise Dayne and her best friend (England's most feared gossip), Lady Withnall who appear as important secondary characters throughout this series. As well, I really enjoyed bringing in Alexander's cousin, Graelem Dayne and his wife, Laurel Farthingale (from *A Midsummer's Kiss*).

I welcome you to all the stories (including several novellas) in the FARTHINGALE SERIES, and if you are in need of even more Farthingales, then please try my Book of Love series where you will meet a host of Farthingale cousins and their friends, all of them sweet and innocent young ladies who cannot seem to keep out of trouble. In fact, they attract trouble wherever they turn, especially when it involves some very hunky heroes. Next release in the Farthingale Series is A Duke For Adela because Miss Adela Swift is next in line to find her true love and he will arrive in the form of Ambrose Thorne, the Duke of Huntsford.

Keep reading to enjoy the first chapter of *A Duke for Adela,* and don't forget to grab your free Farthingale novella after the sneak peek.

SNEAK PEEK: A DUKE FOR ADELA
CHAPTER 1

London, England
May 1824

AMBROSE THORNE, SEVENTH Duke of Huntsford, had been brazenly approached by young women all of his life. In fact, everywhere he turned, young hopefuls would pop up in front of him, sometimes dropping a handkerchief to gain his attention, other times swooning at his feet, or on occasion dispensing with such ruses and openly propositioning him. But until this moment, he had never – not ever in his entire life – been bodily tackled and brought down flat on his back amid bleached skulls and ancient bones on public display.

His head was reeling and shoulder ached from the tumble he had just taken in the Huntsford Academy's newly opened exhibition hall. It was located across the street from the British Museum and ought to have attracted an elegantly academic crowd.

But the mad young woman with dazzling eyes and kissable lips now sitting atop him was no such thing.

Whatever possessed her to fling herself at him?

"Botheration!" she cried, her knee missing his privates by a hair's breadth as she attempted to scramble to her feet and dart away.

"Oh, no you don't." He grabbed the girl's ankle to hold her fast. He'd had quite enough of these brazen debutantes making free with him.

"Let go of me, you idiot! Can you not see that despicable toad is getting away?" She tried to jerk her leg free of his grip. But she had just called him an idiot and he was not about to let her get away with that. "What are you doing? I am not the culprit, you nitwit!"

After a moment, she emitted a soft cry of frustration and stopped struggling. Instead, she cupped her hands to her mouth and shouted across the hall, "Thomas Runyon, you sneaky thief! I'll report you to the Duke of Huntsford! You won't get away with it!"

Ambrose, who happened to be the duke in question, rolled to his feet and now exchanged his grasp on her surprisingly shapely ankle for a grip of her hand. "Come with me," he said with a low growl, his voice laced with as much authority as he could muster after she had flattened him in front of a throng of startled onlookers who were still gawking at them.

Without giving her the chance to protest, he dragged her out of the exhibition hall and up the stairs into the chairman's private office. Her pretty lips did not stop moving the entire time. "You nitwit," she called him again, obviously having a fondness for that insult. In addition, she repeated her conviction that he was the biggest idiot alive.

After slamming the door shut behind them, he plunked her down in one of the soft leather chairs. "Now," he said, his voice laced not only with authority but with fury as he placed his hands on the armrests to keep her trapped between his arms. "Who are you? And what were you doing charging down the exhibit halls like a rampaging bull? Don't you realize you might have destroyed valuable artifacts?"

"I never would! No one appreciates these relics more than I!" Her slate blue eyes blazed magnificently and her equally magnificent dark curls were on the verge of coming undone. He tried not to compare her hair to dark silk, but he could not ignore the fact that her mane appeared surprisingly soft and lush.

If he weren't on the verge of throttling the impudent girl, he might enjoy running his fingers through that massive pile. It threatened to tumble in gorgeous waves if he blew on it with a single breath.

"Who are *you*?" she shot back, looking angry enough to pound her fist into his midsection. To his good fortune, she was not quite as bloodthirsty as she first appeared. Perhaps she was afraid of him and not about to rile him further, especially since she was trapped in his office alone with him. "How did *you* appear out of nowhere like a block of granite?"

No, this young lady was no shrinking violet.

Indeed, although she was small and shapely, she was also full of determination. The sort who could knock him over while running at full tilt despite her diminutive size. Well, she was of average height and rather slender except in her bosom. Yes, her chest was another magnificent attribute of hers, especially as it was now heaving. "Thanks to you," she said with marvelous indignation, "that no-good, plagiarist lizard, Thomas Runyon, has just stolen my latest research findings. Months of work lost! Now he will claim it for his own…and it is all your fault."

"In what way, shape, or form is it my fault? I've never heard of either of you until this moment. And since you seem to know the identity of this so-called thief, he is hardly likely to get away with whatever it is he took from you. What's your name?"

"What's yours?"

"Huntsford."

She stared at him a long moment, and then swallowed hard as understanding dawned. "As in His Grace? The Duke of Huntsford?"

He nodded. "One and the same. Must I ask for yours again?"

She held out her hand as though he was supposed to shake it…or kiss it…or, it struck him that he would rather kiss her lips.

Lord, they were pretty.

She would probably bite him if he tried.

"My name is Miss Adela Swift." She dropped her hand to her

side when he did not reach for it. "Obviously, thanks to your meddling, I was not *swift* enough to catch that crook."

He shook his head as though not hearing right. Was she still berating him? Even now that she knew he was the Duke of Huntsford? He ought to have been outraged. Instead, he threw his head back and laughed.

The girl was priceless.

Completely clueless and befogged.

She cared not a whit for his status.

"You've called me meddlesome, an idiot, a nitwit, and countless other insults. You do realize I could have you banned from this exhibition hall for the rest of your life." He wasn't going to do it, of course. People who spoke honestly to him were rare and not to be lightly dismissed.

She appeared shocked. "But I am a scientist! Well, more of an amateur archeologist, to be precise. But I know my ancient bones and the significance they represent. In fact, I have made some important finds and–"

He groaned.

Dear heaven, spare me.

A bluestocking.

She had the look of one, too. Atrocious clothes. Upswept curls that were more likely to have pencils stuck in them than pretty hair clips. Intelligent eyes.

Yes, he quite liked her eyes that were rather a remarkable shade of blue softened by swirls of gray that added a beautiful depth to them.

Her scent was that of chestnuts warmed on an open fire, rich and sweet when licked off the tongue, soft and delicious to the bite.

Not that he intended to bite into this bluestocking, but he would not mind nuzzling the slender curve of her neck.

"You would ban me from your exhibit hall for chasing a thief?" she asked in utter disbelief. "Where is the justice in that? Um…you do not strike me as an unreasonable fellow, Your Grace. Quite the opposite, your museum has been designed not only with great care and thought, but with obvious love of science.

Particularly that of archeology. Your research library is far better than the public one in the Royal Society, and more than equal to their secret private library."

He sighed and eased away, now settling his large frame in the chair beside hers. "It cannot be much of a secret if you are openly talking about it. Have you seen their private library?"

She nodded.

"Did you break into that, as well?"

She inhaled sharply. "I beg your pardon? I am not the thief here."

"Is that so? The Royal Society Fellows never allow women inside their inner chambers. How did you get in?"

"The Duke of Lotheil gave me a private tour. He and I are kindred spirits when it comes to fossilized bones."

He laughed again, for there was more to the remarkable Miss Adela Swift than met the eye. "You know Lotheil?"

She nodded. "I am very good friends with the Farthingale sisters. Lily Farthingale is married to the duke's grandson. But I am closest to Laurel and Daisy, who are Lily's sisters, and I am also well acquainted with Daisy's sister-in-law, the former Miss Viola Ruskin. She recently married Viscount Ardley. It is through Viola that I met them all. Do you know their husbands?"

"Quite well. We fought together on the Continent against Napoleon's forces."

"You do have the look of a warrior," she remarked. "You are awfully big for a duke."

"I did not realize we came in regulated sizes."

"I only meant that you do not look like a vain and pampered popinjay. Forgive me for knocking you over. I must have caught you completely unaware or else I would have bounced off you and gone flying. Please do not ban me from the Huntsford Academy. I shall be bereft if you do."

He could have given the girl a hard time, but did not have the heart to do it. Her big eyes were shimmering and he feared she might start to cry. "You are not banned," he said with a resigned sigh. "Do you wish for my help in bringing this Runyon fellow to task?"

"You would help me?" She stared at him in obvious confusion mixed with a good dose of hopefulness. "Thank you. Yes, I would. Not only for my sake, but for yours. He also ran off with one of the Huntsford Academy's rare books, although he will probably return it once he realizes what it is he has accidentally purloined. He is too much of a coward to ever dare take you on. But I am merely a woman and not likely to be believed or listened to, so he will walk all over me."

"No, he won't. I will not let him." If this girl was telling him the truth – and there was something in her demeanor that made him believe her – this Runyon character was the sort of fellow who deserved a comeuppance. He felt this way not only for the man's disregard of scientific truth, but also for his pettiness in treating the weaker sex with such arrogant disdain.

Miss Swift cast him a dazzling smile. "I think I am going to like you, Your Grace. I'm sorry we got off to such a bad start. But you really are a good egg."

He was going to laugh again.

He had never received such an odd compliment. Women did not describe him as a good egg. Big. Fearsome. Handsome. But never an egg. "Where do you reside, Miss Swift? I'll need to contact you once I retrieve your research papers."

"I am presently staying with Lady Eloise Dayne at Number 5 Chipping Way in Mayfair. I will happily show you any of my other work. I have a trunk full of notes and sketches of my findings on cave drawings my friends and I have discovered in Devonshire. I'm sure they are similar to the drawings found in the Lyme Regis caves in Dorset and those discovered in France."

Her eyes lit up as she took in a light breath and continued. "I also think I have figured out what those mysterious dots and lines found alongside all of those drawings represent. The realization only struck me today, moments before Runyon – that lizard – stole my notes. Fortunately, I had not written down my hypothesis or he would have stolen it, too. Do you wish to hear it?"

"Perhaps another time, Miss Swift."

"But surely, you must realize how important those symbols are."

Oh, Lord.

Was she going to lecture him now?

"Another time, Miss Swift."

"Oh, I see. You also believe I am just a foolish amateur. This is why no scientific journal will publish my monographs on the cave drawings. They are demanding proof the extinct animals depicted on the cave walls my friends and I discovered ever existed."

"Any reputable journal would require such proof from someone lacking credentials in the field," he said with a nod.

"I understand their concern that it might all be a hoax. This is why I hope to find bones in these caves to prove these drawings are real. But I have turned up nothing so far beyond a few shards of pottery. It is quite frustrating because I think I am very close to discovery. I'm sure the proof is buried deep, I just have to hit the right spot. However, my family will not allow me to return to Devonshire. I am not permitted to leave London for the foreseeable future."

"Why not?"

She cast him a wry smile. "Lady Dayne and her friend, Lady Withnall, are sponsoring my second Season. It is exceedingly generous of them, and my parents will disown me if I muck it up. They insist I put all thought of ancient bones aside and find myself a living prospect to marry."

He chuckled, knowing it was quite perverse of him to like the fact this young woman admired dead things more than the unremarkable prospects one often found on the marriage mart. "You do not appear thrilled."

"Would you be?" She shook her head. "It is humiliating to be paraded in front all those gentlemen, most of whom consider me a country cow."

Ambrose drew in a breath. "Has anyone called you that?"

She nodded. "Several people, in fact. I have a tiny dowry, lack social polish, and am too clumsy and bookish to be considered elegant. I am also no frail, thin creature, as I'm sure you noticed when I landed flat atop you."

He cleared his throat.

Lord in heaven, he certainly had felt that lush bosom of hers mold to his chest and her slender hips grind against his thighs. "No, I had not noticed. I hit the ground hard and had the wind knocked out of me."

Her eyes widened once again, for she was obviously dismayed. "Dear me, how thoughtless. Did I hurt you? Do you wish to see a doctor? George Farthingale is one of the best in London."

He held up a hand to still her fretting. "I am fine. No harm done."

He rose to signal their meeting was at an end and held out a hand to assist her to her feet. "Until we meet again, Miss Swift."

He drew her hand to his lips and kissed it.

Hell, why did he do that?

She was not wearing gloves and his lips had directly touched her surprisingly soft skin.

He could have just bowed over her hand.

But there was something inexplicably appealing about the girl. As she'd said, she was no wispy, waif of a thing, but neither was she built like an ox. In truth, she was nicely formed and her features pleased him. He could not figure out what it was about her just yet. Certainly not her clothes, for they looked like they had been borrowed from a dotty maiden aunt. Nor the style of her hair, which had no style to speak of, although the hair itself was quite spectacular.

She was full in the bosom…he liked that immensely.

And she had a beautiful smile, one that reached into her rather lovely eyes.

There was no way this young woman resembled a cow.

She cleared her throat.

He followed the direction of her gaze.

He had yet to release her hand.

He did so now.

She was still smiling as she backed out of his office, smacking her shoulder against the door jamb on her way out. She made it no more than two steps into his antechamber before tripping over the carpet because she still had her eyes on him and not on where she was walking. Fortunately, it was just a small misstep and she recovered quickly.

The girl was not exaggerating when she said she was clumsy. "A moment, Miss Swift."

He reached her side and offered his arm. "Let me walk you out of the building. Wouldn't want you to fall atop any of our patrons."

She groaned. "Now you think I am an utter peahen."

"No, Miss Swift. To tell you the truth, I find you surprisingly charming."

"You do?" She eyed him warily, as though waiting for him to spring his cruel jest. His heart gave a little tug, for this girl had enthusiasm and intelligence along with decent good looks, and yet no one seemed to view her as a prize.

He would have to do something about that.

Now that the Huntsford Academy was built and open to the public, he was looking for a new endeavor to occupy his attention.

Why could it not be Miss Adela Swift?

Interested in learning more about the Farthingale series? Join me on Facebook! Additionally, we'll be giving away lots of Farthingale swag and prizes during the launches. If you would like to join the fun, you can subscribe to my newsletter and also connect with me on Twitter. You can find links to do all of this at my website: mearaplatt.com.

If you enjoyed this book, I would really appreciate it if you could post a review on the site where you purchased it. Also feel free to write one on Goodreads or other reader sites that you peruse. Even a few sentences on what you thought about the book would be most helpful! If you do leave a review, send me a message on Facebook because I would love to thank you personally. Please also consider telling your friends about the FARTHINGALE SERIES and recommending it to your book clubs.

If You
Kissed Me
Meara Platt
A Farthingale Novella

ALSO BY MEARA PLATT

FARTHINGALE SERIES

My Fair Lily

The Duke I'm Going To Marry

Rules For Reforming A Rake

A Midsummer's Kiss

The Viscount's Rose

Earl Of Hearts

The Viscount and the Vicar's Daughter

A Duke for Adela

Marigold and the Marquess

If You Wished For Me

Never Dare A Duke

Capturing The Heart Of A Cameron

MOONSTONE LANDING SERIES

Moonstone Landing (novella)

Moonstone Angel (novella)

The Moonstone Duke

The Moonstone Marquess

The Moonstone Major

THE BOOK OF LOVE SERIES

The Look of Love

The Touch of Love

The Taste of Love

The Song of Love

The Scent of Love

The Kiss of Love
The Chance of Love
The Gift of Love
The Heart of Love
The Promise of Love
The Wonder of Love
The Journey of Love
The Treasure of Love
The Dance of Love
The Miracle of Love
The Hope of Love (novella)
The Dream of Love (novella)
The Remembrance of Love (novella)
All I Want For Christmas (novella)
Tempting Taffy (novella)

DARK GARDENS SERIES

Garden of Shadows
Garden of Light
Garden of Dragons
Garden of Destiny
Garden of Angels

THE BRAYDENS

A Match Made In Duty
Earl of Westcliff
Fortune's Dragon
Earl of Kinross
Aislin
Genalynn
A Rescued Heart
Earl of Alnwick

PIRATES OF BRITANNIA

Pearls of Fire

THE LYON'S DEN SERIES

The Lyon's Surprise

Kiss of the Lyon

A Lyon in the Rough

DeWOLFE PACK ANGELS SERIES

Nobody's Angel

Kiss An Angel

Bhrodi's Angel

ABOUT THE AUTHOR

Meara Platt is an award winning, USA TODAY bestselling author and an Amazon UK All-Star. Her favorite place in all the world is England's Lake District, which may not come as a surprise since many of her stories are set in that idyllic landscape, including her paranormal romance Dark Gardens series. Learn more about the Dark Gardens and Meara's lighthearted and humorous Regency romances in her Farthingale series and Book of Love series, or her warmhearted Regency romances in her Braydens series or Moonstone Landing series by visiting her website at www.meara platt.com.

Made in United States
Troutdale, OR
04/30/2024

19542324R10174